CYRUS TWELVE

LEONA FOXX SUSPENSE THRILLER #2

TED PETERS

APOCRYPHILE
PRESS

Apocryphile Press
1700 Shattuck Ave. #81
Berkeley, CA 94709

Copyright © 2018 by Ted Peters.
All rights reserved.
Paperback ISBN 978-1-947826-86-1
Ebook ISBN 978-1-947826-87-8

No part of this book may be reproduced in any form or by any electronic or mechanical means, including information storage and retrieval systems, without written permission from the author, except for the use of brief quotations in a book review.

Get more Leona!

Join Ted Peters' readers group
to stay up to date on all things Leona!

Join today and download "Shooter,"
the new Leona Foxx short story at
BookHip.com/NJFLNJ

THANKS

To wordsmith, phrase-smith, brilliant literary critic, and belovéd spouse, Karen Ann Peters, I render humble thanks for polishing this book.

"Thus says Cyrus king of Persia,
'The LORD, the God of heaven,
has given me all the kingdoms of the earth,
and he has charged me to build him
a house at Jerusalem."

—2 Chronicles 36:23

CHAPTER 1

TAIPEI

With his left hand he reached into the terrarium swarming with snakes. After three stabbing motions, he successfully seized a cobra around the neck just under the head. He lifted the serpent, turning it so that he held the adder's head shoulder-high while its undulating five-foot length hung down toward the ground. An angry open mouth thrusted a frantic tongue, searching hopelessly for an object to light on.

With his right hand the diminutive forty-year-old Chinese man in the blood-smudged white apron picked up a large kitchen knife. He placed the point, carefully and precisely, just under his left hand, on the neck of the snake, then punctured the soft under-jaw skin. With a single ceremonious motion, he slit downward, impaling the entire length of the underbelly. The serpent's body throbbed wildly. After dropping the knife, the man inserted his index finger in the snake's neck. With a one sweeping downward motion, he stripped the serpent's interior of its entrails, creating a bloody cascade into the street gutter below. Then he turned and carried his still writhing reptile toward the kitchen.

Leona Foxx stepped over the gutter filled with snake entrails into the open-air section of the night market restaurant. The air was filled with a dank, thick aroma, a curious combination of freshly discarded innards mixed with those swept aside hours earlier. She walked past the tanks holding pythons and poisonous slithering imports. She walked past the cages holding domesticated rats and mice. Snakes eat rodents and people eat snakes.

Leona stood pensively in the middle of the restaurant for a few seconds, visually surveying the customers, not certain who she was looking for. A man, to be sure. But Chinese? Anglo? Other? All she had been told was that he would be an elderly gentleman dining on snake meat and drinking its blood. Numerous customers fit this description. *Now just who might be looking for me?*

Tables in Taiwanese restaurants typically host an entire family, including infants, along with their siblings, parents, and grandparents. The undercurrent of voices, occasional laughter and babies crying throughout the crowded market somehow made her visual task of scanning more challenging. Someone sitting alone should be more easily distinguishable. Leona's eyes continued to dart from table to table until she thought she could see one such individual near the rear of the restaurant's interior eating area. She walked toward his table. It was set for one, but it was flanked by three chairs.

The lone diner was wearing a traditional Chinese red silk embroidered shirt fastened neatly with black cord frogs. It fit loosely, with bulky sleeves that draped onto the table. *Snake on the plate next to his bottle of Taiwan Beer?* Leona thought. *Where's the glass of blood? Is blood even served in glasses?* The graying Chinese senior seemed to concentrate on his food, not noticing Leona intruding herself into his immediate environment. He seemed oblivious to her approach.

Perhaps I'm mistaken. Leona halted and turned to survey the restaurant guests once again. Then she heard a mumbled English phrase—"Cyrus Twelve." It was spoken by the man somewhat under his breath while placing a bite of snake meat into his mouth. He still had not looked at her directly.

Leona slowly stepped around to the far side of his small table and seated herself. At five foot eight, the American visitor to the island Republic of China towered above her average Asian counterparts. Her shoulder-length amber hair set her apart from the native black hair. She had scarcely made herself comfortable when the waiter showed up. "Taiwan Beer and a bowl of sea turtle soup," she said in English without having looked at a menu. Turning to the elderly man across from her, she continued: "Is that what I should order?"

"Whatever suits you," he said, looking up at her. "Do you have anything to say to me?"

"Yes, of course: Cyrus Twelve," responded Leona.

"Now, that was easy," he said. "Are you enjoying your vacation in Taipei?"

Leona felt a certain level of discomfort at this awkward introduction, but she veiled any suspicion behind a warm yet serious smile. She looked directly into the man's luminous brown eyes and was reassured.

The waiter promptly brought a twenty-ounce brown bottle of beer and poured a foamy portion into a six-ounce straight-up glass. Leona took a sip and waited a moment. "I'm not here on vacation, despite what I've told my Chicago friends. Getting down to business right now is okay with me. But first I'd like to ask why you're so fluent in the Queen's English?"

"My father's father fought with the Kuomintang. Once the Republic of China was established in the 1950s and the Americans provided for our security against an invasion by the People's Republic of China, I had the opportunity to serve in the army next to Americans." The man spoke while continuing to chew his snake meat.

"I even spent some time in your country with the army and later in the UK working on my doctorate. I not only improved my English, but picked up the bad American habits of smoking and then chewing gum," the man said with a smile and a chuckle. "I graduated from Fu Jen Catholic University here in Taipei and later earned a Ph.D. in History at Cambridge.

"So, there is the Reader's Digest version of my English acquisition, complete with a reference to Reader's Digest!" he said with an amused tone, looking at Leona to see if she might break her intense stare. She did and smiled back at him.

"Now, are you ready to get down to business?" he asked.

"Of course. Thanks for breaking the ice. Where do I go from here?"

"Okay. Our cutout is a young woman, Katia Rui. Her first name sounds like the Russian nickname for Ekaterina, Katya. She doesn't work for anybody. Well, not for anybody like us. She's a lab technician and courier in a computer components company called TaiCom. It was quite by accident that she stumbled upon the plot and was able to steal a sample chip. Actually, it's more than a sample chip. It's the prototype that will be used later in manufacturing. It tells all. We need it. I can't go for it because everybody knows me. That's why we've asked you to make the connection. All you need to do is look like a tourist. Katia will take care of the rest."

"So, I get the chip from Katia. I give it to you. Then what?"

"Over the weekend we make a copy. Then we get it back before Monday morning. Nobody will even know it was gone."

"You make it sound so easy," Leona said with a hint of disbelief in her voice as she scanned the room with a bit of uneasiness. Out of the corner of her eye she noticed three men seated at an outdoor table under the restaurant's awning. All Asian, perhaps Mongolian. All young and not as talkative as one might expect of three boys out for the evening. One was dressed in traditional Chinese garb; the other two in Western style sweatshirts. Only beer sat on their table. No food.

She gave her attention back to the man across from her. "What is your name?" she asked her new comrade.

"It doesn't matter," he said curtly. Leona responded with a look that scrunched her brow as if to say that it did. But she said nothing.

The waiter arrived with her soup, bowing and smiling and placing the spoon neatly next to the bowl.

"For the sake of Bremerhaven, do you see what I see?" Leona said in a loud whisper. "Over there. Under the awning."

He looked without looking like he was looking. "Asian fecal matter," he muttered. "Pretend you don't notice them."

"Okay. Now, who knows about Katia?" she asked

"No one knows, we hope. But we can't be sure. If she's discovered, she will be in danger. As of right now, however, we think everything's copacetic. Once she has divested herself of the chip, she'll be safe if the rest of us keep our mouths shut."

"Does she know all this?"

"Oh, yes. We helped her devise her plan to pass it off."

"What's the plan?"

"That's where you come in."

"I gathered that."

"She's expecting to meet you at the Lungshan Temple tomorrow morning, Friday, at 11:30. She will find you. She'll be on her lunch hour. Have a pleasant lunch together. Get to know one another. Make it look like a friendship, just in the unlikely event that you'll be watched."

"Will she physically pass me the chip?"

"Yes. But that's not all. She needs to provide you verbally with a conceptual map of operations. She'll explain just what we need to know about the chip. Once we have the chip, we'll copy it. In addition, we'll modify it with a fault, modify it so that it malfunctions. But the change will be invisible. At least we hope it'll be invisible for a while. We'll accomplish all this over the weekend. On Monday morning, you'll give it back to Katia. She'll replace it with this modification, and TaiCom's plan will go forward. But the TaiCom people will confront a frustrating failure. By the time they remedy the fault, our counter technology will be in place to thwart the entire project."

"How did you ever connect with Katia? It amazes me that you were able to find someone so close to the source."

"It's a long story which I will tell you after the switch is complete. Let's just say that the old American saying, 'It's not what you know but who you know' applies here. We connected with her through a third party. Katia has a strong sense of justice and knew she had to turn a 'wrong' into a 'right'."

Out of the corner of her eye, Leona could see that one of the three men she'd been watching had left their table. Two remained seated. *Where had the third one gone? Perhaps to the toilet.* After bringing a few spoonfuls of turtle soup to her mouth and sipping the beer, she addressed her tablemate. "We'll need to decide on a way to contact one another. Do you want my cell phone number?"

Each punched the other's number into their respective cells. Leona noted a text message had arrived from Angie, her BFF in Dearborn, Michigan. She ignored it.

"Just what name should I assign your number to?" asked the American.

"Bernard Lee. You might as well know my name. We'll meet again after you've secured the chip. Tomorrow night. Seven o'clock. Front gate of the Lungshan Temple. Got it? I will tell you the story of Katia."

Just as they were pocketing their phones, the third man from the corner table pulled up a chair and sat at their table.

CHAPTER 2

TAIPEI

LIKE BERNARD, the new visitor was wearing a traditional red silk Chinese shirt, fully buttoned, with draping sleeves. The embroidery was less intricate, indicating a cheaper version of the classic style. On his left hand at the base of the thumb knuckle was a small tattoo, a dragon with a tail as long as a snake that wrapped around the body of the dragon, the tip of the tail pointing down towards the wrist. Under the dragon was a single Chinese character.

Bernard studied the man, carefully inspecting the detail of his tattoo. Leona studied Bernard and noted that his eyes opened wider.

Bernard looked Leona squarely in the eye with an intensity that sent a shiver through her.

The man spoke a few staccato words in Mandarin. His tone clearly spoke anger. Leona did not understand Chinese, but she instantly understood they were in danger. The other two men from the outside table had risen to their feet, walking with a purposeful gait into the restaurant's interior. Then the two separated so they could walk toward the table from opposite directions. Leona figured it was time to act.

She casually picked up the large steak knife her dinner partner had been using on his snake meat. She raised it high, then plunged the knife through the draped sleeve of the uninvited guest, burying it down deep into the wooden table. His arm was now trapped. With all the frogs fastened on his shirt, he would not be able to quickly extricate himself.

Bernard gave Leona a smile of gratitude. "Now run for it!"

The two leaped up and raced through the restaurant door into the narrow street. The two suspicious looking thugs followed, while the third remained temporarily imprisoned at the far table.

"Split up," said Bernard as he raced to his left. Leona took off running to her right. Their two hunters also split, each chasing one of the prey.

Leona in her running shoes raced through the crowd of night shoppers swarming around the alley shops, followed close behind by one of the toughies. Each dodged a myriad of bicyclists and baby carriages. Leona looked over her shoulder frequently but, to her dismay, she had not yet shaken him. Surprisingly, the chase drew relatively little attention from the pressing crowd.

Leona turned a corner and ducked behind a rack over-stuffed with sale clothing. She peered through the shirts to see if her pursuer was close behind. She spied him standing restlessly no more than thirty feet away, anxiously looking from side to side. Leona's heart was beating so hard, she feared its pounding would divulge her hiding place. Good fortune was with her. The pursuer walked on hurriedly, moving his head from side to side to search his environs for any trace of Leona. Leona slipped back into the narrow alley and walked just far enough behind him so that she could watch his moves and still get away if he spied her. She followed him for a hundred feet.

The man passed an array of open tanks filled with octopus, squid, shrimp, turtles, and various fish, a showcase for one of the many seafood restaurants in the market. Leona followed closely and waited for just the right moment. From behind and without warning, she grabbed the thug around the neck. As fast as a lightening bolt, she thrust his head down hard onto the edge of an aquarium, cutting a gash in his forehead. She grabbed his hair and pulled his head up, then followed with a second thrust downward, forcing the bleeding head into the squid tank. She held his head under water long enough for him to swallow and gasp.

At hearing the thud, the screams of the diners and the subsequent commotion, the shop's owner rushed out from the kitchen dressed in a soiled apron and shouting with his arms flailing above his head. He arrived at the scene of the chaos just in time to watch as the tank's water turned red with blood. The restaurant's owner turned mute with disbelief. He froze.

When Leona's victim showed signs of weakening, she released her grip. As his limp body fell to the ground, Leona caught a glimpse of the same dragon tattoo below his left thumb. Leona made a mental note of it, realizing she had to move fast. She stooped to pat him down. Beneath his sweatshirt she found a gun, a Glock 17. She withdrew the bullet clip and threw it into the squid aquarium. Then, she dropped the Glock onto the concrete floor. The thud gave finality to the effort. Within seconds Leona disappeared into the crowd that filled the alley. Immediately a group of stunned gawkers formed to attend to the bleeding casualty of Leona's wrath.

CHAPTER 3

TAIPEI

LIONEL CHANG PULLED his Kymco motor scooter through and around the cars slowing for the traffic light. At the light, he stopped and placed his left foot on the pavement for balance. Impeccably dressed in a black pin striped suit—tailored to his slender physique—with a white shirt and conservative blue tie, he stood out from the other scooter riders, except for the customary and compulsory helmet. Lionel sat in front of the first rank of cars. Momentarily, a party of two on their Keen motorbikes pulled up next to him and stopped. Then another. Still another pulled into line. Soon an array of Yamahas, Suzukis, SYMs, TGBs, and PGO Scooters had lined up and paused in waiting like a herd of cattle. When the traffic light turned green, engines revved and a tide of bobbling helmets swooped into and across the intersection.

Lionel pulled up on the sidewalk in front of Taipei 101 in the heart of the Xinyi District. He was met by a trotting man who took control of the Kymco as well as Lionel's helmet. They exchanged greetings in Mandarin, and the attendant took off to park the scooter in some unknown location. Lionel straightened his custom-made jacket and tugged confidently at his lapels. He stood for a moment and looked up. A cloud hugged the building, preventing him from seeing what lay above the twentieth floor. He headed for the front door.

A golden bolt that had been fastened on July 1, 2003 marked the completion of what was then the tallest building in the world. At 101 floors, the double-paned green windowed Taipei 101 soared to over five hundred meters, scratching the tummy of the stratosphere. The design suggested a postmodernist rendering of a series of inverted pagodas. Owned by the Taipei Financial Center Corporation (TFCC), the skyscraper was designed to withstand earthquakes and typhoons but not to survive rapid drops in the stock market. In more archaic times such a tower would have represented the *axis mundi*, the navel of the world where heaven and earth mate to give birth to the human race. In our more secular modern times, however, Taipei 101 represented Asian *hubris* in the global financial market, going one better than the perfection implied by the number one hundred. It was an economic Tower of Babel on the plane of Shinar, awaiting a heavenly lord more powerful than the dollar to descend and measure its puniness.

The top floor of Taipei 101 is a mystery. There is a club up there, it is rumored. It is a club for only the rich and the privileged and the powerful, it is rumored. But no number button on a publicly available elevator wall will provide the skyward transportation needed to find out for certain. Lionel Chang tapped the button for floor 83, an office floor located among the High Zone Office levels. The fastest elevator in the world rocketed the young executive toward the stratosphere.

On the 83rd floor Lionel passed through the main doors of TaiCom, his computer and communications company. He immediately poked his head into the reception area where Lillian Yang was sitting. "Good morning, Lily," he said in English.

"Good morning, Lionel," she answered, looking up from her desktop computer screen. Her Nine West business suit in a tasteful olive green with short sleeves, belt, and skirt could not hide her distinctively Asian femininity. The thirty-year-old executive assistant looked as alert as she was attractive.

"Do you have the briefing reports prepared for our syndicate meeting this morning?" he asked.

"Yes, indeed. I just placed them on the conference table. Fresh ice water along with pens and scratch paper are also on the table. We're ready to go."

"Great! Have you asked someone to serve tea?"

"Tea will appear shortly after everyone is seated," said Lily.

"Has everything with Mr. Lo been arranged?"

"Yes. Mr. Lo will arrive shortly. I'll escort him in when you tell me."

They smiled at one another, a smile of professional courtesy.

Lionel marched swiftly into his office. He dropped the backpack he had worn on the scooter onto a corner of his massive desk. After taking his bearings he waltzed into the conference room to assure himself that all things were ready. He sat himself in his swivel chair in front of the window.

First he looked out the window. The cloud he had previously seen from below was now visible from above. Looking up he could see the sun; but looking down he could see only shiny white fog. He turned to look at the seat to his left where Lily would play hostess and take notes. Her Latitude laptop was already in place. The LCD on the wall showed just what he wanted it to show: the gated entrance to TaiCom's Development Center. His guests were sure to be impressed.

CHAPTER 4

TAIPEI

By 10:30 am Lionel's guests had all arrived and were busily shaking hands and chattering. After sitting down to receive their respective cups of tea, served graciously by Lily in the traditional Chinese manner, Lionel rose to his feet and asked for introductions.

"You already know that I'm Lionel Chang, CEO of TaiCom. It's good that each of you could be here today. Thank you so very much for taking time from such busy schedules to join me. And most of you have also traveled a very long way. It means a great deal to me and my entire TaiCom family. Hopefully each of you will find this a productive, educational, and engaging meeting. I trust we will have a lively exchange of information and ideas. Thank you again.

"I started TaiCom four years ago in a small office on the other side of the city. I had no financial backing, just my own meager savings of what would be the equivalent of five thousand American dollars. I wasn't exactly poor, but I ate a lot of Top Ramen!"

Lionel said all this with a broad toothy smile, exhibiting the more gregarious side of his personality. He hoped that a short attempt at levity might help to engage this academic, cerebral group seated around the table staring back at him with a curious mixture of intensity and apprehension. A few responded with polite smiles.

"Today TaiCom has twenty full-time employees and a cadre of consultants who help us with specific problems. Actually, I like to call them 'hurdles' since we have never stopped moving forward. We may just take a step back to leap over them."

"Now TaiCom—I am proud to say—has the breakthrough product that will change the world. We will introduce that to you later."

"So, that is *me*. Now let's hear about each of *you*. Each of you has been invited here because you have a critical piece of this greater project. I have spoken and corresponded with each of you individually, but I don't think you all know each other. Let's go around the table beginning at my left."

Lionel sat back down and smiled as he scanned the illustrious group at the table. He had high hopes for this day.

"I'm Lily Yang." Lily stood up, but not quite. She bowed toward the guests, signaling traditional humility and servitude. "I'm Lionel's assistant. If you want anything, just ask for Chang 'n' Yang." The group laughed appropriately and Lily loosened her stance. "Please ask me for *anything*," she pleaded with a broad smile, then sat down once again.

Next to Lily was a prematurely balding fifty-year-old male Anglo with tufts of gray hair sprouting over the arms of his glasses, appearing as if gray and white wings were growing out of the sides of his head. His linen suit coat seemed a bit too large for his underdeveloped torso. The knot of his plaid tie sat off-center under the collar of his striped shirt.

"John Blair here," he said while remaining seated. "I am a professor at Oxford University. Excelsior College, actually. My most recent research puts together neuroscience with nanotechnology. I currently have a grant to work on the possibilities of correcting neurological brain conditions such as Parkinson's through the use of deep brain implants."

Near the end of the table, a young woman with a Russian accent spoke up. "Are you the Doctor Blair we just read about in the most recent issue of *Science Magazine*? Seems you have some sort of public argument with another professor? From Germany perhaps?"

"Yes, yes, I'm afraid that's me. My opponent is Hans-Georg Welker at Heidelberg in Germany. We disagree on the virtues of future machine intelligence. I'm in favor. He's against. Professor Welker whines that the Germans tried once before to create the *Übermensch*, the super-human. And it turned out rather badly, as history records. He fears a repeat of the Nazi era. But I believe he overstates the case. The times are different. We write against one another in scholarly journals. It's all great fun!"

The group concurred with a light air of laughter.

After a pause, the blond-haired American male sitting to the professor's left spoke. "It's good to be here today. Thank you for inviting me."

At no more than thirty, his demeanor displayed a self-possessed, respectful confidence. He wore an open-collared black polo shirt beneath a tan safari jacket with bulging pockets. "I'm Buzz Kidd," he said. "I'm founder and CEO of a small start-up in Sunnyvale, California, OmniNet. We are developing new methods of enhancing human intelligence, something akin to both Artificial Intelligence and Intelligence Amplificiation, but a little different. More about that later. I'm also here as a delegate from TTU, Transhumanist Technical University in Mountain View, also in California."

"My name is Geraldine Bourne," said the person sitting next to Buzz. A stocky brunette Caucasian woman with hints of gray in her tightly pulled-back hair, Geraldine wore a dark blue Ann Klein pantsuit. Her erect posture suggested a woman of composure and competence. "I'm a medical doctor and a neurosurgeon in Toronto. I am especially interested in issues related to memory, memory enhancement, and memory loss. I'm here today representing North American Medical Advanced Technologies, NAMAT for short. This is my second visit to Taiwan." She smiled and childishly flexed her shoulders.

"Do you say 'a-boot' or 'a-bout'?" quipped Buzz Kidd.

"If you listen carefully you'll hear many 'a-boots'," she replied to the delight of the native English speakers in the room. "I do my best to teach my American neighbors to pronounce the word correctly. To no avail, of course."

A smallish man with dark skin and even darker hair was next. "My name is Abnu Sharma. I'm from Mumbai, India. Like Mister Kidd, I too am a computer person, an engineer. And also like Mister Kidd, I claim the title of Transhumanist. I have recently been involved in engineering robots that can safely handle nuclear waste. Just call me Sharma."

All eyes turned to the next in line, a petit woman with spikey, short-cropped blond hair and a disciplined posture wearing jeans, a light green Lake Tahoe t-shirt and a denim vest with countless zipper pockets. An inch of a tattoo surfaced on her neck just above the t-shirt, but not enough was visible to know just what the tattoo was.

"I am Olga Louchakova," she said with a thick Russian accent. "I vas born Saint Petersburg. When I vas born dere, it vas Leningrad. I hack computers everywhere in world from my little office at TTU in California. I paid to do dis. Amazing, yes?. Dis job is designed to help develop computers dat cannot be hacked. Sometimes I get lucky and find computer secrets. Mister Buzz and I share many same interests about future."

The last to speak was a well-proportioned six-foot-two gentleman in his forties with dark, almost black hair, conservatively cut and neatly combed away from his face. His upper lip sported a thin black mustache. He was wearing a deep blue Tom Ford-style double-breasted suit with light blue rope stripes. The medium pink shirt was coordinated with a Nikki Tonal Club Room necktie.

"My name is Khalid Neshat. I'm a physicist specializing in practical applications of quantum theory. I'm Persian. My home is Tehran, but I've been living abroad for the last few years. I'm the president of *Tehran Technologies Incorporated*. We are headquartered in San Francisco, where I live, with a second office here in Taiwan."

Led by Lionel, they gave each other a brief round of applause, accompanied by courteous smiles and brief moments of eye contact.

After Lily finished serving a second round of tea, the group settled in for business.

Lionel Chang chaired. "We are meeting here today to discuss Intelligence Amplification, or IA for short. All of you have been chosen to be here because you have some understanding or connection with this exciting frontier of science.

"We will take this in two stages. First, we will discuss amplifying the human capacity for reason, for expanding rational thought. Second, we will look at the other kind of intelligence, namely information gathering on behalf of governments. One might commonly call this 'spying'."

This scientific assembly appeared both curious and eager.

"Finally, third...well, that will be a surprise. This room may not look like a nursery. But right here, the posthuman species is about to be born. And we are its midwives."

CHAPTER 5

TAIPEI

CHANG CONTINUED: "I've asked Buzz Kidd to open our discussion by describing the role of IA in Transhumanism."

"Thank you, Lionel," began the young, blond American, making eye contact with everyone at the table. He tapped a pair of buttons on his laptop and the LCD wall screen resolved into a picture. Only one item appeared and that was in italics: *H+*.

"I am going to give you a brief overview of our current work and then we can get to the details later.

"As you already know, *H+* is short for Transhumanism. *H+* is a movement alive and well in both the United Kingdom and Silicon Valley. We Transhumanists believe that evolution did not finish its work with the arrival of *Homo sapiens*. We humans are hardly even a rest stop on evolution's highway toward the future. Up until now, evolutionary progress has been guided by the interaction of variation in inheritance and natural selection. Nature has selected us. All by herself. No God. No angels. No interventions. With only one purpose in mind, nature has steadfastly pressed forward toward one very important goal. That goal is increased intelligence. The more intelligent we are, the more fit we are to survive. We human beings in the computer age have finally understood this. We have grasped it. This means we are now ready to take hold of the reins of evolution and, like riding a thoroughbred horse, race toward the finish line."

"Let me add," interrupted Sharma, "that biotechnology is the key to the next stage in evolutionary progress. Natural selection is a long, slow process, taking millions, even billions of years. Rather than wait for natural selection, we will speed things up. We will direct what happens as the human race gives way to its successor, the posthuman species. We will augment and enhance and even redesign biological organisms, including ourselves and our children. Intelligence Amplification through nanotechnology applied to biology is the key, as I have said."

Olga Louchakova cocked her head slightly and looked back at Buzz Kidd. "You said IA. You mean AI?"

John Blair coughed, a sign that he was taking the floor away from the American. "AI stands for Artificial Intelligence. We make computers and robots with artificial intelligence, machines that mimic human intelligence. Some call this 'robotics'. What the Transhumanists in this room are after is IA, or Intelligence Amplification. We want to amplify the existing intelligence of organisms such as ourselves."

"Now, Professor," responded Louchakova, looking at Blair, "you said you are specialist in nanotechnology. Vat is dis nanotechnology?"

"Tiny stuff. A nanometer is one billionth of a meter. A nano unit is about the size of ten hydrogen atoms placed side by side. Invisible to the naked eye, to say the least. We use powerful electron microscopes. We can redesign molecules from the *inside*. Some of my colleagues at Oxford have been making nanobots, little robots that zip around in the human blood stream devouring the bad cholesterol. We can also make nanobots for the bloodstream that increase oxygen, making it possible to swim a mile under water without running low on breath. We're on the way to Superman."

"Thank you, Professor, for shedding light on that aspect of our work. Exciting stuff, isn't it?" stated Kidd, repossessing his role as discussion leader. "We plan to start our research with the human brain, but not stop there."

Kidd had their attention. "You've heard the professor describing how nanotech can be used for improving physical health. If stem cell research leads to the regeneration of deteriorating organs and if nanobiotech increases physical capabilities, we can expect the human life span to increase dramatically. Perhaps we'll live to be a thousand years old. Maybe longer. If old age or diseases no longer kill us, we just need to stay away from moving buses and avoid war to have eternal life. We call this radical life extension, or RLE."

Chang offered a follow-up. "Now, RLE in the West might simply mean more and more of what we're used to. It might just mean more ski trips, graduate diplomas, and stints in the PTA. It could sound boring, unattractive. But to us in the East, it could have a powerful cultural effect. We Chinese Confucianists and Taoists, for example, highly regard age. As a person grows older, his or her wisdom grows. In fact, his eternal spirit becomes more and more genuine and creative. Younger generations revere this and ritually celebrate their elders on their sixtieth birthday or eighty-eighth birthday. When these elders die, their wise spirits move to the next world and share their wisdom with struggling souls. So I ask: why not keep these wise elders with us? If we keep the senior savants alive for a millennium, think of the growth in wisdom that will accrue to our entire civilization. With RLE, Asian culture might lead the world to a new level of appreciation and reverence for age."

The group paused to digest what had just been said.

"If we are able to extend life to a thousand years as you say," Bourne began slowly, "then what about the population of our planet? Will we have room for everyone to live this long? After all, people who die leave space for the next generation to have a place to live. We'll run out of room on Earth, won't we?"

"RLE is not for everybody," said Khalid Neshat as he took the floor. "Remember that we believe evolution wants increased intelligence. We want to speed up the increase in intelligence. So perhaps we should extend people's lives selectively. Only those with an IQ above, say, 150 would be encouraged to live these long lives. We might find a way to shorten if not eliminate the lives of the masses of average people, those with lower IQs. Perhaps we have to face it: some people deserve to live on this planet, while the others....?" Neshat just quit speaking as he shrugged his shoulders.

The room was silent.

CHAPTER 6

TAIPEI

"Let's get back to the brain," said Bourne. "That's my field. So, Mr. Kidd, where do I fit in here? I can do brain surgery. That's simple. But what else?"

The expression on Kidd's face communicated a sense of gratitude for the opportunity to finally say what he had originally wanted to say. He coughed briefly into his hand.

"We believe IA will come in two phases. Phase One will combine memory augmentation with increased computational capacity. Then, in Phase Two, enhancement of our capacity to reason should follow. After all, reasoning consists of rearranging our memories and computing connections. If we have a full inventory of complex data available to our memory, we will be able to assemble the parts to create whole new concepts."

"Are you sure this is what constitutes human intelligence, Mr. Kidd?" quizzed Bourne. "Doesn't intelligence require insight, something beyond computation?"

"Please let me continue," said Kidd. "We're here today because we are about to enter clinical trials on memory enhancement. Mr.

Chang...Lionel...has engineered our first memory enhancement implant. Lionel, perhaps you could explain what comes next."

"The implant is a microchip smaller than a watch battery," said Chang, making eye contact with each individual around the table, including Lilly Yang. "We've been working on the circuitry for two years now, and we believe we have it right. Our plan is to implant this chip in the human brain. The chip's memory will contain more information than *Wikipedia* and *Google Search* combined. The chip will be so wired into the brain that certain thought cues will activate it. Once activated, the person will be able to quiz his mental encyclopedia and receive an informative answer almost instantly. It will provide a sensation similar to reading, but this will be strictly an invisible mental reading. In conscious conversation, a person with our chip implant will be able to access an enormous library of data."

"What will this do to established memories, the ones we've developed through life experience?" Louchakova asked Chang, picking up on Bourne's hint of skepticism.

Kidd interjected, "Our established memories won't go away, at least not right away. Our memories are kinda like a deposit in a savings account. If we don't withdraw anything, the money's still there. We might even make some new deposits from time to time. However, the chip memory will contain invented life experiences and integrate them into its encyclopedic knowledge bank. The person with the chip will be unable to distinguish between actual past experiences and the ones we have added. The two sets of remembered experiences will grow together for a brief period. But then, quickly, the chip memory will grow so powerful that, well frankly, our natural memories will atrophy from diminished usage. The chip recipient will become a different person, the one we have preprogrammed. But so be it! It's not unlike trading in an old Ford for a new Lexus."

CHAPTER 7

TAIPEI

Leona taxied to the Manka district in Taipei, arriving at the Lungshan Temple late in the morning. As she walked through the main gate she looked up at the near tropical sun. Her eyes also caught the symbol of the sun on the temple roof: two celestial dragons playing with a large red ball.

The sun was unusually intense for a late spring morning and there was little shade in the open area outside the temple. Leona sauntered toward the forty-foot waterfall to the right of the main gate. The wafting spray provided a pleasant cooling effect on her face and on her bare legs below her shorts.

Leona checked her watch. Eleven-twenty. No sign yet of Katia. Pious Buddhists and Taoists bustled past her, most entering rather than departing the forehall through the right front door, nicknamed the dragon's mouth.

Eager to meet this new "friend," yet appreciating that her often-impatient self was not anxious, she decided to check her voice mail. One message from Gerhart Holthusen, Director of the CIA, calling from his office in Washington, D.C. All she heard was, "Have a good day, Lee." Nothing from Graham.

Shortly after half past the hour, Leona heard a soft voice hesitantly calling, "Leona?" It was the voice of Katia Rui. At five feet and less than a hundred pounds, the slender Katia was petite by Western standards. Her short dark hair framed an expressive face with a gently jutting jaw. She walked comfortably in high heels and wore a yellow flowered sun dress. She smiled at Leona with a smile that communicated a genuine warmth and eagerness to meet her.

"Katia?" exclaimed Leona, turning to give the newcomer her undivided attention.

"Yes, I'm Katia. Sorry to be late," spoke the Chinese woman. "A last minute matter at the office."

"It's been pleasant here. No problem. I'm just glad we could meet."

"I have something to do here. It won't take long. You might even find this place interesting. In a few minutes we'll catch some lunch and get down to business. Please, come with me."

The two women marched through the dragon's door into the forehall, a roofless courtyard. Worshippers ambulated to and fro, holding burning incense sticks between folded hands. Smoke from sensors hung like a low cloud above tables of offerings, offerings of fruit and packaged food. Leona's nose caught the fragrance of freshly cut flowers mixed with the wafting fumes of glowing incense.

"Although the temple has been located here for nearly three centuries," lectured Katia, "this ornate building was completed in 1924. The main hall with the roof in the center is dedicated to the bodhisattva Quan Yin. Legend has it that Quan Yin practiced sincere spiritual discipline and approached the door of salvation. She was holding her empty water bottle. The Buddha told her that with each act of self-renunciation, drops of water would begin to fill her bottle. When the bottle became completely full, she would then be admitted to Buddhahood. However, a drought occurred in China. People were dying of thirst. It was an emergency. So, Quan Yin offered the people drink from her bottle, depleting her own supply and depriving herself of Buddhahood. Today we think of her as a goddess of grace."

"What are these people with folded hands and incense praying for?" asked Leona.

"They pray for what people all over the world pray for," said Katia with a slight tone of impatience.

"Well, just what do *you* think people pray for?"

With a puzzled, almost perturbed expression, Katia proceeded to say, "They pray for wealth and good health and the success of their children. What else?"

"I was just wondering," said Leona wishing to drop the subject.

CHAPTER 8

TAIPEI

"I HAVE A QUESTION." The group turned to give the Persian their attention. "Look at the modern *Wikipedia* or even the old *Encyclopedia Britannica* for that matter. It's out of date the day it's published. Information is exploding constantly. Even if our brain can access this encyclopedia with an implant, we could be accessing out-of-date data. So..."

Chang smiled. "What I'm going to say next will speak to your question, Mr. Neshat. And more. You're right. Whatever data we place into the chip memory prior to implantation will be finite and limited in many respects, regardless of the quantity. Even if it's the most up-to-date possible, it will quickly become out-of-date. So let me ask: might there be a way of updating the chip? The answer to that question is: yes, indeed."

"How? Plug it into my computer and download updates?" asked Neshat with a sarcastic grin.

"We've got a much better method," said Chang with a note of glee in his voice. "The chip includes a two-way radio signal linked directly to a geosynchronous satellite. We at TaiCom will periodically send new material for each chip to download. The data library will grow constantly. Previous information thought to be erroneous will be erased and replaced with what is new and accurate."

All eyes lit up: a few chins scrunched slightly upward, forcing the lower lip to protude, signaling both delight and approval. Lilly took this moment to offer another round of hot tea. She respectfully walked around the table and refilled each person's porcelain cup.

"Dis is ingenious idea," said Olga, "but just how you plan for dis implant to integrate with human brain? One thing to have implant. Another to make connections."

"This *is* very complex, as you can imagine." Buzz Kidd spoke. "Recall what we said earlier about nanobiotech. We will obtain a sample of the recipient's DNA. This DNA will be integrated into the chip's circuitry. Certain genes will be turned on or off by nano-switches. Once the chip is surgically implanted, the chip will itself become a tissue in the person's body. Gradually, with just the right genes turned on, a new set of nerves will grow that connects the chip with the targeted regions of the brain. We will target especially the hippocampus and the prefrontal cortex, the hippocampus for long-term memory and the prefrontal cortex for rational thought."

The expression on Olga's face turned from curiosity to puzzlement.

"Really?" she paused in thought. "Wait one minute. What about short-term memory? Individual memory occurs in region of brain affected by sensation, where originally perceived. If I look at you and see you, for example, my visual cortex and neural structures involved in dis sensation of seeing remain active for several seconds. Short-term memory can involve parts of the brain other than hippocampus, maybe even entire brain. You forgetting dis?"

Kidd continued. "No, of course, not. We focus on the hippo because it collects what's happening elsewhere in the brain. Sensations—sights, sounds, scents, touches, spatial location—all register in the hippo. It collects and connects these sensations, establishing networks of memory and trains of synthetic thought. The long-term memory is formed in the hippo; and this long-term memory is needed for enhancing rational thought, for making us smarter. So, the hippocampus becomes our main region of concern."

"But, if I may object, what about working memory? Working memory takes place in prefrontal cortex, not hippocampus. We can keep only four to seven items of memory active for quick reference; and dis takes place..." She pointed her finger to her forehead and tapped.

"Ah, yes," responded Kidd. "Did I mention that the prefrontal cortex is our second target? Here we find the brain's executive function: planning, problem-solving, and such tasks. The interaction between the hippo and the prefrontal cortex is what we're trying to augment, or amplify, or control."

"So why you keep all this secret from me, Mister Buzz. I see you back in California, and you never say nothing about such project."

"Well, my friend, I wanted to surprise you, and Mr. Chang here wanted me to keep it hush-hush until today."

"Well, that's all good to hear. Still, there's so much more," insisted Bourne, shifting the conversation to the group. "What we think of as the rational capacity emerging from brain activity includes unknown interactions between the prefrontal cortex and the insula—for emotional salience in decision-making—or the anterior cingulate cortex—for cautions and inhibitions and such. Then there's the amygdala. I... Oh, never mind. I'm willing to provide the surgical procedure, but I'm not sure you can accomplish everything you're planning."

"Actually," said Chang addressing the group, "this is why we invited Dr. Bourne here. At our invitation she has already developed the appropriate surgical procedure for us. In fact, she has provided us with a prototype."

"I have?" Bourne's eyes opened wide with a touch of surprise.

Chang continued. "We expect this to be a very minor in-office procedure with only a local anesthetic. A small incision would be cut just behind the right ear. The chip would be implanted and the incision closed. While healing takes place, the chip's nano-programmed DNA will precipitate cell growth and establish a new neural circuitry that connects the chip with the targeted regions of the brain. We expect this growth process to take two to three days. To be safe, four. After four days we will activate the chip and train the recipient on its use. Doctor Bourne already completed a first implantation surgery on one selected recipient to help establish the best practice. Once we have confirmed its efficacy, we'll package it and distribute it to the medical clinics we designate to perform implantation surgery."

"I was not aware that the simple procedure I performed would have such far-reaching effects. I am amazed, actually, and excited by the prospects," Bourne stated in a tone that moved from doubt to assurance.

Louchakova nodded. "I see. I presume reason you obtain DNA sample in advance is you avoid immune rejection after implantation, right?"

"Yes," said Chang. "And More. We need to trigger exactly the right genes for neuronal growth. That's how we make each chip patient-specific."

Bourne mumbled for all to hear, "Yes, this what we have begun to experiment with."

Louchakova continued her interrogation. "I suppose chip shape hard, fixed, unbendable. Means you must limit application to adults whose crania are already at maximum growth, right?"

"No," responded the surgeon. "The chips are flexible. Rather than covalent bonds, we use hydrogen bonds. The polymer chips can change shape within the brain without compromising their conductivity. We could, if appropriate, place one in the brain of a child and it would, in principle, remain operative for the child's entire life."

Then Louchakova spoke a bit more loudly. "But I still have theoretical problems. You first talking about intelligence amplification, IA. Now I listen to you—and I think you offer ingenious technique. Make no mistake, very exciting. But I not see how dis relates to Phase

Two. Don't see how amplified access to data has any effect on intelligence per se."

"One step at a time," interjected Professor Blair. "If I have understood Mr. Chang and Mr. Kidd correctly, today we're only working on Phase One. Once we've successfully increased mental access to data, we can then take direct steps toward IA. Here is the big assumption we Transhumanists make: the human mind is an information pattern. It's exactly like software in a computer. Imagine that our physical brain is the hardware. Then, our mind is the software. We know how to track and duplicate computer software. By the time we get to Phase Two, we will be able to copy a given person's information pattern, duplicate it, manipulate it, and—using this chip technology—enhance it. Once we have amplified the intelligence of a number of individuals, *they* will collectively take over the process and design the next stage of IA. Our present generation can then step out of the picture. Amplified intelligence will continue to amplify and amplify and amplify. It won't be long before we will have given birth to a new species, a posthuman species of cyborg intelligences that surpasses what we've ever seen before."

"Gentlemen!" Bourne's voice intoned both impatience as well as professional authority. "Louchakova's doubts are worth listening to. I'm a brain surgeon. I've taken apart and put back together brain after brain on the operating table. And, I need to say frankly, I just don't know what intelligence is. Now this is not because I'm stupid. It's because human intelligence is a mystery. To liken the human mind to the information pattern in computer software fails to comprehend this mystery. The mind does all kinds of things that go way beyond mere manipulation of information. Insights, for example, are creative leaps in understanding that leave data in the dust. The mind analyzes and synthesizes and imagines whole new realities. Something's missing in your assumptions. Where do you place the human soul?"

Blair responded slowly. "We Transhumanists tend to avoid using the word 'soul'. No one has ever proven we have a soul."

Bourne studied Blair's face. She looked at Kidd and Chang. She sat back in her chair and dropped her right hand on the table top. "Count me in for Phase One. But that's all."

"It's too late, Dr. Bourne. You have already gone well beyond what your assumptions might have previously permitted."

Bourne's face registered bewilderment.

Sharma took advantage of the temporary lull in table talk. "I'd love to hold the chip prototype in my hand. If it's the engineering marvel you say it is, this could be a moving moment."

The biggest smile of the morning covered Chang's face. He nodded to Lily. She got up and left the conference. Small talk ensued and a low hum of indistinguishable voices filled the room like white noise. Blair helped himself to the last of the tea.

When Lily returned, she was accompanied by an erect Chinese man, an athletic-looking twenty-year-old. After whispering something to the newly arrived guest, Lilly asked for the group's attention. The assembly went silent.

"Now I'd like to present Phase Three. This is the surprise Lionel mentioned. Please meet Mr. Choong Lo."

CHAPTER 9

TAIPEI

"We'll walk past Quan Yin's hall," said Katia, pointing down an open-air aisle to the right. "We're going to a corner in the rear hall. The rear hall was added at the end of the eighteenth century when the Taiwanese became successful at trade and prosperous in business. On the far left we pray to Matzo, a goddess that protects traders as they sail on the sea to the Chinese mainland. But that's not where you and I are going."

"So, where *are* we going?"

"I want to visit the altar to Wen-Chang, the god of literature. I'm tired of my job as a lab technician. I'd like to go to the university and study, but I need to pass the entrance exam. I've got a copy of my entrance exam application here in my purse. I'll put it on Wen-Chang's altar, and he will help ensure that I get a passing grade."

Katia pulled a photo copy of her exam application out of her purse. The two walked toward the far right corner of the rear hall. As they approached the waist-high gate protecting the Wen-Chang altar, a man in a traditional gray robe received her offering. In turn, he handed her a ball point pen. Katia took it enthusiastically. She turned to Leona. "This pen is blessed by Wen-Chang. If I write the exam with this pen, then I'm certain I'll pass."

"Has this worked for you previously?" asked Leona.

"Every time," Katia answered. "It's a sure thing."

CHAPTER 10

TAIPEI

CHOONG LO TOOK the chair at the far end of the conference table, facing Lionel at the other end. Choong gave the appearance of a comfortably seated business man displaying a congenial yet professional smile.

"Thank you for coming to meet our scientists today, Choong," stated Chang. "We will not keep you long. Please remind me, where did you grow up?"

"I grew up in Hong Kong," he responded. "My parents were educators. When they moved to Taipei to teach, I was only twelve years old. I've been living here ever since. It is my plan to major in biology at Fu Jen University. I'm grateful that TaiCom will provide a laboratory internship site for me."

"Now, Choong, please tell us why you are here."

"Of course, Lionel. I'm a guinea pig, so to speak. I volunteered to undergo a chip implant so that Lionel—that is, Dr. Chang—and his colleagues could experiment with some new device they're working on. Nice to see you again, Dr. Bourne," he said, nodding in the surgeon's direction. "I do not know the details, but I have been happy to cooperate. After all, it's science, you know."

With an intrigued expression on her face, Geraldine Bourne leaned forward to speak. She began, "Mr. Lo, do you..."

"Please stop right there," interjected Lionel, simultaneously tapping a key on his computer. "Please, Dr. Bourne, remember exactly what you were going to say. In a few minutes, I'll signal to you by rubbing my right eye. At that point, I would like you to resume your present posture and then complete your sentence. Can you remember to do this?"

"Why, of course, but..."

"Thank you," said Lionel, again cutting her off. As eyes around the table drifted toward Choong Lo, they noticed how still he was sitting. Choong Lu's eyes were open, but he certainly was not seeing anything. His face was expressionless.

Then, the clicking of Lionel's laptop computer keys filled the quiet of the room. Suddenly, Mr. Lo's face regained expression as he looked around the table making eye contact.

"Wie heissen Sie?" asked Lionel.

"Ich heisse Helmut Klein," answered Mr. Lo. Odd. Out of place. His German seemed perfect. But Mr. Lo appeared thoroughly Chinese. How could this be?

"Wo sind Sie geboren?" Lionel inquired.

"Ich bin in Heidelberg geboren, Doktor Chang. Aber, Sie wissen das, nicht wahr?"

"Können Sie Englisch?"

"Genau," answered Mr. Lo, as Helmut Klein. "Of course I can speak English. But you know this, don't you, Doctor Chang."

"Where did you learn your English?"

"In the gymnasium. When I was a young person in school in Heidelberg I had English lessons every day. Now, at the university, much of our reading is in English language texts."

The faces of those sitting around the table were aghast with surprise. Just what was happening here? It appeared that this one body held two entirely different people.

With a touch of flair, Lionel pressed a key on his laptop. Mr. Klein's face went into immediate rigor mortis. Although he continued breathing, Mr. Klein's body seemed to be in suspended animation. Lionel typed in another code.

When Mr. Klein's face regained its expression, he looked around the room to acknowledge his surroundings and make eye contact with those in attendance.

Lionel began, "And what is your name?"

"Why, Charles Worthington. But you know this already, Doctor Chang," responded a third personality inhabiting the body of Choong Lo. "Oh, I guess you want these good people around the table to know too, eh, mate?"

"Where were you born, Charles?"

"In Adelaide, Australia. I'm now attending Charles Sturt University in Canberra. Studying biology. I'm visiting Taiwan on holiday."

The conspicuous finger of Lionel once again punched a laptop key. Charles froze in position. Lionel addressed his incredulous guests.

"As we said a few minutes ago, we can send updates to the *NeoEncyclopedia Britannica* and into the memories of those persons with chips. With this capacity, we can actually do more. We can temporarily erase the brain's existing memory completely and substitute a new one. In fact, we can create an entirely new identity through memory substitution. Because of the well-known principle that *neurons that fire together wire together*, the substitute memory controls muscle usage so that the person gets the correct childhood pronunciation of words. Previous athletic and musical skills return in rough form, so that only a little practice raises them to their previous performance level. This amounts to a virtual personality transplant with the same technology we would otherwise use for IA."

Mouths dropped around the table. Questions were fired at Lionel and impressive answers given. The room became electric.

Neshat asked as if thinking out loud, "Does this mean we can order assassinations via satellite? Can we finally make our own Manchurian Candidate?"

Lionel launched into yet another brief dissertation. "Assassinations are the old-fashioned way of doing things. A new era is about to dawn. By refining the technology, we need not fully replace a memory. We can alter it slightly, diminish it, enhance it or add new material. By strategically placing persons with TaiCom implants around the world, we could become very influential. From our satellite control center we could influence debates on the floor of the U.S. Congress or the U.K. Parliament. We could direct bank executives in their decision-making. We could direct the decisions generals make on the battlefield. We could...well, you get the idea."

"But I still want to know about assassinations," pressed Neshat. "What if..."

"We have learned one thing so far, even though our research is by no means complete. What we have learned is this: even with an altered memory, a person's moral character remains basically unaltered. Even if you substitute a new memory and ask a person to carry out an immoral deed, the moral law within retains its hold on that person's conscience. When we use the TaiCom implant for espionage, we can only expand on the moral commitments a person has already made; we cannot compel someone to violate their conscience. Here is the implication. If we wish to foster violence, then we must select an original brain already wired for violence, or better, an original brain already so committed to some noble cause that the individual has already considered violence against his or her opponents. In the latter case, it'll only take a little push to get the job done."

Lionel seemed to interrupt himself by turning to Geraldine. "Now, Dr. Bourne, do you recall what you were going to say? If so, finish it when I rub my eye." Lionel then pressed the computer key and rubbed his right eye. After a second's pause, it was clear that Choong Lo was back in the room.

Geraldine continued. "...have any pain associated with your

implant? Do you think about it very often? Does it affect your daily life?"

"No pain," said Lo. "Because I can't feel it, I don't think about it. Anyway, it's not been activated. Lionel—I mean, Dr. Chang—has not yet turned it on. So, I simply remain myself."

The room itself seemed to gasp.

"Do you know Helmut Klein?" asked Geraldine with intensity.

"Who? No, I don't recognize the name," answered Lo.

"How about Charles Worthington?" asked Buzz with a knowing smile.

"No, I don't believe I know that person either," was Lo's answer.

CHAPTER 11

TAIPEI

LEONA AND KATIA walked casually through the press of worshippers and stepped up to the front porch of the main hall. Through the drifting smoke, the larger than life gilded statue of Quan Yin appeared, seated in lotus position with her right hand raised in benediction. Ordinarily she would be holding an alabaster water jar in her left hand. In this case her empty left hand simply indicated meditation. Her serene face was encircled by a halo, which was in turn engulfed in a penumbra of flames. The Quan Yin statue exuded mercy and peace.

Leona and Katia crammed themselves between others praying at the fence protecting the statue from her devotees by a distance of twenty feet. The two women could feel each other's shoulder as they whispered reports of what they were viewing.

"Well, I think...." Katia's voice stopped mid-sentence. Leona, still staring at Quan Yin, no longer felt the press of Katia's shoulder. Leona turned to learn why. Katia's head had dropped so her chin was resting listlessly on her chest. To her bewilderment, Leona watched as Katia's body fell limp. Her yellow sundress was now red, stained with the flow of blood. In Katia's back, a knife.

Leona, simultaneously confused and alert, visually scoured the crowd while grabbing for Katia's body and lowering it gently to the ground. Leona's eyes caught a quick snapshot: a male foot below a loosely-fitting gray pant leg, shod in a dark brown sandal. That foot was too close and seemed out-of-place. Leona dove through the crowd. The man to whom the foot belonged ran toward the large brass incensory with Leona only a few feet behind. Soon he found himself in a garden apron at the balcony's edge.

Without hesitating to look, the man leapt, landing on the pavement eight feet below, somewhat unstable in his sandals. He was caught by a husky Buddhist monk in a mustard yellow robe. The monk grabbed the man and pulled him safely to his feet, continuing to hold him. Yelling from the balcony to the monk, Leona said, "He's a killer! Hold him for me!"

The expression on the monk's face registered that he did not understand English. Leona was now able to fully see the face and form of Katia's attacker: medium height, dark complexion, round face with broad features, perhaps Mongolian. A large bandage covered his forehead over the right eye. *I'm sure I've seen this thug before,* Leona addressed herself in a fraction of a second. *He's wearing the red badge of honor I gave him last night.* The assassin wiggled in his captor's arms. Soon he was free and running toward the front gate. The monk stood there perplexed. Leona quizzed herself, *Do I chase him? Or, do I return to help Katia?* She decided on the latter.

Leona knifed back through the crowd and knelt at Katia's side. The dying Katia could not talk. She grasped Leona's hand desperately. Into Leona's palm she pressed an object, a small round object wrapped in a tiny plastic bag.

CHAPTER 12

TAIPEI

Lily, who had left the room briefly, returned. She leaned over to whisper into Lionel Chang's right ear. The smile disappeared. His face became red. His eyebrows curled inward. The muscles in his jaw tensed up.

Lily whispered a second time.

Without looking at his guests, Chang stood and hurried toward the exit.

Lily addressed the group with a plastic smile. "Mr. Chang has been suddenly called away. I'm terribly sorry. Our meeting is concluded. We will stay in touch via cell phone. Check your text messages. We will continue discussing the business plan on Monday. Ten o'clock. Right here."

CHAPTER 13

TAIPEI

LILLIAN YANG STOOD by the elevator door, head bowing, her left arm gracefully stretched to direct each departing guest into the cab. Last in line was Khalid Neshat, who hesitated and looked directly into Lilly's eyes.

"Don't you want to get in, Mister Neshat?" she asked.

"Oh, no. Let them go," he answered while stepping back from the elevator door.

Lilly watched while the elevator closed and began its descent.

"Thank you for a well-organized meeting, Lilly. I'm sure Mr. Chang properly appreciates your skills."

"Oh, he does. What more may I do for you, Mr. Neshat?"

"Please call me Khalid. You certainly like to please Mr. Chang's guests, don't you?"

"Yes, of course. What more may I do for you, Khalid?"

"Let me show you something." Khalid Neshat led Lily down the hall away from the TaiCom office. After turning two corners they arrived at a large door, perhaps a service door, almost flush with the wall. Neshat removed a blank credit card from his pocket and swiped it on the electronic receptor affixed to the wall. What appeared originally to be a service door was actually two doors that split open, revealing an elevator. Neshat extended his hand, welcoming the executive assistant aboard the gondola. She complied with a mixture of trust, curiosity and courtesy. Once in the elevator, Neshat swiped the card again, pressed the button for Floor 101, and stood still looking at the young woman.

"I did not know this elevator was here," remarked Lily.

"Be ready to learn much," responded Neshat. He reached tenderly toward her left ear. "What lovely earrings," he said softly, while his right hand momentarily lifted the delicate jade Yin-Yang swinging from her pierced ear. Lily shyly lowered her eyes, experiencing an unfamiliar melding of flattery and embarrassment.

It took only seconds for the elevator to reach 101. The two stepped out onto a floor Lilly had never seen before. The entry area was dimly lit and devoid of furniture. Lily observed several doors around the perimeter, each labeled with letters and numbers with no particular sequence or pattern. Walls, doors, and ceiling were all painted a non-descript off-white. The floor was industrial gray. *Strange, thought Lily, for such an exclusive floor.* Neshat escorted her down a long corridor to the right of the elevator, stopping in front of one more plain doorway with a sign in Chinese, Farsi, and English —"Khalid Neshat." The magic card opened this door as well.

Behind this ordinary door was a wondrous world of the rich. Lily was awestruck as she slowly stepped into the expansive room, as if matching the tempo of an exquisite adagio. She moved around the room, admiring the aesthetic accouterments of every detail, including the soft lighting. It was combination office and private personal nest, complete with a large television screen, antiques, brocade upholstery, and a well stocked bar.

"Might I pour you some cognac?" asked Neshat.

"No, I don't drink alcohol," she responded. "But you go ahead."

"I shouldn't, you know. I'm Muslim. Yet, when in Taipei...do as the Romans do." He poured Martell cognac into a snifter, then a drew a glass of sparkling water for his guest.

The Iranian walked slowly toward the Taiwanese woman, staring into her eyes. Her eyes locked on his. Neshat handed her the glass of sparkling water. She took a sip, her eyes never leaving his. Neshat gently set his cognac on the table and placed his expansive hands on her delicate shoulders in one artful movement.

"Do you really like to please?" he asked.

"Yes, of course. But, Mr. Neshat, I don't...."

"Khalid, I said." Then, while holding her firmly, he planted his lips on hers. At first she stood motionless, receiving but not reacting. His left hand moved slowly down her back while his right hand massaged her shoulder in rhythmic circles. He leaned forward, his lips still touching hers. Khalid's lips undulated gently against hers until she responded in synchronized movements. He then plunged his tongue passionately into her mouth.

He removed her lightweight jacket, never allowing his lips to leave hers. He ran the fingers of his right hand down the center of her half-exposed back. With his left hand he cupped her small, firm right breast. He gripped her now taut nipple between his third and fourth fingers. Her body moved, swayed, undulated.

He pulled her dress straps off her shoulders, slowly, one at a time, dropping the dress onto the floor. Still kissing her, he unsnapped her bra and let that fall. His face fell to her neck, kissing gently yet firmly. Sweeping his lips downward he paused to suck briefly on each breast nipple. Soon he was on his knees, removing her dainty panties, and burying his face in her bush.

He felt for his own belt buckle. He opened his front and let his trousers fall. Then he sat down on the couch and drew the now pliant female body toward his. In moments she was astride him. He went deep within her. Her now energized body whirled clockwise, then counterclockwise. Up and down. In and out. Like lava surging up from within a volcano, he could feel an eruption coming. So could she. He screamed. So did she. He thrust upward. She downward. Both screamed as ecstasy erupted.

CHAPTER 14

TAIPEI

THEY LAY flat on the sofa for a few minutes. Lilly's eyes were closed when she heard Neshat gruffly say, "Get dressed." It sounded like an order to a soldier from a general.

She had finished dressing when he again handed her the water. She thanked him. She took a long, thirst-quenching swallow. Neshat's facial expression acknowledged nothing. She sipped again from her glass.

"Let me show you something special about this room," he said pedantically. "Set down your glass and come with me."

She walked toward him. She stumbled slightly when bumping into the arm of a chair. Lily regained her composure and followed his gesturing hand. He led them both toward an exterior wall.

"The air pressure in here is three PSI greater than what is outside. This means I can have a window that opens."

Khalid placed his own glass of cognac on an end table. He approached the wall of green double paned windows and pressed a button. One five-by-five foot pane slowly slid sideways into a sleeve like a pocket door.

She approached Neshat to look out into the mysterious clouds shrouding the building's middle floors. The two bent down to see the cloud girdling Taipei 101.

"Ahh," she said, turning toward her host with eyes big in amazement.

The Iranian smiled. He reached his left hand toward her right ear. He briefly fondled the earring before yanking it, tearing through the skin and shredding her earlobe. She screamed as his left hand slammed onto her right ear. She could feel the blood gushing.

Then Neshat stretched out his arms. One went down between her legs, the other around her shoulder, gripping her back. In one seamless swing her body went up. He thrust the now astonished and horror stricken woman out the window. He watched briefly as her body flailed helplessly and then disappeared into the cloud below.

Neshat closed the window. He straightened his clothes. He walked to the hallway door. He turned to survey the room, then walked back and placed the two drinking glasses in the wet bar sink. He rinsed them and stood them upside down in the drainer. Returning to the hallway door he flipped out the lights and departed.

Because I can.....

CHAPTER 15

TAIPEI

AT THE AGREED upon time Leona paced back and forth just inside the Lungshan Temple gate. It had been hours since the murder. Leona had been questioned by police as a material witness and then released. Very few visitors to the temple this Friday evening were even aware of the dramatic events earlier that day.

The temple was lit up as colorfully as a Fourth of July fireworks display. Pilgrims sauntered past her, entering and departing in a way that was simultaneously casual and purposeful. Most walked upright, but some in wheelchairs were being pushed, while still others limped slowly with a cane or crutch.

Leona's cell phone buzzed in her purse. *Another text from Angie,* she said to herself. *I've got a lot to report. But I need to talk now with Bernard Lee, not Angie.* But she saw no such person in the temple apron.

Time passed. *Might this Lee guy have suffered the same fate as Katia?* she quizzed herself. She studied her surroundings. *Maybe he'll never come. Then what do I do? Maybe I have been duped.*

As she turned her head she noticed a wheelchair in her vicinity.

An elderly woman with a scarf covering most of her head was sitting quietly, unmoving. Beneath the tatters of her ragged skirt Leona noted what appeared to be strong, muscular legs, leading her to wonder just what had crippled her. The elderly woman smiled at the American visitor and beckoned her with a slight hand movement. Fearing confusion should she try to talk with an invalid unable to speak English, Leona walked over and gently placed a hand of affection on the sitting woman's shoulder.

Leona could hear an indiscernible mumble. She leaned down and in a strong whisper said, "I'm sorry. I don't speak Chinese."

Then Leona heard the voice speak in a forceful whisper, "Cyrus Twelve," in unmistakable English. "Push me, Miss Foxx. I'm Bernard."

Leona's face remained expressionless, but her chest pounded with the feeling of unexpected surprise. "For the sake of Breslau," she mumbled. Soon she was pushing the wheelchair out the temple gate and along the sidewalk. No conversation took place. Leona simply pushed forward, awaiting the next directive.

It came at the corner. "Here," said Bernard. "This van is waiting for us."

Leona could not read the red Chinese characters painted on the side of the white van. A large sliding door opened. Down dropped a hydraulic platform. Leona pushed the wheelchair into place. Bernard Lee was hoisted into the vehicle. Leona found a seat near the rear. The side door closed and the van entered the traffic.

CHAPTER 16

TAIPEI

"What's it say on the side of the truck?" Leona asked the man in the wheelchair.

"This is a Presbyterian transportation service for disabled persons," responded the man in a normal tone of voice.

"Why the disguise?" she asked.

"After last evening, it's clear that one of us, if not both of us, have been identified. The secret's out. I don't know for certain what secret, but at least one of us might be followed from time to time. Even if you were followed this evening, you'll look like a kindhearted American visitor helping a stranger. No one will suspect." Mr. Lee began to take off his disguise, revealing his jean shorts and t-shirt underneath.

"You're handy with a snake knife, Miss Foxx. I wonder if that goon is still fastened to the tabletop?"

Both laughed.

"Now, just how should I address you, Mr. Lee?"

"Huh? Oh. Just call me Bernie."

"No, I don't think so."

"Why not?"

"Well, you're nearly twice my age. And you've got a doctorate. Out of respect I should address you as Dr. Lee, right? Or, would you prefer Mr. Lee?"

Dr. Lee laughed with a look of opportunity on his face. "We're colleagues, aren't we? You've got a doctorate. Biology, is it?"

"Yes, biology with a special focus on astrobiology."

"Well, then I should call you Doctor Foxx, right? You can call me doctor and I'll call you doctor. We'll never be able to say anything because we're wasting time with formalities."

"This is getting ridiculous," said Leona. "I simply wanted to show appropriate deference to my honorable senior."

"Okay. You call me Bernie. I'll call you Leona."

"But my nickname is Lee."

"So should I call you Lee and you call me Lee?"

Both laughed.

"Bernie and Lee!" he said emphatically. "That's it. If you want to show me senior deference, then simply obey me: Bernie and Lee."

"Okay. Gotcha, Bernie."

"Do you have the chip with you?" asked Bernie.

"Yes, of course," answered Leona.

"May I?" He held out his hand.

Leona loosed the laces on her left running shoe, a New Balance 967. From a hidden pocket just under the arch, she withdrew a tiny plastic pouch and placed it into Bernie's open palm.

From under his t-shirt, Bernie turned on a miniature flashlight hanging from his neck on a lanyard. He studied the object carefully. He nodded with satisfaction. Then he placed the chip into his right front pocket.

"I'll give this back to you tomorrow or Sunday, Lee. Then you'll pass it to Katia and she'll return it to its rightful place at TaiCom before Monday morning."

"I have some bad news for you, Bernie. Very bad news." Leona recounted the details of Katia's murder.

Bernie displayed an almost uncontrollable disturbance. He put his head in his two hands and sobbed. "Poor Katia," he said repeatedly. "This just shouldn't have happened!"

A few minutes passed as Bernie attempted to gather his emotions. Leona sat quietly resting her hand on his in an effort to provide some consolation. Bernie eventually forced himself to sit up straight.

"Did Katia have a chance to pass on details? Such as the exact location at TaiCom where she would return the chip?"

"No. I'm afraid she had no time to say anything. I received the chip. That's all."

Bernie shook his head in dismay. Silence followed.

CHAPTER 17

TAIPEI

"Where are we going?" asked Leona. The van droned on, halting occasionally for traffic lights.

"Actually, I'm not going to tell you," said Bernie. "It would be good for you not to know some things, such as the location of our lab. Nevertheless, you're coming along. You'll get to see everything, even if you won't know where you are. You and I will need time to debrief one another. We've got a lot to talk about."

Bernie glanced at the driver. Leona looked past Bernie through the windshield, but she saw nothing to aid her in ascertaining her location. She shrugged her shoulders in compliance.

A half hour later, Leona heard a downshift and then felt the van ascending a hill on a curved road. Her body rocked from one side to the other with each curve. Bernie smiled at her.

"Kinda like a Disneyland ride," he said.

Leona nodded. She then felt the vehicle slow to make a sharp left turn, then stop abruptly. The driver rolled down his door window. A guard approached to speak with the driver. The two exchanged sentences in Chinese. Through the windshield Leona watched as a large garage door opened. The driver then entered the garage with the door closing behind them. When the engine had been killed, the side door was opened for them. Both Leona and Bernie exited, this time with Bernie walking.

In the spacious garage Leona noticed two other parked vehicles, one a Toyota Camry and the other a three-wheeled mini truck. A uniformed guard, a young man, bowed and gestured for them to follow him. He led them as far as an open door, then stopped while Bernie and Leona entered the building proper. The two visitors walked down a lengthy hall with closed doors on either side. No decorations. No door labels, save for one exception. Midway down the hall hung two pictures, one on each side facing the other. On the left hung a picture of Chiang Kai-shek. Directly opposite hung a picture of Mao Zedong.

Toward the end of the hall, a door opened. Out stepped a young woman dressed in a white lab coat, standing stiffly to hold the door open, assuming that Bernie and Leona would know they should enter. She bowed her head slightly as they passed her.

Leona found herself in a small nondescript room with only a wooden bench against the wall to the right. In front of them stood a large metal door with a frosted glass window. Once the woman in the lab coat had secured the door behind them, she walked around to place her hand on the handle of the second door. Then she looked at Bernie and spoke in Chinese. Whatever Bernie said in response communicated understanding.

The woman pressed down on the handle and opened the large metal door. Leona felt a slight blast of air as the door opened. She and Bernie stepped into an even smaller room, about the size of a large closet. The door closed behind them. Bernie looked up at Leona.

"This is a low pressure chamber," he said. "The next room is high pressure. We don't want to take any contaminated outside air into the lab with us."

Leona studied the tiny chamber, finding nothing interesting or curious to fix on. It was painted gray and looked as sterile as the air was pure. Though she was not prone to claustrophobia, this suffocating space could provoke it.

After thirty long seconds, the second door opened. Leona eagerly stepped through. Bernie had done this routine multiple times, so he was nonplused. Again, Leona felt the slight blast of pressurized air rush past her. It was refreshing. They were now in one of the favorite playgrounds of the spy world—the analysis laboratory.

CHAPTER 18

TAIPEI

THE LARGE ROOM had a warehouse feel about it, high ceilings with visible joists and ducts. Every inch was painted or furnished in white. It was immaculate and obviously well-maintained. The research stations were lined up in rows, separated by artificial walls head high. The one row fully visible to Leona was lined on each side by computer terminals interspersed with additional equipment such as printers, microscopes, oscilloscopes, freezers, a walk-in Faraday Box, and some unidentifiable machines on desktops.

The two new arrivals were greeted by a young Chinese man—slender, bespectacled, with random tufts of hair standing straight up. *Geeks look the same the world over,* Leona thought. The geek bowed perfunctorily and Bernie responded. Leona added her bow.

Bernie passed the chip in its clear plastic pouch to the geek, who immediately held it up to background light to get a good look. He smiled and started to turn away. Bernie spoke in Mandarin and pointed his arm and hand toward the right. The geek nodded and then hurried to his workstation, where he placed the chip under an electron microscope.

After following Bernie for a hundred paces or so and then through a door, Leona found herself with him in a smallish lounge area. Comfortable, colorful divans lined the walls, accompanied by floor lamps. Bernie motioned that they sit at the dining table.

"We've missed our dinner, Lee. I trust you're hungry."

Leona nodded affirmatively. Bernie called over his shoulder, again in Chinese. Soon a woman appeared in a kitchen apron, smiling and bowing. After a few seconds of interchange, the woman disappeared back into her kitchen, returning with two large soup bowls, which she placed before the two dinner guests, along with napkins and soup spoons. On a second trip she brought a pot of tea, two handleless cups, and a small bamboo dish with six hard boiled eggs. The eggs were shelled and dark brown in color. She placed the brown bomb-like globules between the two diners.

"What's this, may I ask?" Leona said to Bernie.

"Oh, these are hundred-year-old eggs. We bury them in the ground, leave them for a century, and then dig them up to eat. Appetizing, eh?"

"Really?"

"No, of course not. They're buried for only one year."

Bernie turned and addressed the kitchen woman, who was watching as the meal commenced. She exited and returned with two twenty-ounce bottles of beer and small drinking glasses. "The beer will help wash down all tastes," Bernie said with a knowing smile.

Leona looked at the miscellany swimming in her dark-colored soup. A shrimp was identifiable. Maybe some seaweed. But what was that? A chicken's foot?

Bernie was busily eating. Leona asked, "Where's the rice?"

"Rice?"

"Yes, rice. I always have rice with Chinese food."

"Oh." Bernie called for the kitchen woman to bring some rice. Momentarily she appeared and placed a small cup of white steamed rice in front of Leona, along with a pair of chopsticks. *I suppose I should forget the idea of asking for brown rice*, she thought. She dipped the spoon into her soup just deep enough to siphon off the surface liquid, which she sipped gingerly. *Now, how can I appear gracious and still avoid eating those repulsive eggs?*

"THIS IS AN EXPENSIVE CHIP," said Leona. "It's already cost at least one life. Why's it so valuable?"

Bernie sipped his soup much more joyously than Leona. "It's a brain implant. TaiCom's been working on it for some years now. Its alleged purpose is Intelligence Amplification. But that's a misconception, because nobody knows how to actually enhance intelligence. What it does is provide artificial memory, access to data through thought. It may also extend the range of computational capacity, just like your laptop."

"Would you call this an advance in medical research?" asked Leona.

"If that were all it was, then we wouldn't be trying to steal the design," said Bernie.

At that moment the lab door opened and the geek walked in. He joined the two soup eaters at the table and requested the kitchen help to bring him a beer.

"Perhaps introductions are in order," said Bernie. "Leona, this is Pang Boo Wah, or Boo Wah Pang for you, a Westerner. Boo Wah, this is Leona." They shook hands. Boo Wah then poured himself a glass of beer and drank through the foam.

"What've you learned?" asked Bernie. "Can you copy it?"

"It's copying right now," said Boo Wah. "My computer is tracing the circuits as we speak. I have not analyzed it completely yet, but it's quite a device! I found a segment coded for DNA interface. It includes nano-activators to stimulate DNA replication with special promoters for specific genes. What I think this means is that TaiCom plans to implant it surgically and have it grow into the recipient's brain tissue, just as if it belongs there. If they pad it with sample

DNA from the recipient, they'll avoid immune rejection. Clever." He took another slug of beer.

I suspect this geek's been to an English-language university, Leona told herself. *Perhaps American, given the accent.*

"I believe we suspected this," added Bernie. "What else?"

"I haven't found the thought trigger yet, but I expect I will. The memory is finite, as one would expect in a device this small, yet it has the capacity of an encyclopedia. What will be both necessary and desirable, of course, is to update it constantly. That way the recipient can have access to the best data."

"How will they update the memory?" asked Leona.

The geek smiled. Bernie smiled. "Now, Lee, we're getting to what our concern is. Tell her, Boo Wah."

"What Bernie suspected and what I have just verified is this: the implanted chip will be wirelessly connected to an orbiting satellite. The satellite can send signals that will be received directly by the person's brain."

"That sounds efficient to me," added Leona.

"Now, Leona," said Bernie, "let's think this one through. What are the implications?"

"What I have confirmed and Bernie had predicted," Boo Wah said, looking at Leona, "is that the receiver and transmitter will have multiple functions. The satellite can send signals that will erase portions of the artificial memory and substitute new material. In principle, this exchange and alteration could take place at any time, perhaps even many times per day. On the one hand, it could mean that the human person on the ground would have uncanny access to mountains of information that could make him or her function like a genius in relevant situations. On the other hand, the entire setup is ripe for abuse."

Bernie was nodding his head, acknowledging what Boo Wah was saying. His smile had that I-told-you-so expression. He turned to look straight at Boo Wah. "What about tracking? Do you think the chip will enable the satellite listener to discern what the recipient is thinking? Will mental eavesdropping be possible?"

"To me, the chip looks like it will have this capacity," said Boo Wah.

Bernie turned toward Leona. "Now consider this. Once the chip has been implanted in an individual, the satellite beam will track that person everywhere, twenty-four seven. The eavesdropper could sit by a monitor and track this person's location and—now get this—and even read the target's thoughts. Read the target's thoughts!"

"Wow!" exclaimed Leona. "Every thought?"

"No, only those thoughts connected to the chip. But there's more," added Bernie. "By manipulating the content of the memory card, the tracker could introduce material that would contribute to the very thinking of the recipient. The recipient might even confuse what's been sited in the memory with his or her own thoughts. This positions the tracker on the verge of thought-influence, almost at the point of thought-control. With this system in the hands of our enemy, each person with a chip implant would become a Trojan Horse, or even a guided missile."

CHAPTER 19

TAIPEI

"I can imagine," said Leona, "a diabolical plot unfolding when an implant recipient in a security force is suddenly told to assassinate a prime minister, or a president, or even the Queen. But I can think of something even worse!"

"What's that?" asked the two men.

"What would be worse would be to go commercial. Sell the chip on the open market. Millions of people would purchase implants, and then the guy you call the tracker would put advertising directly into everybody's brains. We couldn't even bury our head in a pillow to escape advertising."

The three chuckled together. Leona added, "I'd really like to see this thing work. I would love to be the guinea pig."

"You'll never get the chance," said Dr. Lee.

CHAPTER 20

TAIPEI

Boo Wah rose from his chair and disappeared back into the lab. "I'll see how the copying is going," he said while the door was closing.

"So, what's our plan?" asked Leona, turning toward her new partner.

Bernie's smile seemed to be engraved on his distinctive face. "After Boo Wah is satisfied with his copy, he will alter the original. This will cause it to malfunction. Then you will replace it at TaiCom. At some point in the future, when TaiCom is about to activate it, a surprise will interrupt them. They won't know what's wrong. This should set them behind a few months in their clinical trials. This will provide us with the time we need to formulate a counterstrategy."

"But why are you suspecting anything sinister at all with TaiCom? Maybe TaiCom simply wants to sell a new product that could have great commercial value."

"Even if that were the case, we would still need to monitor what's going on. Actually, the situation is a bit more ominous. This week TaiCom is holding meetings with technical people and investors who represent the Transhumanist movement. Transhumanism is an ideology that seeks to improve the human race through a technological increase in the speed of evolution. To date, Transhumanism is not political, even though a strong endorsement of global capitalism is at the center of its belief system. There was a transhumanist candidate for the presidency of your country in a recent election, but he did not gain much in the way of votes. As soon as the movement becomes political, it could turn fascist. Not necessarily, of course, but with this technology the temptation might be just too great to resist."

"Are they really bad guys?"

"Oh, no. They're not bad guys at all. Just idealists, as far as I can tell. What we're trying to do here is anticipate the future. Look at the possibilities. We want to head them off at the pass, as you used to say in the old Western movies."

"Not bad guys, eh. What happened while you were eating snake the other night? What happened to Katia? For the sake of Bremerton, Bernie, the storm clouds are already on the horizon."

"We don't know who's responsible for this violence. But we'll find out."

CHAPTER 21

TAIPEI

THE LAB DOOR opened and Boo Wah came back in. He resumed his seat and picked up his beer. "Done!"

"Were you able to copy it?" asked Bernie.

"Completely. No problem." Boo Wah opened his hand and threw a half dozen peanut-sized circuit chips on to the table. They spread out like dice.

"What about the alteration?" Bernie pressed.

Boo Wah selected one chip from the table. He held it up and then responded. "That turned out to be easier than I had anticipated. I simply severed one microconnection. This disables the interactive transmission capacity. This will still permit TaiCom to download information prior to implantation and to integrate the chip with a person's DNA. It will even permit additional satellite input. But those guiding the operation will be unable to read the thoughts of the implantee. The flaw will not be discovered until they test transmission. This should befuddle them." Boo Wah chugged a glass of beer as a celebration. Then he placed the altered chip in front of Bernie.

"Is there any reason we cannot give the chip back to Leona right now?" asked Bernie.

"No. It's hers."

Leona's face looked wan, but her eyes marked the location of each chip on the table. She reached with her right hand for the altered chip, while her elbow covered a second chip. She swept both up into her left hand, closing it before anyone could see she was holding two chips, not one. "Well, I just don't know how to thank you two boys for such a lovely gift," she said sarcastically. "How did you mark the altered chip, Boo Wah?"

"You'll see I've marked the edge with a blue felt-tipped pen—virtually invisible unless you're looking for it."

Leona did not look in her hand. "Now just how do you expect me to slip this back into TaiCom's inventory without being discovered?"

"I'm just a lab geek," said Boo Wah. "How would I know? You're the spy."

"It's got to be Monday morning," said Bernie, addressing Leona. "Katia worked at TaiCom, on the 83rd floor of Taipei 101. She had planned to return it on Monday before office hours, hoping that nobody would have missed it over the weekend. But now we have a problem. Just where at TaiCom is the chip's home? Katia knew, but we don't. If you put it in the wrong place, then it will be obvious that it had been moved. But maybe that's the best that we can get away with."

"Why wait until Monday? Why don't I try to break into TaiCom tonight?" Leona quizzed her comrades.

"Because weekend security is impenetrable. All who come and go are registered. Records are kept. Even Katia would not have tried it on the weekend, and she has...or had...official clearance. The building is unlocked Monday at 6:00am. Most offices don't open until 8:00am. So that's your window, Leona. Do you think you can handle it?"

"I guess I'll have to make it work," pined Leona.

CHAPTER 22

CHICAGO

A HANDSOME AFRICAN American man wearing a white alb without a stole approached the front of the chancel at Trinity Lutheran Church. "Good morning," he said.

"Good morning," chimed those in the pews. A sense of quizzical tension pervaded the congregation because they did not see the familiar face of Leona Foxx in front of the altar.

"No doubt you were expecting to see Pastor Lee here this morning," he continued. "She is in Taiwan at the moment. She's there on a brief vacation, eating plenty of Chinese food. She sends you all her warm greetings and best wishes." A sense of relief overtook the assembly. There was nothing to worry about—their pastor would soon return.

"For those of you who have not met me, I'm Graham Washington," said the black man in the alb. "You may call me Pastor Gee. As you know, some months ago I was sent to Trinity by our presiding bishop, Justin Hurley, as a Parish Listener. The bishop wanted to learn more about Trinity's mission and activities here on the south side of Chicago. Because I know your parish well now, Pastor Lee asked if I would conduct the worship service with you this morning in her absence. She also asked if Hillar Talin would serve as acolyte." He turned with his hand directing all eyes to the teenager sitting in the rear of the chancel. Hillar was a lanky teenaged boy with liberty-spiked hair and a twenty-gauge stainless steel nose ring. Hillar stood briefly, blushed, and sat down again.

"Today is a special Sunday. Tomorrow is Memorial Day, so perhaps we should take a moment to honor those of us in this room who have served in America's armed forces. Those of you who have served in the U.S. Navy, would you please stand up." Three healthy young men rose to their feet, two Anglo and one African American. All three had worn their uniforms for the occasion.

"Remain standing please. Now, those of you who were or are soldiers in the Army." One stood up, a woman. She reached down to aid her pew partner, a man. As he gained stability, all could see him leaning on a crutch. One leg was missing. Both smiled.

"Do we have any Marines?" Three men rose and were added to those standing. A fourth waved from his wheelchair.

"Coast Guard?" Two young men stood.

"Finally, what about the U.S. Air Force?" This added two more.

"These men and women have served our country. The rest of us owe them gratitude, because they have defended our freedom as Americans. They...."

"What about Sven Fiske?!" an anonymous voice shouted. Other voices blended in. "Yes, what about Sven?"

An elderly troll-looking man in the front row sporting a large hearing aid, perhaps a centurion, was struggling to his feet. He gripped his cane with two hands. Graham smiled and directed his attention at the senior. "Sven, where did you serve?"

"I fought with the Norwegian insurgency against Nazi Germany," he uttered. Because it was difficult to hear, his daughter, Lena Fiske Brandt, repeated it loudly and proudly so the entire congregation could hear.

"That's marvelous," Graham added, his eyes still on the elderly veteran. Then he turned to the congregation. "Let's show our appreciation for our men and women in uniform." Applause broke out. Some clapping rose to their feet. Then the entire room was on its feet. The applause lasted much longer than Graham expected.

Graham motioned for everyone to be seated. "As part of our memorial, I've asked one member of Trinity to say a few words. Orpah Tinnen knows firsthand the sacrifice a military family makes. Orpah?"

Mrs. Tinnen made her way from a pew to the chancel. Graham handed the African American woman a wireless microphone. She took it in hand, paused, and began to speak with unanticipated clarity and poise.

"The cost of freedom is high. I know. My family and I have paid the price. My father and my husband served in the U.S. Marine Corps. My father was killed in the first Iraq war. My husband died from an IED in the second Iraq war. Last year my son, Magnus, a Navy Seal, died while deployed in Afghanistan. These three men in my life sacrificed their lives so that we could live in freedom with democracy and security."

Graham's inner mind stirred. He could hear what no one else could hear rising up from within his disturbed conscience. *What bullshit! And Mrs. Tinnen believes so firmly in military sacrifice for freedom. Her father died for Texarab Oil Company. Her husband died for Houston's windfall profits. Her son Magnus died not in Afghanistan but rather in a secret war in Iran. All she got from the Pentagon was a flask of ashes, probably from a burned fence post. But she believes this was a sacrifice for freedom. I guess when human lives get wasted, it's better to believe there's some sort of meaning that blesses them. Now I've got to stop this pessimism*, Graham told himself. *I've got to lead worship, goddamit.* Graham struggled to regain his composure and his public face.

Following Mrs. Tinnen's personal reflections, the congregation stood to sing, "America the Beautiful." When the descant kicked in on "God shed his grace on thee," Graham's double-mindedness disappeared and he sang with gusto.

CHAPTER 23

CHICAGO

"Go in peace. Serve the Lord," Graham called out after arriving at the front door of Trinity Church following the recessional hymn. The congregation shouted back in unison like soldiers at attention: "Amen." Then Graham took the pastor's customary place on the church's porch to greet the exiting parishioners.

As the slow line of worshippers filed out, Graham shook hands, exchanged niceties, and complimented countless women on their hair or broach or dress. For the smaller children, Graham knelt as if for prayer to ask each child's name and provoke a laugh. He gave a humorous salute to those military veterans whom he had recognized, accompanied by, "Our nation thanks you for your service."

Many of these vets responded with something like, "Thank you for remembering us today." The eyes of more than one glistened with an uncontrolled tear.

One vivacious young African American woman presented herself to Graham as if she were auditioning. She was wearing an eye-catching Caribbean print dress with white quilted peep toe pumps. Graham's Y chromosome immediately directed his eyes to the filigree cross dangling from a golden chain. That cross was nestled snugly in the woman's cleavage. Graham nearly missed her hand when reaching for the handshake.

"Good morning, Pastor Gee," she sang out like a rooster at dawn.

"And, a good morning to you too," he replied with eager courtesy. "I don't think I've had the pleasure of meeting you. Welcome to Trinity Church, Mrs....?"

"That's Miss! Pastor Gee. I'm Trudy Lincoln. This is my first visit to your lovely church."

"Lincoln, eh. Did Henry Ford name a car after you?" Graham asked while trying to seed an exchange of smiles. When a quizzical look appeared on her face, indicating that she didn't get the joke, Graham continued almost without interruption. "Please feel welcome to come next Sunday and learn to like us."

"Actually, Pastor Gee," she said in a loud whisper, "I'd like to approach you about some questions I have about God and the Bible and my faith and things like that. Do you ever...." She broke off speaking. Then, she resumed, "Might you be available some time for a personal conversation?"

"Yes, of course," he responded with unusual alacrity.

"Should I make an appointment?"

"I don't have my appointment book handy. Perhaps we could exchange phone numbers and then make contact later in the week. Would that work for you?"

"That's a plan!" she exclaimed. Immediately she reached into her clutch bag and removed her cell phone. "Smile," she commanded while lifting it to her field of vision. "I need your photo for my directory." After snapping the picture and obtaining his mobile number, she dialed his number. He could feel the cell phone vibrate in his pocket; but he shied away from digging under his alb to pull it out.

"Now, you can call me, or I can call you," she said. Then, Trudy departed with an over-the-shoulder, "You'll be hearing from me."

CHAPTER 24

CHICAGO

ONCE THE CROWD had dispersed and Graham could catch a breath, he sensed he was still not alone. He was right. Hillar approached him slowly from the sanctuary, accompanied by someone Graham had never seen before. Graham took the initiative. "Now Hillar, just whom have you brought with you today?"

"Graham, I'd like you to meet my brother, Jaroslav. We call 'm Jerry," said Hillar, stretching his arm toward his sibling.

"Older or younger?" asked Graham, extending his hand.

"He's my older brother," interjected Hillar.

Jerry stared for an awkward moment at Graham's open hand, then after an embarrassing delay quickly engaged in the meshing of hands.

Hillar spoke. "Jerry's just moved in with Mom'n me. Right, Jerry?"

"Yeh," the older brother said, breaking his silence. "Yeh, I'm gonna bunk at home for a bit." He forced a smile.

"Jerry's a vet too," Hillar announced. "He fought in Afghanistan and against ISIS in Iraq. Secretly, ya know."

Graham could not recall Jerry standing up when he asked the veterans in worship to stand and be honored. "When did you get back from overseas?" he asked, looking Jerry straight in the eyes.

"Long time ago," Jerry mumbled. "Year or two, I reckon."

"What've you been doing since your discharge?"

"Nuthin' much. Hanging out with some of my military buddies," he muttered.

"Jerry's been living with his friends up on the North Side. Now, he's decided to come back home. Mom and I are glad he's back," said Hillar with a note of feigned victory in his voice.

"So, you're coming home!" added Graham, trying to maintain the victory tone.

"Actually," Jerry went on with his head now cast downward. "Gotta go somewhere. Our household broke up. One of my buddies...well....he hung himself last week. The other three of us...well...we just thought we couldn't live there in that place any more. So we went our own way."

"Jerry's got PTSD," interjected Hillar.

"That right, Jerry?" asked the pastor.

"Yeh. That's right." Jerry paused. His eyes looked around, as if to find a safer location. He shuffled his feet.

"Bad, eh?" muttered Graham, keeping his eyes on Jerry's. A moment passed. Hillar twitched. Graham maintained the stillness of a statue.

"How bad, Jerry?" asked Graham.

"I got to see a psychiatrist at the vet hospital. Said I got moral injury. That's the worst type of PTSD, ya know. Said it comes from battle trauma, or something like that."

Graham decided to conduct an interrogation. "Well Jerry, certainly you know better than a psychiatrist how you feel. Just how do you feel?"

"I feel bad. Real bad." This was followed by an interim pause.

"Is this why you didn't stand up during worship, when I asked all our vets to stand up?"

Jerry turned to look Graham in the face for the first time. "Pastor, I know you meant well. I know you meant well to honor all of us in the military. And I know you meant well when you thanked us for fighting for America's freedom. But that's just not the way it is."

"What do you mean, 'that's just not the way it is'?"

"I mean, nobody gets free because of our fighting. We'd sweep through a village about four in the morning, looking for insurgents. We'd knock down a house door and stomp in. Then, we'd shout in English, 'freeze or I'll shoot!' Hell, those people don't know English. They'd git up outa their beds to find out about the ruckus, and we'd pepper them with bullets. We'd kill children waking up. We'd leave children without their parents, cause we'd shoot their parents. Sometimes it seemed better just to shoot the whole family, so nobody'd be left alone. Then we'd go on to the next house. Nobody gets freedom from our merciless killing. Nobody. Not the Afghanis. Not the Iraqis. Not the Americans either."

Graham, Hillar, and Jerry remained standing like gravestone sculptures. Jerry continued. "I feel like I should be punished for what I did. But I'm not punished. I'm just put on a plane and sent home, back to this life in Chicago. Most o' those people in worship today got no inkling of what it's like to be over there, in the war zone, destroying people's homes and wasting the people who lived in them. But I know. I know the truth."

Graham and Hillar remained mute, waiting for what else might erupt. Jerry stared at his shoes. Then he lifted his face. "There's no justice, Pastor. I thought there'd be justice. I need to be brought to justice. All my buddies'n me need to be brought to justice. But there's no justice. There's only...nothing. I go home. We all go home. Except those whose homes we destroyed. Justice doesn't chase after us. If there were such a thing as justice, it would be chasing us. If there were such a thing as justice, it would chase after me like a greyhound chases a rabbit. But..."

Jerry looked at the horizon. "There's no God, Pastor. Your God is not there. Or, at least your God's justice is not there. And if there's no

God, then there's no me." At that, Jerry walked down the church porch steps to the parking lot. There he turned right and headed down the street toward home.

Hillar looked at Graham and shrugged his shoulders, communicating that he couldn't explain what had just happened.

CHAPTER 25

TAIPEI

At 6:05 Monday morning the cab dropped Leona off at Taipei 101. She entered the tower's main door wearing her New Balance 967s, Bermuda shorts, a t-shirt covered by a tennis sweater, carrying a canvas bag decorated with a large green 'S' monogram against a white background. Her sun glasses sat atop her head. Anyone looking at her at this time of day would quickly surmise that she was an American tourist suffering from jet lag.

The forlorn tourist wound her way past the arcades and up the escalator to the elevator floor. After smiling at sanitation workers and an occasional security guard, she sent herself up to the 83rd floor. When the elevator doors had closed behind her, it became obvious she was alone on the floor. Nothing was open. Everything was still. She wandered past office suites until she found the doors to TaiCom International. Two large sliding doors met in the middle, flanked with matching frosted glass side panels.

Leona looked carefully in both directions. Seeing no one, she reached into her canvas bag and drew out a small electronic device not much larger than a cell phone. She flipped the on-switch and studied the wiggling needle in front of the frequency register. She adjusted the dial. The needle on the frequency register settled. Leona pressed a switch. The doors unlatched and then slid open.

At first Leona did not enter. She held her scanner through the opening to find the wireless frequency for the alarm system. In a moment she had disarmed it, entered the suite, and closed and relocked the doors behind her.

The invader surveyed the situation. A traditional style reception desk held a computer monitor and an intercom station. A spacious reception room sat to her right, complete with comfortable couches and a tea table in the center. A hall to the left led to offices and perhaps even a lab. Directly behind the reception desk was the door to the president's office. The name, Mr. Lionel Chang, stood out in both Chinese and English characters.

If it were me, I'd keep the chip in the president's office. Maybe under lock and key. Or maybe under camouflage in a very ordinary location. Hmm.

She tried the president's door handle. Locked. *Is it an electronic or mechanical lock?* She jiggled the handle. *Ah. Mechanical.* From her bag she drew a small ring of keys, prepared in advance for just such occasions. In seconds the door was open and Leona entered the office.

The interloper walked slowly around the desk and sat in Mr. Chang's chair. From this vantage point she scanned the office with her eyes. A second door to the left. On the desk a massive computer screen. The keyboard with both Chinese and English characters. *Now, where would I put such a chip if I sat here day after day?* She took plenty of time to think.

Too much time. *Are those noises coming from the hall doors?* She heard the glass doors sliding open and human voices entering the suite. She glanced at her watch. Only 6:30 am. The president's office door was slightly ajar. *Do I have time to close it before being noticed? No!*

The volume and pace of the new voices increased. Even though the language was Mandarin, Leona could guess they'd discovered that the security system had been turned off. Excitement seemed to explode in the reception room. *Are those footsteps coming this way? Where to hide?*

Leona dove under the desk and scrunched herself into the kneehole. *I can't believe that I'm under a desk. How infantile! Why don't I...*

It became clear that the voices belonged to three men. They had switched to English. All three had entered the president's office, without noticing or at least without mentioning the fact that the door had been unlocked and ajar. Evidently they were standing facing one another, each chattering and competing for the others' attention.

"Two deaths?! At the same time?! Friday?!" This voice sounded to Leona like that of an American.

"Yes, Mister Kidd," responded a second voice with a distinctive Taiwanese accent. "This is what I am trying to investigate. Now Mr. Chang, clarify for me just how these two women were related to you?"

Chang spoke. "The first one was Ms. Lillian Yang, my executive assistant and receptionist. Her office is right in front of this one. We passed it on the way in."

"Is this the body we found on the ground Friday morning, a few minutes before one o'clock?"

"Yes. She must have thrown herself out of one of our windows," said Chang.

"Oh, I don't think so, Mr. Chang," said the police investigator. "Not from this office anyway. Her body was found on the other side of the building. What window might she have used? Is it not the case that all windows in Taipei 101 are sealed? Were any windows here on Floor 83 tampered with?"

"I don't know," muttered Chang.

"We will investigate this. Now tell me about the other woman."

"You know who it is," continued Chang. "Katia Rui. You told me your department is investigating her murder."

"That's right. She died by knife wound at the Lungshan Temple shortly after 12:00 o'clock noon on Friday. There were many witnesses. Now, this is just about the same time that Ms. Yang fell to her death, is that right?"

"You know better than I do," said Chang.

"Mr. Kidd?"

"Sorry, Officer, I am just learning about this for the first time. I met Lily Chang. I liked her a lot. But I simply don't know this second woman. I don't recall having met her."

"You didn't meet her, Buzz," said Chang. "Ms. Rui worked in a different office. One down the hall. She was a lab tech, a messenger from this office to our various lab sites around the city."

"Was she carrying a message when she was killed, Mr. Chang?" asked the investigator.

Chang paused. "No, she was taking an early lunch hour."

Leona sensed that one of the three was now sitting on the desktop, one foot still on the floor. Most likely, President Chang. She held her breath.

"Gentlemen," said Chang addressing his guests. "Perhaps we should continue this conversation in the reception room. We can make ourselves comfortable there. I might even be able to find us some tea."

"I'm ready for breakfast," said the American.

Leona heard them depart, closing the president's door. She breathed a long sigh of relief. *Now I have to make my decision immediately.* She stood up and looked around once again. She reached down into her left shoe and removed the pouch containing two microchips, the good copy plus the one with the altered circuit. She unwrapped the good copy and placed it on the computer keyboard above and between the F5 and F6 keys. She grabbed a Sharpie from the pen cup and removed the cap. She placed the open Sharpie lengthwise along the top of the row of F keys with the point only an eighth of an inch from the prize. She dropped the cap into the pen cup.

Now what? Leona studied the second door, the one to the left. She opened it and stepped into a small vestibule with three more doors. She closed the president's office door behind her. She opened the door to the left just a crack, then all the way. It was a toilet room, complete with wash basin and shower. After closing the bathroom door she opened the center door, revealing a cozy boudoir with a bed, plasma TV screen, and a wet bar. After closing this up she turned to the third door, the one on the right. She opened it just a crack, enough to peak. It led back to the reception room. It was at the far end, away from the reception desk and central doors. Leona listened.

The men were chattering again, but Leona could also hear a woman's voice. Eventually Chang explained to the other two in English. This new woman had graciously agreed on short notice to come into the office and serve as receptionist for the day. He would personally train her, but only after the three had eaten breakfast together and satisfied the gentleman from the police department. Would she mind remaining in the office for an hour until he could return? Yes, of course she would be willing. He told the temporary receptionist to keep the front doors closed until 8:00. Soon all was quiet.

Leona slipped through the door and silently sat herself on one of the lounge chairs. She picked up her cell phone to text Angie in Michigan. The young woman behind the reception desk looked around her new space and gave the desk chair an experimental spin. When her eyes caught sight of Leona, she was startled. Seeing that her guest was an American, she spoke in English, "Have you been waiting long?"

CHAPTER 26

TAIPEI

"You're done here in Taipei," Bernie told Lee over midmorning tea. "You can book your flight back to the States. But please, one more assignment."

"I'm done?" quizzed Leona. "That was pretty easy. You brought me all the way across the Pacific just to return a chip?"

"Actually, Lee," continued Bernard, "there's much more to it."

"I thought so."

"The reason Holthusen called you for this assignment has more to do with the long-term agenda. Your background in biology could be valuable. We thought you should start with us here in Taipei so you could get introduced to the players in this game. We fear this Transhumanism game might take quite a while to play out. We wanted you in with the starting gun."

"So, just who are these players?"

"Well, you've already met two, sort of. You just overheard Lionel Chang and Buzz Kidd. These are the two techie geniuses. They're committed Transhumanists, and they know their stuff. With these two as pilots, IA will take off at Mach One speed. Right now, as we're speaking, they're conducting a meeting at TaiCom with an international group of supporters, both techies and funders. What I predict is that they'll lay the groundwork for their first clinical trials. What I further predict is that somehow the clinical trials will involve the espionage community. We'll have to wait for details. Wait and watch. That's my job. And it's going to be your job too, even if you're only a part-time spy."

"What about the two dead women? I only got to know Katia for a few minutes, but I came to like her immediately. I find her murder most unsettling. And is there any connection with that poor woman who fell from high up Taipei 101?"

"The second woman was Lillian Yang, Chang's executive assistant and just as knowledgeable as her boss regarding the chip. As of now, I don't see any connection between the two murders. And they were both murders. Rule out suicide."

"Whom do you suspect?"

"Two possibilities. On the one hand, I suspect someone is trying to torpedo Chang's operation, steal the chip, and divert its use. But, on the other hand, Chang himself might be responsible for the hit on Katia Rui. It's quite likely that he discovered the chip was missing, deduced who had taken it, and ordered her immediate elimination. If this is the case, then it doesn't matter where you left the chip in Chang's office. He will simply think it had been moved, most likely by someone inside other than either Rui or Yang. He might even breathe a sigh of relief, thinking that no one outside TaiCom has seen it. We can only hope."

"But the Chang possibility does not explain the death—I mean murder—of his assistant."

"No, it does not, unless Chang suspected collusion between the two women. We can only speculate. Regardless, the chip is back where it belongs and we have done our job. At least for the time being."

"For the time being only?"

"Time never stops for us. Here's what you need to know. The

week after next, on Thursday evening, a meeting will take place in Silicon Valley, just south of San Francisco. It's a follow up to what's happening at TaiCom as we speak. NASA will host the meeting on behalf of a new joint venture between NASA Ames and a new institution, Transhumanist Technical University. Buzz Kidd is a big deficant at this so-called university. Somehow they've persuaded NASA scientists to throw in with them on shared research. I don't know the details. I suggest that you show up to meet some of the principals. This knowledge might come in handy later, even though we can't predict just how."

Leona smiled. "'Defecant'? I've never heard that word before. Is this Ph.D. level discourse?"

"In common English, I mean 'turd'."

"Thanks for the clarification. Back to this event. They certainly will not invite me into their strategy meetings."

"No, of course not. However, Thursday evening they'll hold a reception. All the hot shits will be there. So will you. Simply shake hands, measure smiles, and get noticed. Didya hear me: get noticed! This is the way we'll put money into the bank, so to speak. I'm giving you your official invitation and security clearance right now." Bernie slipped an envelope across the table. Leona placed it into her S bag.

"Can you find your way to O'Hare, to San Francisco, and to NASA?"

"That I can do, for the sake of Brussels. I've got an old friend who works at NASA. I'll try to connect."

"One more thing, Lee," said Bernie. "You didn't by accident take one of the viable chips, did you?"

Leona coughed briefly into her left hand. The two smiled, shook hands, and went their separate ways.

CHAPTER 27

TAIPEI

Lionel Chang was holding up the microchip in his right hand as the group assembled in the TaiCom conference room. It was housed in a fresh transparent plastic pouch. "I'll pass it around so each of you can feel the future in your own hands."

Members of the group expressed satisfaction as they felt the miniature treasure and passed it along. Chang demanded their attention and introduced a new member of the planning committee.

"I'm Wu Phee Seng, from Beijing," he said as he stood. He was unusually diminutive, short and skinny with a burr hair cut and glasses. "You Westerners may reverse it to Phee Seng Wu. I'm with the China Aerospace Corporation. The CSAC along with the China National Space Administration, or CNSA, are state-owned companies. Indirectly, I represent the government of the People's Republic of China. It is a pleasure to be present with you today." He sat and smiled.

"I have invited Dr. Wu to join us," said Chair Chang, "so he can help us with the transmission portion of our project. We plan to make use of NASA's satellite system for our communications. Dr. Wu will provide the expertise we need to negotiate with NASA and set up the system." All those around the table nodded in minibows. Dr. Wu responded in kind.

"Why not simply attach our TaiCom transmission capacity to a Chinese satellite?" asked Sharma. "Why NASA?"

Doctor Wu smiled with a knowing almost condescending smile. "Let me explain in strictest confidence. In order to secure our cryptography from surveillance, hacking, or piracy, we are using quantum transmissions. Perhaps you have heard of 'entanglement,' what Albert Einstein called 'spooky action at a distance'? When photons are entangled, what happens to one photon also happens to the other no matter how far apart they are. There is no causal connection. That's why the great physicist thought this is spooky. The Chinese Academy of Sciences in collaboration with the Austrian Academy of Sciences has put a satellite into orbit that can transmit two quantum signals to two locations a thousand miles apart, independently and simultaneously. Each quantum transmission will be unique but with one and only one duplicate—the duplicate available to the monitor. At Mr. Chang's invitation, I am here to offer this technology to TaiCom."

"There is no way the Chinese government will allow us to use their most advanced quantum key distribution," interjected Chang. "So we are inviting the very scientist who developed it, Dr. Wu, to work for us and to provide an upgraded version for the NASA satellite. Because we are paying NASA, we will get what we want." A gasp could be heard around the table.

"Unfortunately, Lily Yang will not be with us this morning," continued Chang. "Taking her place is Kang Yen Yen. You may call her Yen Yen." Turning to the new employee, Chang added, "Thank you, Yen Yen, for coming on such short notice."

The new receptionist bowed delicately, then departed to prepare the tea.

"Over the weekend I spent considerable private time in conversation with Dr. Bourne. I am pleased to report that we have devised a plan and a timetable for developing a scalable implant surgical procedure."

"Yes," said Geraldine Bourne. "I will arrange for experiments on DNA sampling and implantation procedures at my laboratory and hospital in Canada. I believe we can safely agree to begin implanting at scale by September 1. If I should run into unforeseen difficulties, then we'll stretch it to October 1. In the meantime, I believe you all can identify the first recipients and make appointments."

The group applauded, exhibiting high spirits.

"Who will be our guinea pigs?" asked Sharma.

"We have already established proof of concept and have successfully implanted versions of our chip in actual guinea pigs and, of course, Mister Lo," said Chang. "What we need now is to establish two further things: first, can we avoid immune rejection with our matching DNA plan? And second, will our implants lead to just the right neural circuitry? Only further human trials can answer these questions."

"I mean: which human beings will we test?" asked Sharma.

"Ah. Good question. We will limit our human subject pool to a very select market: spies."

"Spies?" gasped the group.

"Yes, spies. If anybody is ready for IA and willing to pay for it on a gamble, it will be espionage organizations. Here's our starting list: MI5 and MI6 in the UK; the Canadian Security Intelligence Service or CSIS; the Australian Security Intelligence Organisation or ASIO; France's *Direction Generale de la Securité Exterieure* or DGSE; Russia's *Sluzba Vneshnei Razvedka* or SVR; Germany's *Bundesnachrichtendienst* or BND; the CIA and FBI, of course; and perhaps our most hungry customer, Israel's Mossad. They will have the hunger for our products and the authority to command participation among their agents. In addition, they will take care of the monitoring for us. They know how to track a spy and garner the information we will need to watch what happens."

John Blair was quick to add, "And we have the added benefit of competition. Once one spy organization learns that this product will be available to the others, it will not want to be left behind. We might even find ourselves in a bidding war. They'll fight to be in on the ground floor."

"It could become a cyber arms race," said Buzz Kidd. "And we'll turn out to be the winners of the race." His smile was matched by the victorious smiles around the table.

"If it becomes a cyber arms race," asked Sharma, "what's to prevent our competition from removing our implant, duplicating it, and manufacturing a competing brand?"

"We've thought of that," said Chang. "The chip includes a self-destruct mechanism. As soon as the satellite discerns the chip's surgical removal, it signals it to malfunction. By the time our competitor puts it under an electron microscope, the circuits will look like spaghetti."

More grins of satisfaction.

Kidd offered a contribution. "What we're doing here is taking a baby step up the long path to creating posthumans, the intelligent species which will surpass us. This will be expensive. We will need large amounts of capital. By selling this technology now, we will build up the reserves we need for future R and D."

Heads nodded.

CHAPTER 28

TAIPEI

KHALID NESHAT LEANED FORWARD and entered the conversation. "Did I hear you mention Mossad?" he said to Chang. "Has Mossad shown interest?"

"Yes, indeed," emphasized Chang. "We have not yet begun a systematic marketing to all such organizations, but our preliminary conversations with Mossad representatives indicate a high level of interest."

"What then would be our plan?" asked Neshat. "Would Mossad provide a handful of individuals for the clinical trial? Would Israel be the only provider?"

Kidd took over. "Here's our strategy. Suppose we say we need twenty individuals to volunteer for the first clinical trial about September 1. This means, of course, that they will already have amplified data access and be prepared for highly sophisticated operations. We will have instantly created a cadre of superspies. Our buyers will be motivated to pay just for the clinical trial opportunity. We might even expect some buyers to cough up extra dollars for the privilege of being the only contract, providing all twenty guinea pigs.

An exclusive contract, so to speak. That's what Coke does to Pepsi, and vice versa. We can capitalize on spy jealousy."

"Is Mossad likely to outbid the CIA?" asked Neshat.

"It could happen," responded Kidd. "Let's go fishing with our idea and see who bites."

"Before we continue much longer on this topic, let me remind you of what's coming." Chang took the chair again. "In two weeks, on Thursday afternoon and evening, we'll reconvene at NASA Ames in Mountain View, California. I believe you already have the details. Yen Yen will provide each of you with your invitation and security credential on the way out. Buzz's friend Alan Kurz will host us on behalf of TTU, Transhumanist Technical University; and Chris MacDonald will host us on behalf of NASA. It will be a splendid event. And we will move our entire project along. See you in California."

As chairs slid and bodies meandered toward the conference room exit, Neshat approached Wu. "If you need a partner in setting up the satellite transmission component, I'm willing to help. I'm a quantum specialist."

"Thanks. Please remind me of your name. Doctor…?"

"Neshat. I'm Dr. Khalid Neshat."

"I look forward to working together."

CHAPTER 29

CHICAGO

THE PARSONAGE PORCH just off South Burnham Avenue in Chicago was crowded. Midnight the black cat sat regally on the door threshold surveying her kingdom. Pastor Leona Foxx sat on the top step, petting Buck the Siberian Husky, who lay unmoving so as to not disturb the affection. Cupid, the six-year-old girl who lived three doors north on South Burnham, sat like Sitting Bull helping the pastor to pet the dog. Jerry Talin leaned on the fence; he looked vacuously away from the assembly toward infinity.

Hillar Talin sat on the bottom step concentrating on his laptop, furiously moving his fingers from key to key. Graham Washington bent forward, looking over Hillar's shoulder to watch his movements on the screen.

A moment earlier the lounging porch party had noticed the approach from the northeast of what at first appeared to be a small object in the sky. As it drew closer, it became clear that a drone was surveying this South Shore neighborhood.

"I think it's a quadracopter with an HD camera," said Hillar to the group. He continued to monitor the interloper's location and movement on his screen. "Now I can find out if it really works."

"If what works, Hillar?" asked Graham.

"My radio interception device. I've been working on it in my garage. I plan to knock anything out of the sky guided electronically," he announced with the confidence of Mark Zuckerberg.

"How does it work?" quizzed Graham.

"First, I scan with radar to see if any electronic waves are pulsing in the area. Then I jam 'em. I make them malfunction. Nobody's gonna spy on me!"

"For the sake of Bridgeport, Quaz, what do you have to hide?" asked Leona.

"Why are you still calling me Quaz?" protested Hillar.

"Because I always liked Quasimodo, and I like you too."

Hillar frowned. "I've got nuth'n to hide, of course. It's the principle of the whole thing. Nobody's gonna spy in our neighborhood. I wanna outsmart the smarties. This is a reality video game. This is war!"

For the first time, Jerry turned to look at the group. Then his expressionless face turned away again.

The invading drone had crossed to the west side of Burhnam and was flying slowly over the Trinity Church parking lot at a height just above the maple trees. The drone seemed to be studying the parsonage porch assembly.

"Watch this," exclaimed Hillar. "It's my first real test." The teenager pressed a computer button.

The quadracopter's engines sputtered. The craft twisted ninety degrees and dropped to one side. Then the engines shut down. It fell onto the parking lot blacktop with a clacking sound. Hillar walked over to pick it up. Then he walked back toward the porch holding the crashed drone high, looking like a fisherman who had just caught a largemouth black bass.

"Now you've got a problem, Hillar," announced Graham. "Whoever flew that drone has taken your picture. They'll come looking for you."

"Bring 'em on!" muttered the teenager.

CHAPTER 30

CHICAGO

LEONA along with Noel Freeman stared at the computer screen image attached to the electron microscope. This state of the art microscope belonged to the research division of the University of Chicago Medicine Center in Hyde Park. It was midnight. The hospital hall lights were low, even though the interior of their research lab was well lit.

"Here is where your Chinese friend severed the circuit," said Doctor Freeman, pointing to a spot on the screen with her pencil point. "See the break?"

"If I put this chip in my own brain, Noel, will it make me smarter?" asked Leona.

Noel laughed. "Nothing like this can make you smarter. It might give you access to information, but it won't increase your IQ. Anyway, Lee, you're already too smart for your own good."

"Thanks for the compliment, but I want to become my own guinea pig. Could we experiment by implanting the chip in my own brain?"

"Why in the world would you want to do that?"

"Because, for the sake of Brooklyn, I want to monitor what the TaiCom syndicate is doing. I would like to gain access to TaiCom transmissions, but I want to avoid any impairment of my own reasoning capacity. I don't want to lose my mental independence."

"If we wired it to your pre-frontal cortex, you should be able to read the chip but make your own decisions regarding its content. If we place it just right, you will maintain your own mental control."

"It must be patient-specific, you know," said Leona. "It's gotta connect with my DNA without rejection."

"Yes, of course," said Noel nodding. "That'll be automatic the way I implant it. No problem. But, Leona, as your friend and as a neurosurgeon, I hesitate to recommend such a treatment if it's not going to be therapeutic."

"This is not therapy for me. It's therapy for the world, so to speak. I gotta get inside the TaiCom mind without TaiCom getting inside my mind."

The two women refilled their coffee cups and stared at one another.

"Do you believe in brain-mind identity?" Leona asked her friend in the white lab coat.

"No, I don't. Here in the lab or in surgery I am a scientist. I think scientifically. I think rationally. I am utterly impersonal, dispassionate, logical, and systematic. But, as you know, I also write poetry. There is nothing scientific about poetry. So, when I'm ready to be a poet, I tell my brain to shut off the science and open up room for poetic thinking. Did you get that: I tell my brain what to do. My brain does not tell me what to do. I give my brain orders and my brain obeys."

"If my mind is more than my brain, then there is no risk that this brain implant will overtake my mind, right?"

"Well, sorta. Your mind can't do without your brain, obviously. So, I think it may depend on just how we connect the implant. If we wire it to the prefrontal cortex, I believe you'll get just what you're asking for."

"You *believe*?"

"I can't be sure."

"Why can't you be sure?"

"Medicine is an art, Leona, not a science."

"But you just said that you're a scientist as a neurosurgeon."

"There's more than one meaning of *science*, Leona. You know that."

Leona paused. "Yes, of course. What do you think are the chances that we'll get it right?"

"Very good. And, if it doesn't work, just come back and I'll remove the implant. Don't worry."

"Now, who is talking to me: the scientist or the poet?"

CHAPTER 31

CHICAGO

THE MEMORIAL SERVICE was scheduled for 11:00am.

It was now 10:00am in Chicago. Graham sat upright in the La-Z-Boy in Leona's living room, in the parsonage behind Trinity Church. Buck the husky sat erect on the floor, watching. Midnight the black cat sat with her tail folded under her, also watching. Cupid sat on the floor with her left arm around Buck. Her face registered seriousness combined with bewilderment.

Hillar was stretched out on the couch with his head in Leona's lap. His eye sockets were swollen, pink, and puffy from crying. Leona gently kneaded Hillar's hair. Grief, sadness, and desperation hung in the air like mountain fog in the morning.

"Why? Why did he do it, Pastor Lee?" Hillar pined.

Leona continued massaging Hillar's head in silence. Eventually she broke the silence. "Let me tell you a story, Hillar. Once when I was still a child, my mother and I stayed up late to watch a re-run on television. It was called 'High Noon.' The chief character was a nineteenth century marshal played by actor Gary Cooper. He was

Marshal Will Kane in Hadleyville, located in the New Mexico Territory. He had just married a woman who was a Quaker, played by Grace Kelly. That means she was committed to non-violence. Now get this: a Quaker marries a marshal! Can you see the plot coming?"

"Yeah, I get it," muttered Hillar.

Graham began to sing softly, "Do not forsake me, O my darling."

Leona's frown shut Graham up. Leona continued, "At high noon on his wedding day, a train was scheduled to arrive in Hadleyville. That train would bring four outlaws who had previously announced they were coming to kill the marshal. They wanted revenge, because the marshal had previously arrested the gang's leader, Frank Miller. At high noon, everyone feared the town would be overrun with gun fighting.

"So the townspeople told the marshal to get out of town. Get away! Take the violence away. And of course, the marshal's new wife, the Quaker named Amy, wanted him to get away as well. As you can imagine, the conscience of the marshal was torn between standing to fight and running away to avoid the fight.

"Marshal Kane and his new wife left town in their buckboard. But then came an important moment, literally a turning point. Marshal Kane stopped the buckboard. He thought. Then he turned around and headed back to town. Amy protested and threatened to leave him. Yet he continued back to town to fight the bad guys."

"Why did he go back?" asked Hillar.

"We'll get to that in a minute, Quaz. When Kane got back to town he had to fight the gang on his own, because nobody else wanted to get mixed up in the violence. During the gun fight, Amy picked up a gun and shot one of the four. By shooting this man, Amy was declaring that her marriage to Will Kane was more important than her commitment to non-violence.

"When the movie ended, Frank Miller's entire gang was dead. Marshal Kane threw down his marshal's badge, ending his career in law enforcement. He and Amy drove off into the sunset, so to speak."

"Again, Pastor Lee, why'd Marshal Kane go back?" pressed Hillar.

"That's the very question I asked my mother the night I first saw this movie. I demanded that my mother explain to me why Marshal Kane went back to face possible death. Do you know what my mother said?"

"No, what did she say?"

"She told me that I was just a little girl; and that I couldn't understand until I was grown up. Then, my mother told me a story. This is a story within a story now, Quaz."

Hillar broke into a smile. Graham continued to watch and listen understandingly.

"My mother told me that when 'High Noon' first appeared in the movie theaters in 1952, she went to the theater with her mother and father. That would be my grandmother and grandfather. After she saw the movie, my mother asked her parents: why did Marshal Kane go back? They told her that she would have to wait until she grew up before she could understand. Going back to face danger is kind of a grown-up thing, I guessed."

"When your mother grew up, did she get the point?" asked Hillar.

"Yes, she eventually got the point."

"When you grew up, Pastor Lee, did you get the point?"

"Yes, I got the point. I now understand why Marshal Kane went back to Hadleyville."

"So, what you're trying to say is that Marshal Kane and my brother Jerry are the same, right?"

"No, not at all. I'm trying to say they were opposites. Marshal Kane had a strong sense of self. He believed in justice. He believed he had a duty to enforce justice and to protect Hadleyville in the name of justice. He had integrity. By 'integrity' I mean he was integrated. Who Marshal Kane was was integrated around justice. He was so committed to justice that the townspeople could not persuade him to shirk his duty. His Quaker wife could not persuade him to forsake his duty. Even the threat of death itself could not disintegrate him."

"So, Jerry didn't have integrity. Is that what yer saying?"

"I don't mean it in the way you think. I'm not saying Jerry was dishonest. In fact, he was more honest than most of us. Rather, I'm saying that his struggle was that he couldn't integrate his self around justice. This is because justice evaporated and disappeared. At least, this is what Jerry thought. Once justice disappeared, his sense of self disintegrated. He fell apart, so to speak."

"So, if my brother Jerry were in that buckboard, he would not have decided to go back to Hadleyville, right?"

"If Jerry were in that buckboard, he could not have decided to do anything. Going back to Hadleyville to do his duty to justice would not have made any sense to him. Driving on to a new life with Amy would not have made any sense either. After losing justice, your brother Jerry lost himself. He was dead long before he committed suicide."

Graham looked at his watch. "Leona, it's getting to be that time."

"Graham, would you mind doing the service alone?" asked Leona. "I think I'd like to sit in the pew with the Talin family. Would that be okay with you, Quaz?"

"Oh yes, Thank you, Pastor Lee."

"Cupid, would you help Hillar go find his mommie? Hillar, find your mother and get the family to sit in the front pew on the pulpit side. I'll join you shortly." Hillar stood up. As Cupid stood up, she began to point up at Leona.

"What is it, Cupid?" asked Leona.

The little girl continued pointing upward. Leona bent down. Cupid began to finger her hair. Momentarily a bare clearing on Leona's scalp became visible in the forest of her auburn hair.

"I saw the doctor, Cupid," said Leona. "The doctor fixed my owie."

Satisfied, Cupid reached for Hillar's hand. The two exited the parsonage hand in hand.

Leona went to the rest room. Graham went to the sacristy to robe.

DURING THE MEMORIAL SERVICE, Graham stepped into the pulpit to deliver a brief homily. After reading his scriptural text, he opened his sermon. "If I recall correctly, the last words I heard Jaroslav Talin say were these: 'If there is no God, then there is no me.'"

CHAPTER 32

CHICAGO

Leona finished packing her Briggs and Riley Spinner and closed it up. "I'm ready if you are!" she shouted to Graham. She pulled the spinner down the hall, then picked it up for the carry down the stairs to the front door.

Once Graham had loaded the bag into the CR-V, they set out for O'Hare airport. "Thanks for taking over the funeral for Jerry, Graham," whispered Leona in a mournful tone. "And I'm especially grateful for the pastoral care you showed to Hillar and the Talin family during this crisis. You've got a pastor's heart, Graham."

Graham drove without saying anything. Leona softly removed Graham's hand from the steering wheel, drew it to her mouth, and gently kissed it. She then replaced Graham's hand on the wheel somewhat ceremoniously.

"Now, why again are you going to San Francisco?" he asked impetuously.

"I'm going to NASA Ames in Mountain View, California. I'm going to become bait in a honey trap. It's my high noon, and I gotta git the bad guys."

"Honey sticks two ways, you know," muttered the driver.

"Grammy, darling, are you worried about my safety or about something else?"

Graham continued driving in silence. After a period, Leona picked up the conversation. "As I told you, my assignment is to meet the Taiwan cabal and their Transhumanist friends in the Bay Area. I need to get to know them. I need them to get to know me. Washington—that's Uncle Sam, not you—wants to monitor these brain bruisers. While I'm serving our country, you can stay here in Chicago and serve our Lord. See what good partners we make?"

"Somehow things have gotten turned around, dammit. I'm the guy who works full-time for the CIA, not you. You're only a....what are you...an asset? a consultant? a honeycomb? I'm the one who should be doing the spying. You, my dear Leona, are the pastor of Trinity Church. Why don't you stay in town to do your job?"

An empathic smile broke out on Leona's face. With a patient cadence she continued. "We together are doing *our* job, Mr. Washington. We're being good stewards of our talents. While I'm called away for this short time, you can keep the sheep in the fold. When I return, then you can go after the wolves and I'll tend the sheep. How's that?"

A smile emerged on Graham's lips as well. He reached over to grasp Leona's left hand. He gave it a tender squeeze. Small talk and practicalities occupied the conversation for the remainder of the drive to O'Hare.

After a warm good-bye hug at the United departures terminal, Graham put the CR-V into gear and headed back to Chicago's south side. About ten minutes en route, his mobile phone sounded. He glanced at the screen. It was a strange number. No, he'd seen this number before. *I wonder if that's the number for...what's her name...ah, Trudy Lincoln?*

CHAPTER 33

CHICAGO

ALTHOUGH NICKNAMED THE WINDY CITY, without the wind on a hot day Chicago should be named Convection Oven City. The sun burns you from the top. The sun's heat is then reflected by street asphalt upward, cooking you from the bottom as well. And unlike other parts of the country, the heat does not dissipate during the night. Like rocks in a campfire, the pavement keeps the city roasting all night long. Graham fought back by donning his sandals, cargo shorts, and Tommy Bahama shirt.

Trudy Lincoln had said she'd return home from work about six, and that Graham should arrive about seven. Questions about faith were bothering her. And Graham saw it as his duty to pay a pastoral call. Had he been a member of the German clergy, he would have referred to his work as *Seelsorge*, care of souls. Yes, care for Trudy's soul was his motive for paying this call. *Yes, it's my only motive for making this pastoral call,* he tried to persuade himself.

Graham walked five blocks south and walked up the five porch steps of a bungalow on South Burnham near 85th Street. He rang the bell. He could hear high heels approaching on a hardwood floor.

Then the front door opened. A smiling Trudy stood there, shimmering in a full length white silk robe.

"It's a scorcher today, Pastor Washington. I mean, Pastor Gee. Come into my air-conditioned home and cool off!"

Graham entered, closing the door behind him. It indeed felt better inside, where the temperature was only seventy or so. Trudy swished and swirled as she bid Graham to sit on the divan while she sashayed to the kitchen for two glasses of iced tea. Graham could hear every step as her high heels tapped on the oak floor. Upon returning and placing the condensate drinking glasses on the coffee table, Trudy prepared for her three-point landing in the arm chair directly across from Graham. This included the lifting of her left leg over her right, causing the silk robe to flap open. This revealed that she was wearing only a bra and panties, both hot pink. The near iridescent glow of Trudy's brassiere and scanty panty intensified the color contrast with her delectable chocolate skin. With false modesty she quickly covered herself up again. Then she stared into Graham's eyes.

Graham could feel concupiscent impulses warring with his spiritual self-discipline. He covered his internal conflict by saying nothing.

Placing her chin in her left hand with the elbow on her left knee, she continued to stare into Graham's eyes. "Thank you for coming to call on me, Pastor Gee. I've been looking forward to your visit ever since I attended worship at Trinity Church." Trudy seemed not to blink as her eyes bored into Graham like an electric drill. All Graham could muster was a nod and a grunt while feigning the compulsive need for a sip of tea.

Keeping complete control of the situation, Trudy continued. "I did appreciate the way you conducted worship, Pastor. You speak so boldly, yet so kindly. I think I can hear a strong relationship with God along with a genuine caring in your voice. And the way you introduced our soldiers the Sunday prior to Memorial Day! Such a nice gesture, Pastor. We need to honor our men and women in uniform, don't you think?"

Graham nodded affirmatively at this trivial truism. Still, he refrained from speaking.

"I'm new in the neighborhood," Trudy continued. "I just moved here from the Loop. How long have you been pastor at Trinity?"

"Actually, I'm not the pastor at Trinity," he confessed. "The senior Pastor is Lee Foxx. I simply play the role of assistant pastor; I take leadership when circumstances require it. Pastor Foxx was out of town the first Sunday you visited. I'm a 'pinch pastor.' I come to bat when the real pastor isn't hitting."

"You certainly know how to hit, Pastor Gee. You hit a home run, as far as I'm concerned." Trudy laughed at her own joke. "But are you trained'n everything? Did you go to seminary or something?"

"Oh, yes. I have an M.Div. degree from Princeton."

"Are you Presbyterian then?"

"I'm kind of a hybrid, Reformed and Lutheran. If I lived in Germany, I'd be a unionist."

"I don't know what they do in Germany," said Trudy. "I was raised in a National Baptist church. Sang in the choir'n everything. I gave my life to Jesus when I was sixteen. That's a year after I gave my virginity to Albert. Albert directed our choir." Trudy laughed.

Graham laughed with her. Trudy shuffled in her chair, unobtrusively opening and then re-closing her silk robe. *Revelation followed by concealment is what Heidegger would call this,* Graham conjectured to himself. *Truth is found in the unveiling, the disrobing.* Then, Graham silently scolded himself and thought, *I gotta concentrate here.* He spoke. "So, you've got some questions."

CHAPTER 34

CHICAGO

"Yes, that's what I told you after church. I'm so glad you were willing to come to my home to talk. I've been doing a lot of thinking recently. Actually, thoughts come into my mind uninvited. They're alarming thoughts. They terrify me, and they kind of rule my mind for long periods of time." Trudy's countenance had become earnest, sober. This placed Graham at ease, oddly enough; because now he could respond pastorally to an authentic question rather than to his own secret desire to get seduced. "Tell me about these thoughts."

"Well." Trudy looked right past Graham and out the front window. "Well, I just wonder if what we say about God is right. What if we're wrong?" She paused. Graham waited without speaking. She continued as if not noticing the time gap. "What if we're wrong? What if there is no God? Or, what if God is really different from what the Bible says?"

Graham focused his attention on her eyes. Eventually, she turned her head slightly and was once again looking directly at him. A blushing smile recognized the eye contact. She looked downward.

"I bet something is prompting you to entertain these unwelcome thoughts," commented Graham.

Trudy looked back up. "It's my boss. I recently took a job in the Loop with a startup company. I'm a computer engineer. I specialize in monitoring and tracking and such. My new boss is a Muslim. Well, actually, he's an ex-Black Muslim. He says he doesn't believe in God anymore. But he keeps pestering me about my Christian beliefs. He says I'm just a fool for believing what Christian churches teach."

"So, he's an unbeliever who can't leave your beliefs intact, eh?"

"Yeah, that's right. He says I will go to hell because I don't believe what is right about God. He calls God *Allah*. Even though he doesn't believe in Allah any more, he tells me Allah will send me to everlasting hell. Pastor Washington, I don't want to go to hell."

"Can you be more specific? Just what is it about your Christian belief that allegedly warrants eternal damnation?"

"He keeps saying Allah is one. Allah is one! Because we believe in the Trinity—that God is Father, Son, and Holy Spirit—I am stubbornly refusing to believe that Allah is one. That's what he tells me. Now, Pastor, we believe the Trinity is only one, right? Three-in-one, or something like that. Right? Well, I get kind of confused here."

"You're not the first in the history of Christianity to get confused about the Trinity. Christians believe that God is one, almost like the Muslims do. Don't get uptight. Relax. We'll sort this out. Yes, indeed, Muslims do not like what we Christians teach about God as Trinity. But curiously, Muslims are utterly confused about what it is they are rejecting. Take the Qur'an, for example."

"Did you say the Qur'an?"

"Yes, of course."

"My boss actually gave me a copy of the Qur'an to bring home and read. But I can't read it. I open it up and, well, I can't find my way around."

Graham began laughing. "That's because the Qur'an is written backwards. Like the Hebrew language, Arabic is written from right to left. So...well, just bring me your copy of the Qur'an."

Trudy stood up and left the room. In a jiffy she was back and handed the book to Graham. Graham did not watch for the now habitual flash of the white robe revealing the hot pink scanty panty. Rather, he immediately placed the Qur'an in his left hand and opened to the first pages with his right. *The Holy Qur'an* in both Arabic and English was published in Tehran, Iran. He then began to thumb his way through the text. Turning to Sura 4:171, Graham read out loud: "'Say not Trinity; desist. It will be better for you, for God is one God.' Perhaps this is what your boss was referring to: God is one, and the idea of the Trinity violates this. If you violate the thought about God's oneness, then you commit *shirk*. *Shirk* is a grievous form of sin."

Graham flipped some more pages. "Now, I want to show you something else, something really odd," he said, turning to Sura 5:116: "Here, Allah mimics Christians who 'worship me [Jesus] and my mother, as gods in derogation of God.' Look at this carefully. The Qur'an assumes that the Trinity is made up of Jesus, God the Father, and Mary the Mother. Now, you know that this is a gross misinterpretation of what we Christians actually teach. We never place the human mother of Jesus, Mary, in the Trinity. No wonder the Muslims object to the idea of the Trinity! We Christians would reject this as well."

Trudy studied the text one more time. "That's right, Pastor Washington. The Trinity rejected here is not the Father, Son, and Spirit." She turned to look again at Graham. She smiled as if she was experiencing an insight. "If a Muslim understood what we Christians truly think, then this difference about God would just go away. Right? Maybe these two religions could get together. Right?"

"Not so fast. Islamic theologians in the centuries after the Qur'an was written listened to Christians who tried to correct their mistake. Once the Islamic scholars gained an accurate understanding of what Christians think, they still rejected the Trinity as polytheism. They still think we commit *shirk*. So, I have little hope that we Christians and our Muslim brothers and sisters will become a single happy family very soon."

The conversation turned to small talk. Eventually, Graham rose, excused himself, and headed for the front door. As he reached for the doorknob, Trudy ran her right index finger down his left arm. "Certainly I wouldn't be committing *shirk* if I kissed my favorite pastor good-bye, would I?"

Graham stood motionless. Trudy arched up on her toes to reach his lips. The two embraced. Graham thought this kiss could be interpreted as a "hello" rather than a "good-bye." He elected the latter interpretation and swiftly walked five blocks north to the Trinity parsonage.

CHAPTER 35

NASA

"Leona!" Kelly hollered exuberantly, waving with arms outstretched high over her head. "Lee, Lee. Over here!"

"Kelly!" Leona spotted Kelly Latham Compton, the younger sister of her best friend, Angelina Latham, on the steps of the visitors center at historic Moffat Field, crowded this night with finely dressed couples and abuzz with unaccustomed social activity. Leona gave an acknowledging nod and hurried her pace towards the young woman, whom she hadn't seen for close to a decade. The two women hugged in the kind of warm embrace that only those who know each other well can share.

"Leona, you look *fabulous*. This crazy life you lead seems to be good for you."

"Well, it keeps me trim, I guess, but thanks for the compliment. And you...you...YOU look *amazing* for, what? Two kids? Wow. How many years has it been? Five? Ten?"

"Before the kids, I'm sure. Maybe eight years? Yes, eight. It was at the wedding."

"I remember when you were little and used to sit by Angie's door and listen to our private girl talks," Leona recalled with a chuckle in her voice. Kelly smiled back, enjoying the recognition.

"And, look at those earrings!" Leona tilted her head to examine the cubic zirconium stud supporting a fine silver chain connected to a second identical stone hanging from Kelly's right ear.

"Yes, you are now looking at the very earrings you gave me on my wedding day. I remembered. That's why I wore them this evening."

The two linked themselves together, arm in arm, and chattered away, randomly talking over each other and listening, recognizing there were a lot of years to catch up on. Yes, Angie is just fine. Yes, Kelly's husband, three-year-old son and five-month-old baby are just fine. Yes, Leona enjoyed her brief vacation in Taiwan.

CHAPTER 36

NASA

KELLY LATHAM COMPTON. She had added Compton when she married Alexander Compton, founder and owner of a chain of pharmacies in the South Bay. Kelly had grown up in Dearborn, Michigan, with her older sister, Angelina Latham, and Angie's best friend, Leona, of course. Bradley was her son; her baby daughter was named after her aunt Angie, affectionately nicknamed Angel.

It was seven in the evening. Leona and Kelly walked together through the large glass doorway of the NASA Ames Research Center at Moffat Field in Mountain View, California. NASA space scientists were playing host to the lab rats from TTU, Transhumanist Technical University, an elite institute adjacent to the NASA Research Park. TTU selects only the brightest of the brightest for its students and provides full-ride scholarships, funded by donors in Silicon Valley. The students in the lab carry out the experiments designed by the faculty. Kelly had been such a student.

Kelly and Leona turned more than a few heads as they strolled through the door, to the tables covered in white linen where drinks were being served. Kelly had shoulder-length, sandy blonde hair, wore very little make-up and had a bright and fresh look about her that always attracted appropriate attention, even when she wore a practical, nondescript beige pantsuit as she did this evening. A yin-yang medallion hung from a gold chain around her neck, resting where one might otherwise expect to see cleavage.

With hair in a feathered pageboy, Leona wore a simple yet sleek navy blue dress that clung gently to the curves of her athletic body. Around her neck, she wore a hand-crafted silver necklace from Taiwan with a likeness of the Buddhist goddess Quan Yin. Leona had an uncanny ability to stay within a conservative fashion milieu, yet add a touch that made her unique and stylish. Navy blue was Leona's black, at least out of the pulpit.

Kelly listened carefully as Leona quizzed the bartender behind a large table of neatly arranged bottles and glasses. "What are your whites?"

"We have a Chardonnay and a Sauvignon Blanc," he responded with a plastic smile.

"I mean: what labels? Who makes them?"

The man behind the table in the black tux reached into a tub full of ice and picked up a bottle of Chardonnay. "It looks like a...a Dragon Tooth Vintners. Do you recognize it?"

"Yes. It comes from Mainland China. If you light your cigarette the entire building will explode!" Leona tossed the line to him without looking to see if he cracked a smile.

"What's the Sauvignon Blanc?"

He pulled up the next bottle. "The label reads, 'Domaine des Justices.'"

"That's French. It's passable. But here we are in the heart of California's wine district, and NASA is buying foreign turpentine and passing it off as the fruits of viticulture. I'll have a Perrier, also French."

"You haven't asked about the reds. I've got a Field Stone Cabernet Sauvignon."

"Sold! Fill up my glass, but please leave something for nose."

The man with the black bow tie filled Leona's stem glass nearly three quarters full, leaving just an inch to sniff the bouquet.

"I'll have what she's having," said Kelly in a way that revealed an indifference to what she was drinking.

As the two young women turned to move into the party, they realized they needed to file through a thick group of cocktail seekers now bellying up to the bar. The man immediately to Leona's right was talking on his Nokia cell phone. He hurriedly whispered "goodbye," then nearly shouted, "Kelly! It's me, Doug."

"Oh, Doug!" responded Kelly. She turned to Leona, introducing the tall, pale man with a nervous demeanor and a twinkle in his eye.

"Lee, this is Doug Valentine. He's an exobiologist, works in the NASA lab with me. Three microscopes to the left."

In order to shake hands with Leona, Doug set his Nokia on the bar table. He grabbed Leona's right hand with both of his. They exchanged 'glad-to-meet-you's.'

"Leona's an astrobiologist too," Kelly added, intentionally making the profession seem current.

"Oh, great!" said Doug. "What do you look for? Microbes or brains?"

"I want to talk with ET," responded Leona with a quick sideward glance at Kelly, eyebrow slightly raised. "I would love to find intelligent life on extra-solar planets. But, I must confess, right now my science is on the back shelf. I'm not an active researcher."

"Just give me a worm that eats methane on Titan, and I'll be happy," said Doug with quirky grin.

"You'd better get your drink," said Leona, noticing the crowd was building.

Doug turned toward the bow tie behind the bar table, and nonchalantly ordered two glasses of chardonnay. Hearing this, Leona grimaced to Kelly. Kelly smiled.

As this distraction was playing out, what neither saw was another hand moving surreptitiously over the cluttered table to pick up the

Nokia. Doug took the chardonnay, one glass in each hand, and like a cat with a mouse in its mouth proudly walked away from the table to show his prey to his date, his wife.

CHAPTER 37

NASA

LEONA AND KELLY found a quiet five square feet of floor space to stand, chat, and imbibe. As attractive as an oasis to the thirsty, these two would not be alone for long. In moments they were approached by three wide-eyed men.

"Good evening, ladies," said the youngest of the trio, one of the few in jeans and a polo shirt. "I'm Buzz Kidd."

"I'm Leona Foxx."

"I'm Kelly Compton."

"I know you," interrupted the tall one. At six-foot-eight and lanky, he towered over the group. Out came a right hand the size of a shortstop glove. He grabbed Kelly's hand. "You work in the bio lab, don't you? I'm Chris MacDonald. I work here at NASA too."

"Oh, you're the Mars guy, right?" asked Kelly.

"Did I see you interviewed on Sixty Minutes?" asked Leona.

"Yes, I'm the one with the plans to terraform the Red Planet."

"Do you mean you'll plant life on Mars that looks like Earth? How will you do that?" Leona began an interrogation. "With only fifteen percent of Earth's volume, eleven percent of Earth's mass, and thirty-eight percent of Earth's gravity, how will you grow anything that looks like Earth's life? And how can you get life going if you have only iron oxide for soil?"

"Wow. You're just a Gatling gun of facts, aren't you?" replied Chris. He was about to continue the conversation when he was interrupted by Buzz, speaking in a loud voice.

"And this is Abnu Sharma," said Buzz, directing his open hand toward the shortest of the three.

"Please just call me Sharma," said the Indian dressed in suit and tie, as he shook the hand of each of the two women.

The bubbling of introductions included a toast with wine glasses and queries directed toward the two head-turning damsels. Who are you? Why are you here?

"I'm a pastor in Chicago," Leona announced.

"A pastor? Aren't you in the wrong celestial sphere?" asked Chris. "Why, in heaven's name?—that's a lame attempt at humor, by the way—why would you be interested in space travel or nanotechnology or Transhumanism or any of this stuff?

"I'm just interested in everything," she told the group while smiling and sipping. This left them to wonder if she were a dumb blonde with colored hair or playing with them.

"I'm a lab rat, just as Chris said," added Kelly. "My specialty is exobiology. I'm looking for biomarkers that indicate life within our solar system."

Twenty feet from this animated conversation, Lionel Chang stood sipping a Dragon Tooth Chardonnay. He starred at Leona. Then from the right pocket of his blue blazer he withdrew his iPhone. With dexterous thumb movements he went to a sub-gallery. He settled on one photo. He looked at the photo and then at Leona. Then back to his iPhone. Satisfied, he dropped the phone back into his pocket as he took a lengthy drink of the white wine.

CHAPTER 38

NASA

"There's life right here," said Buzz, raising his glass for another toast.

"I know," said Kelly, as if she failed to get the joke. "But I'm looking for signs of life on the moons of Saturn and places like that."

Two other men walked into the group. One spoke. "My name is Khalid Neshat. This is Phee Seng Wu." They shook hands with the two women and learned their names. Of the men, only MacDonald was new to Neshat, so he offered his right hand. They shook and exchanged names. The eyes of the conversation group shifted away from looking at one another and toward what had become the center of attention: someone with a microphone.

TTU's Allen Kurz took the floor and introduced the dozen or so researchers who were accompanying him. Included among those introduced were Olga Louchakova. He paused. He raised his wine glass in his left hand. Then, he raised his right hand with thumb only a half inch below his index finger. "We're that close!" he announced. The room broke out into applause, accompanied by drinking and toasting.

Six-foot-tall Kurz wore what his compatriots thought to be his veritable uniform: five-pocket relaxed fit Hudson jeans and a black Carhartt mock turtleneck. He continued his address. "The final chip will be smaller and lighter than a watch battery. And here is the genius: it will be patient specific. It will rely upon the DNA specific to each person with an implant, thereby avoiding immune rejection of this foreign object. We will surgically place the chip in its raw state into the left temporal lobe. As the intruding device makes its home in the surrounding brain cells, it will draw a DNA nucleus into its circuitry. In short, it will establish its own bio-nano symbiosis. We expect this process to take two to four days following implantation. Maybe even sooner in some cases. But in any case, we will refrain from signal activation until the symbiosis is complete."

The room broke into a second round of applause, a quilted applause interweaving the moving hands of scientists and investors. Kurz continued. "I've designated Dr. Phee Seng Wu to represent TTU and our Transhumanist colleagues to work with NASA on establishing the satellite network."

Neshat, who was standing next to Wu, gripped the Beijing scientist by the elbow.

"Oh!" he responded. Then he raised his right hand. "Dr. Kurz," he hollered. "Dr. Khalid Neshat will work with me and NASA on the satellite connection."

"Thank you, Dr. Wu," Kurz continued. "And thanks also to you, Dr. Neshat, for your willingness to pursue this important work. Now, let me turn things over to our NASA friends."

Eventually the microphone was handed to Chris MacDonald.

"We here at NASA are pleased to enter into a cooperative agreement with TTU. It will be our task to place in orbit a satellite with direct communication to the implanted chips. It will be an exclusive channel with two-way access. Only two days from today the satellite will be launched and orbiting." A new round of applause broke out.

As the brief program came to an end, Khalid turned to look directly at Leona. "My, but you're awfully pretty to be a scientist."

"Most scientists I know can't tell what's pretty and what's not," Leona said. "They only know if the path of an electron is elegant or not." She sipped her wine. Kelly watched the conversation.

Khalid offered a diplomatic laugh, uncertain whether this was a rejection or come-on. He thought he should try again. "If you were an electron...did you say your name was Leona? I'd certainly want you in my cloud chamber."

"I'm not sure you and I share the same inertial reference frame. I'm actually a biologist, an astrobiologist to be more precise. So is Kelly here."

"I'm a nuclear physicist," added Khalid. "I specialize in energy production, fission energy production. I also dabble in astrophysics. I'm sure I would not know anything about what you biologists talk about. So if you want to lose me..."

"Oh, no, we don't want to lose you," interrupted Kelly.

Khalid smiled. He turned his eyes back to Leona. "What lab do you work in? Are you here at NASA?"

"No. Actually, I don't work in a lab right now. I'm a pastor in Chicago."

"Pastor? What's that?"

"I'm a clergywoman. You know, sort of like an imam. I serve a Christian church."

"You're a woman and you lead a church!"

"You're a Muslim, and you drink wine!" responded Leona with a tone of friendly sarcasm. She gave him a wink.

"I like wine. If this room were filled with other Muslims, then I would be drinking tea. But as long as I'm in the company of Westerners with lax morals, no one will tell me that Allah will judge me."

"We Christians would describe you as a sheep straying from the fold. I'm a shepherd. I look for lost sheep."

"Your work must be very...very...interesting." Khalid was stumbling, but Leona seemed to respond to his charm. Khalid continued. "I would love to come and see you at work sometime."

Leona laughed. "You're not serious. I work in Chicago."

"I get to Chicago occasionally on business. After I leave here I'll go to Chicago and then on to Detroit. Could we meet for lunch?" Khalid reached into the inside pocket of his double-breasted suit coat. "Here's my card. It has my email on it."

Leona opened her clutch and pulled out a business card for her new acquaintance. "Please call me when you get to Chicago. I'll invite you to my church on the south side. But right now, I'm afraid I need to depart. I'm flying home on the red eye, I need to head for SFO."

Leona turned to Kelly. "I've got to return my rental and check in. So I'll say goodbye here. I'll tell Angie we've had a great time connecting."

The two women hugged one another and repeated good-byes. After shaking Khalid's hand, Leona disappeared out the building's front door.

Khalid watched Leona depart, his eyes dancing to the rhythm of Leona's hip swing. Then he turned to Kelly. He smiled so that his mustache exuded an extra dose of sophisticated charm.

"Shall we find somewhere to sit down and talk?" Kelly asked.

CHAPTER 39

NASA

"It's too noisy," said Khalid. "Let's sit closer." They arranged their chairs on one arc of a small round table. Looking Kelly in the eyes, he asked her about her NASA work.

"I'm in the lab that examines evidence for microbial life within this solar system," she told her attentive partner. Although she worked to maintain eye contact, she could not help but notice and admire his carefully groomed hair, meticulously trimmed mustache, square jaw, and effortless speech.

He spoke. "Tell me what you think. Are we alone? Or do we on Earth have space neighbors?"

Kelly continued. "We have neighbors. Here's what I think. The universe is 13.82 billion years old, or so you physicists tell us. The Earth was born 4.5 billion years ago, making it one-third the age of the whole shebang. Our planet was lifeless until 3.9 billion years ago, when microbes appeared. Microbes were the only living things for nearly two billion years. They breathed methane and excreted oxygen. Eventually the proportion of oxygen in the atmosphere grew. Natural selection then selected species that would breathe oxygen and excrete methane. Think of it: you and I and the cows drink in oxygen and excrete methane. Quite a reversal, eh!"

"So, we eat and drink oxygen and then we, shall we say, shit and piss methane, is that right?"

"Are you making fun of me?"

"Oh, no. This theory is very intriguing. Please go on."

"Do you really think so?"

"Yes, indeed. Tell me more."

"Well, Saturn has moons, the largest of which is called Titan. Titan is similar to Earth: it has an atmosphere, changing weather, seasons, lakes, mountains and valleys with flowing rivers. Like Earth, Titan's atmosphere is dominated by nitrogen. It does not have the oxygen we have. Where we have oxygen, Titan has methane—giant sporadic releases of methane in the form of rain. So I ask: why couldn't there be microbes somewhere on Titan that breathe or drink methane just like our microbial ancestors on Earth?"

"Good point."

"That's what I'm looking for."

"I think that's just great. How's your research going?"

"Well...I just don't know. Doug Valentine thinks my ideas have merit. But nobody else does. My colleagues listen to me but then walk away and whisper derogatory things to the other lab rats. I'm only a post-doc. They just don't take me seriously."

"I take you seriously, Kelly. And I'm a scientist too."

"Thanks, Dr. Neshat.'

"Khalid. Please call me Khalid. We're friends now, aren't we?"

"Yes, Khalid."

Like a perfect gentleman, Khalid volunteered to make a trip to the beverage table. He brought back fresh tasty treasures of viticulture. Kelly treated him as her hero, having slain the dragon of a crowded room to protect their relative privacy.

"Tell me about your family," he said.

"Thanks for asking. I've got a son, still in pre-school. I've got a darling baby daughter, the love of my life. I miss them each day I'm in the lab. I just can't wait to get home to see them."

"Why are you here this evening? Why aren't you home with this lovely family?"

"Well, I was told this social event would be important. After all, NASA and TTU are getting together. So this is just one evening away from home. It's unusual."

"You've not mentioned your husband. Are you happily married?"

"I'm married. Let me say that much."

"Does your husband understand your lab work? Or your Titan theory?"

"No. This is not his field. He doesn't understand my work. Or me."

Khalid smiled and sipped his wine, maintaining eye contact.

Kelly followed suit. Silence followed that. They each drank a second time. The silence continued in a slightly awkward fashion that both understood and appreciated. They exchanged smiles.

"I'm overnighting at the Hilton Santa Clara, not far from Great America," said Khalid. "So are the others from out of town. Would you like to visit me tonight?"

Kelly moved sideways on her chair. "I have to go home. My family, you know."

"Why don't you go home? Check on your family, then come to the Hilton?"

"Let me think about it." She smiled. She took a drink. "I've thought about it. Okay."

"Why don't you phone me with an ETA?"

"Okay. What number?"

Khalid reached into the left side pocket of his suit coat. He started to remove his iPhone. He let go of it and shifted the action to his other hand. He removed a Nokia from his right pocket.

"Dictate your cell phone number to me," Kelly requested. Khalid hit a button, looked at the phone, and dictated an area code and phone number. "I'll put it in my directory under KN, under 'Handsome KN'."

Kelly stood up. She dropped her hand on his and squeezed it. Without saying a word she disappeared through the crowd and out the front door.

CHAPTER 40

NASA

An hour later Khalid was back in his hotel room. The Nokia was lying on the dresser as if waiting for an assignment. He dialed the operator on the house phone. "Would you please connect me with Phee Seng Wu."

No answer.

"Now, I'm trying to remember his room number. Is it 340 or 440?"

"We're not supposed to divulge...Oh well. It's 342."

"Thank you very much. I appreciate it." Neshat hung up.

A moment later the Nokia sounded. Khalid picked the phone up, pondering whether this was the call he was waiting for. He tapped "answer," then hesitated, waiting for the caller to speak first.

"Khalid? This is Kelly."

"Oh, Kelly. How wonderful!"

"I'm in my car. I'm not sure why I am doing this. I told my husband Alex I needed to go back to the lab because I thought I left my computer on in my hurry to get to the reception. That's against the rules. That's the kind of thing he understands. He'll go to bed soon. The kids are already asleep. I am feeling a little uneasy about meeting you. So let's just talk when I get there. Okay? It should take me only ten more minutes to reach the Hilton."

"Of course. I will enjoy some good conversation. Just park. Come straight to room 221. I'll be waiting."

WHEN KHALID HEARD the soft knock on the door, he abruptly ended a conversation on his iPhone. He walked with an air of confidence towards the door. He opened the door slowly and saw the youthful, fidgety figure of a woman who was attempting to look calm.

"Kelly. How nice you are here." He spoke with a sophisticated composure. Then he closed the door behind her. With the smoothness of a magician, he locked it with the chain.

"You look a bit nervous, my dear. May I get you a glass of wine or perhaps a brandy? It seems the people at NASA love to give non-practicing Muslims gifts of liquor."

"Well, maybe a glass of white wine, not too much. Any kind will do."

"Good. I will join you."

Kelly stood there stiffly, breaths shallow, wondering what she could possibly be thinking? *I am a mother, a good mother. I take care of my children—I have never even left them alone in a car with the engine running. And I'm a wife, a pretty good wife. I have never cheated on my husband or even considered it. I don't think Alex has ever cheated on me. I have never even been tempted before.*

Her eyes closely followed Khalid as he walked across the room to a small wet bar where he uncorked a fresh bottle of wine and took out two glasses. *Maybe a drink will give me some time to think. I have been working in this lab since before Bradley was born. Maybe I am just bored and have never admitted it to myself. Alex is the kind of husband every woman wants.*

Khalid poured the wine and set the glasses down on the small coffee table in front of a hide-a-bed sofa on the wall directly opposite the bed. *There is just something about this man with eyes so brown they are almost black. There's something about the glowing color of his skin. Exotic, sensual. He talks and moves like no one I have ever known.*

"Come sit here, next to me," Khalid invited her as he sat himself, and then gently patted the place next to him.

Kelly smiled and sat down and reached for her wine. Khalid took his and raised it, offering a toast "to new friends." Kelly responded in kind, her awkward smile relaxing as she took her first sip.

They talked for a while about little things, nothing. Where she grew up, more about her kids, where he went to school, when did he come to the U.S. He was interested in her work, or so it seemed. That pleased Kelly. Most people outside the lab had no clue what she did or why she did it.

But they both knew it was simply verbal foreplay. Kelly was becoming more and more comfortable; her body language showed it. Khalid had an eerie ability to zero in on what was important to a woman, to listen to her without judgment. Kelly felt herself letting down her guard, sinking into his dark hypnotic stare.

Offering her a second glass of wine, Khalid moved over to the wet bar, grasped the bottle, and walked towards Kelly with the neck of the bottle pointed towards her. He tilted it downward and poured. He set the bottle down and with one movement reached for her hand and drew her up to him. Kelly exerted no resistance, and rose to stand as if being invited to dance. Khalid drew her close to him and gently pressed his lips to hers. Kelly felt herself sink into his body.

In a matter of seconds, the gentleness of the first kiss moved to passion, their arms moving up and down each other's back, and their kisses reaching deep into the other's mouth. Khalid removed her beige jacket one sleeve at a time, allowing it to drop at her feet while he carefully unbuttoned her blouse, one button at a time, interspersing his sensuous movements with kisses that made Kelly impatient. Khalid led her, naked, to the bed. As she lay there, he looked down on her with an intensity that Kelly had never experienced before. It sent a bolt of excitement through her now trembling body. Khalid disrobed without ever losing eye contact, knowing just how to use his trim, fit body to get what he wanted.

The next moments seemed to speed by. Khalid came down on her with a force that startled Kelly, but she was wet and ready for him. He wrapped his arms around her body and began to kiss her, moving from place to place on her body as if he could read her mind. Kelly groaned with delight, and returned the kisses, exploring his entire body, ending with his hard, erect penis. Khalid pulled her to him and went into her easily, moving rhythmically in and out of her, then in circles stimulating her and allowing her to move her own hips in synchronized motion. Kelly came with a powerful rush; Khalid followed by just seconds. Both groaned and screamed with passionate gasps. Then they lay still, quietly savoring their pleasure, staring straight upwards at the ceiling. After a few minutes, they turned their heads towards each other, gazed into each other's eyes and laughed.

"You are an exciting woman, Kelly. There's a magnificent shower in the bathroom. Large enough for two. Would you like to join me?" Khalid's words flowed like melted butter.

"Hmmmm......Sounds perfect."

"Why don't you get started? Set the temperature just the way you like it. I'll join you in a moment."

Kelly rose quietly from the bed and walked slowly to the bathroom, suddenly aware of her nudity. She wondered about Eve in the garden. *What just happened? Oh my God, it was amazing.* She felt a chill come over her body as she opened the shower door and turned the faucet to hot. As the steam billowed up, Kelly adjusted the temperature and stepped in, allowing the streams to relax and cleanse her, and pull her back into her own reality. *No one will ever have to know about this. I certainly can't believe there is a future in this relationship. Maybe every woman needs to do this once. What a handsome man and wonderful lover. But this is not me, not my life.* Kelly put her head under the pounding stream, rotating it back and forth while lathering her hair until it frothed up like marshmallow.

CHAPTER 41

NASA

THE SHOWER DOOR CREAKED OPEN. Kelly giggled, anticipating an overture from Khalid. She apologized for being lost under a mound of suds, but invited her lover to enjoy the luxury with her. She scooped up a handful of lather and playfully offered it to him, intending to decorate his chest. As she did, she moved her hand down his arm, and discovered a strange object in his hand—cold and hard, large, metal, sharp-edged.

Kelly let out a chilling scream, quickly muffled by the strong sinister hand of Khalid. The scream was abruptly interrupted as he severed her larynx with the precision of a surgeon. *Oh God. Brad-baby, Angel, Alex....I don't want to leave you. God forgive me.* She could not fight back.

The butcher slit her throat from nearly one ear to the other. Her eyes bulged with terror, but only momentarily. Blood gushed from her mouth, streaming down her chest, flowing downward, mixing first with water and then with semen. As life left her, her body slipped in staccato movements along the shower wall until it slumped lifeless onto the tiled floor.

Khalid's knife had a ten-inch blade, smooth on one side, saw-toothed on the other. After stretching Kelly's body as far as he could on the shower floor, he made an incision just below the navel. Blood flowed like the Mississippi. Into the incision he pressed the knife, cutting through tissue. Once he'd reached the spine, he severed it, using the knife as a saw. The corpse was now in two pieces. Khalid looked down at Kelly without emotion. He turned the shower temperature to cold and left it running.

Khalid had already planned what would happen next. He opened both of his suitcases. He removed the contents, placing clothes and sundries in large sealable plastic bags he had brought along. He assembled his computer and deskware, closing them in his large brief case. He returned to the bathroom to check on the severed body on the shower floor. Nearly all of the blood had been washed down the drain. He studied the matter for a moment after shutting off the water.

He tamped the lower half of Kelly's corpse with one of the hotel towels. Then he moved the legs toward an open plastic trash bag. Once they were stuffed in the bag, he sealed it. He placed this full bag into another, top in the bottom, and sealed that. *This should prevent blood seeping out.* He lifted the double bag up and fit it into one of the open suitcases. Then he returned to the bathroom and repeated the procedure with Kelly's torso. Soon he had two suitcases, each bearing half of a human corpse.

His eyes scanned the room. *Have I forgotten anything?* He walked to the closet. Out of the left pocket of his suit coat he withdrew the Nokia. Then he threw the Nokia into one of the suitcases and closed both lids. He locked the combination locks on both.

CHAPTER 42

NASA

WHEN HE HAD FINISHED DRESSING and combing his hair, Neshat put tight plastic surgical gloves on his hands. He removed the plastic liner from the sitting room waste basket and shoved it into his pants pocket. Then Neshat left his room and walked up the fire stairs to the third floor. He knocked lightly on Room 342. No answer. Then, he knocked harder. Finally, the door opened a crack.

"Oh, it's you," said Phee Seng Wu, dressed in his sleeping clothes. He opened the door and let his late night visitor enter. "My, but it must be important at this late hour."

"Quite important, my friend," said Neshat while chaining the door. He sat. Wu sat. Neshat spoke. "How far have you gotten in developing the hookup between our transmission program and the satellite system?"

Wu smiled. "I've made considerable progress. Our program is ready. Once the satellite is in orbit, I expect it will take only a short time to establish our communications link."

"Where do you keep our program?" asked Neshat.

"Right here." Wu picked up a USB thumb drive and waved it with a smile.

"Thanks," said Neshat. "That's all I need to know. Without a further word, Neshat grabbed the slightly built Chinese man and threw him down upon the bed. Neshat leaped up onto his back and placed his right knee squarely between the prone man's shoulder blades, rendering him helpless. From his pocket he withdrew the plastic bag and forced it over Wu's head. Wu struggled. He began to yell, but the bag muffled his sound. Wu's head turned to the side. When his mouth opened to inhale the bag was sucked in. When he exhaled he coughed. After two minutes the struggle lessened.

Neshat kept pressure on his back and made sure the bag was tightly sealed. Time passed. Activity ceased. The Beijing scientist was breathing no more.

Neshat released his pressure and removed the bag. He carefully arranged Wu Phee Seng's body with his face in the pillow. Some drool spilled onto the pillow case. Neshat smiled. He pulled the blankets over, making it appear that Wu had died in his sleep.

Neshat put the USB in his pocket and departed.

CHAPTER 43

NASA

BACK IN HIS OWN ROOM, Neshat picked up the house phone and dialed the front desk. "I have changed my travel plans. I need to drive to San Luis Obispo for a breakfast meeting. So I need to leave now."

"But it's only two o'clock in the morning," said the desk clerk.

"I know this. But I think prudence dictates that I get on the road. Would you kindly ask a porter to come and get my luggage? I'll check out and then pull my car up to the front door."

"Certainly, Mister Neshat."

Leaving the suitcases and bags in the room, Khalid slung his briefcase strap over his shoulder and took the elevator to the first floor. After checking out and placing his folio in his inner suit coat pocket, he went to the parking lot and pulled his rented Cadillac Escalade up to the front door. The porter placed all the luggage, including the two suitcases, into the car through the hatch door. Khalid placed a ten-dollar bill in his hand and drove off into the night.

He had no intention of driving the Escalade south to San Luis Obispo. Rather, he drove northward on US 101 toward the city. In the Bay Area, "the city" means San Francisco. At San Antonio Avenue he exited and looked for a closed grocery store or filling station. He pulled into a Safeway parking lot and drove to the rear of the store. He stopped at the dumpsters. He removed the two suitcases and deposited them with the other trash. Soon he was back on US 101, again heading north.

CHAPTER 44

CHICAGO

LEONA'S PLANE touched down at O'Hare at 6:45 am. Minutes later she walked through the Arrivals door pulling her convertible carry-on. She spotted Graham's waiting CR-V and approached it. Graham exited from the driver's door and came around to the sidewalk. The two kissed briefly but held the embrace for a much longer time. Leona looked up into Graham's eyes and spoke. "Grammy, I've missed you."

"Ditto," replied Graham. He then opened the right front door and invited his passenger to get in. He placed the suitcase in the trunk and soon they were on the road.

"Did you check your voice mails?" asked Graham.

"No. What's up?" asked Leona.

"Better call Angie right now."

"It's early. She's probably still in bed, even if she's an hour ahead in Detroit."

"Just call her immediately."

Leona hit speed dial and connected. "Angie, what're you doing up so early?"

"Leona," said Angie, "did you spend time with Kelly last evening at NASA?"

"Yes. We had a some great moments reconnecting. It was so good..."

"Leona, Kelly's missing."

"What?"

"I got a call during the night from Alex. He said Kelly didn't come home. When did you last see Kelly?"

"Well, it was just before I left Moffat Field for the airport. Maybe ten o'clock."

"Alex told me she came home and then said she needed to return to the lab to turn off a computer or something. I think that was later. Do you know anything about this?"

"No. Nothing. Sorry."

"Alex is worried sick, as you can imagine. He called the lab. Nobody saw her. He then called the police. I'm worried too."

"That makes both of us."

The two continued their exchange for a few minutes and then hung up with promises to keep each other updated.

Graham pulled his car into the parking lot adjacent to Trinity Church. He stopped right in front of the parsonage, situated right behind the church building. He carried Leona's suitcase up the porch steps. Both Leona and Graham nodded to the black sentry through the picture window—Midnight the cat watching all parking lot activity from her lookout post atop the couch. Graham held the door for the lady to pass into the house. Buck, the Siberian Husky, had heard the door unlatching and was already waiting to see who might be entering. The two humans were greeted by a wagging tail and an undulating Husky torso, signs of welcome on the part of *canis familiaris*.

Soon the coffee was poured and Graham brought Leona up to date on activities involving the life of the church, including a description of the previous Sunday's worship service. Graham then asked for a debriefing of events at NASA. Leona had much to tell.

Graham listened intently, asking questions to get his picture in focus.

"Now, why the hell did Director Holthusen give you this assignment? You're only a part-timer. So, you run off to China to play spy and I sit here in Chicago babysitting your congregation. You run off to NASA, and again I just babysit. I'm available for a new assignment. Why didn't Holthusen ask me?"

"He asked me because of my background in biology. What did you do your doctorate in?" Leona was speaking rhetorically and loudly. "New Religious Movements! What? New Religious Movements! Now, who gives a flying fuck about New Religious Movements?"

Graham frowned. He picked up a pillow and threw it at Leona. She raised her left arm to parry the pillow thrust. Then she leaped over the coffee table and onto Graham's lap, her knees pressed into Graham's thighs. With both arms she embraced Graham in a headlock. He wrapped his arms around her lower back and squeezed. They tipped to the side and rolled off the couch, crashing into the coffee table. Two nearly empty coffee mugs went flying. Both wrestlers lay on the floor, tussling.

Upon hearing the commotion, Buck came running from the kitchen. When he saw the human combat on the living room floor, he began to growl. Then he whined. He did not bark. He shifted his weight from one front foot to the other, growling and whining. It was clear Buck was trying to decide unsuccessfully who the aggressor was. The growl was a warning to the aggressor. The whine indicated that poor Buck was undecided as to what action to take. He walked up on top of the two prone bodies. He wanted to put a stop to the violence, but he did not know how.

Leona and Graham were now doubling up with laughter. Simultaneously they both reached up to scratch one of Buck's ears. Upon seeing a cease-fire between the two warring humans, Buck's tail began to wag and he showed signs of relief.

"Let's try an experiment," said Graham. "I'll pretend to hit you. You scream in pain."

"Okay," said Leona.

Graham lifted his left hand and pretended to strike Leona's shoulder. She yelled, "Ouch! Ow!"

Buck's mouth opened with fangs bared. He lurched forward, snapping at Graham's offending arm with a loud and vicious growl. Graham immediately ceased his arm movement and relaxed back onto the floor. Buck gave out one more warning growl and then backed up a short distance.

"Well, now I know where I stand with Buck," said Graham, chortling.

Leona was also laughing. "Oh, Buck! Thank you for protecting me." She reached up to pet Buck on the head. So did Graham. Buck looked utterly confused, but relieved once again.

Leona's iPhone signaled that a text had arrived. She stood up, found her phone, and checked. "Lunch 2morrow. 1:00. Hilton Michigan Ave. Khalid."

CHAPTER 45

CHICAGO

LEONA BOARDED the Metra at 79th Street / Cheltenham in the direction of Chicago's Loop. She arrived downtown with sufficient time to enjoy a casual springtime walk through Millennium Park to the Hilton. Khalid greeted her upon entering and ushered her to a luxuriously appointed dining room with white tablecloths.

"I had thought I might have just a sandwich or a salad," she remarked on her way in. "This is a bit much just for lunch."

"Not too much for such a beautiful woman," responded Khalid, following the maître d' to his reserved table, a table for two by the window facing Lake Michigan. Leona smiled. She enjoyed being treated with such charming deference.

With menus in front of them, Khalid asked, "Now, Reverend Foxx, I know you like wine. What is your favorite?"

"Oh, just the house wine will do," she said with a head shake.

"No. I know better than that. You have a cultivated palate. Please tell me, what is your favorite wine?"

"It's not going to be on the menu. And even if it were on the menu, it'd cost too much."

"Let me ask again: what is your favorite wine?"

Leona shifted slightly in her chair. "Silver Oak."

"Did you say Silver Oak?"

"Yes. It's a cabernet sauvignon. That's all Silver Oak makes—cabernet."

Khalid requested the wine steward. When he had arrived and greeted the dining room guests, Khalid asked, "Do you have Silver Oak?"

"Why, yes, of course," said the steward. "Napa or Alexander Valley."

"Napa," said Leona quickly.

Khalid smiled. "That's what we'll have: one bottle of Napa Valley Silver Oak with two glasses."

When the steward was departing, Leona whispered loudly. "Mr. Neshat, you didn't even ask for the price."

"Price makes no difference. We will enjoy our lunch today, Reverend Foxx. We will enjoy Silver Oak as well as the silver crests on Lake Michigan's waves."

Leona sighed and looked out over Millennium Park and the Great Lake beyond.

"What brings you to Chicago?" asked Leona.

"Tomorrow I fly to Detroit. I've got a meeting Monday with a small computer peripherals company," said Khalid.

"But what brings you to *Chicago*?"

"You, frankly."

Leona blushed. Small talk ensued. Khalid spoke of his youth in Iran, his education, his interest in both nuclear physics and astrophysics. He said nothing about his connection to Lionel Chang and the newly formed Transhumanist syndicate. Leona spoke of her Michigan childhood; her studies in biology and astrobiology; and her work as a parish pastor. She said nothing nor even hinted that she had once been incarcerated on death row in a Tehran prison. To the Persian suitor, she appeared to be a hometown girl, a hometown girl with pulchritude and aptitude.

The Silver Oak was tasted, sipped, discussed, and enjoyed. So was the lunch that followed.

"I find it curious," began Khalid, "that you, with all your education, would dedicate your life to religion."

"Actually, Mr. Neshat, I don't care much about religion per se. What I care about is God and my service to him. I serve God by loving my people. That's where my heart is. That's where my life is. Well, most of the time. Right now I'm certainly enjoying the Silver Oak. And I'm enjoying our lunch together."

Khalid smiled. "If you are enjoying this lunch as much as you say you are, might I make a recommendation?"

"What's that?"

"Please call me Khalid. I've heard enough of this Mister Neshat for the day."

Leona laughed. "Okay, Khalid. And stop with the Reverend stuff. I'm Lee to my friends. And I'd like to think of you as such a friend. So it's Lee. Okay?"

"Okay, Lee."

They toasted.

"Do you believe we human beings should be moral, Lee?" asked Khalid in a baiting tone.

"Certainly," responded Leona.

"Why do you think we should be moral?" he asked, now sipping his wine.

"Because this is what God wants us to do," she said. Then she added, "God is love. If we abide in love, we abide in God. Or maybe it's the other way around. If we abide in God—then we'll look for ways to love one another."

"Nah. I think it's all in the oxytocin," he blustered.

"What do you mean?" Leona's nose was sniffing her wine's bouquet.

"Oxytocin is a neuropeptide that influences brain activity. It enables mothers to bond with their babies. When it's active we want to make friends. It's what makes the two sexes attracted to each other.

Without oxytocin, you'd be a loner. We'd all be loners. Oxytocin rewards us: doing good makes us feel good. Morality is just the way oxytocin dictates that we live in groups, live in community. It's simple, isn't it? We don't need a supernatural explanation such as God. Just look at how our brains work."

"I know what oxytocin is. But if our morality is simply the result of neural activity, why do we get the sense of obligation, the demand to do what is right or good even if we don't will to do it?"

"I don't feel any sense of obligation. I just do what feels good. Have you thought that maybe religion and belief in God's demand is a mistake? Maybe it's a mistake in human evolution. Maybe oxytocin doesn't require religion or belief in God to make us bond with one another for survival. Maybe morality is less important than you think it is. What do you think about that?" Khalid took a sip from his glass.

"I think that love is the ultimate. It's divine," responded Leona. "When we love or receive love, God is present. Even if your oxytocin theory could be confirmed scientifically, this would not alter the metaphysical part of it. God is co-present in our neurons and in our relationships. Well, Khalid, that's what I think." Leona smiled and took another sip.

"I'm glad we're talking about love, Lee." Khalid winked.

Leona's iPhone signaled. She checked the incoming text. Her facial expression changed. Her face read: terror. "Khalid, I must get a taxi immediately. I'm sorry, but I can't continue our delightful conversation at the moment. Please call me again."

Leona disappeared from the dining room on the run. Khalid watched her depart, helplessly.

CHAPTER 46

CHICAGO

"To O'Hare! I'm in a hurry," exclaimed Leona as she slammed the cab door.

"Which airline?" asked the driver as he pulled south on Michigan Avenue and then turned west.

"United."

Leona hit speed dial. "Grammy?" The voice on the other end had only enough time to breathe loudly before Leona continued. "I'm on my way to O'Hare. Gotta get to San Francisco. Angie left me a message. She says her sister Kelly has been found dead. Her body was dismembered. I can't believe it. I saw Kelly just two nights ago."

Graham started to speak. Leona interrupted him.

"Can you take over Sunday's duties? Sorry to ask this once again."

Leona could not see Graham stomping his feet. His feet said, "No, dammit!" But his voice squeaked, "Of course, Lee. You can count on me."

"Gotta hang up, Grammy. You're a peach. Love you. Oh, and please feed Buck and Midnight." Click.

CHAPTER 47

MOUNTAIN VIEW

It was 8:30pm PST when Leona's flight touched down at SFO. Angie's plane from Detroit arrived half an hour later. The two met at the baggage claim, even though Leona brought no baggage. The two women rented a Prius and raced south on Highway 101 toward Mountain View. Angie had arranged by phone to meet her brother-in-law, Alexander Compton, at the Compton home only a mile from Moffat Field. They arrived shortly before 10:00 Saturday evening.

Once in the living room, Angie raced to Alex and they hugged. Tears flowed. Leona approached more cautiously. A giant of a man stood up from the sofa and stretched out his hand. "Chris MacDonald from NASA, Reverend Foxx. We met..."

"Oh, of course, Doctor MacDonald. Thanks for being here at this dreadful moment. Was today the day the satellite was launched?" Leona asked.

"Yes. Everything went up just as planned," answered Chris.

A second man stood and introduced himself as Alan Kurz from TTU.

"Yes, I saw you from afar at the NASA reception," said Leona courteously. "Nice to finally meet you."

When MacDonald and Kurz had retaken their seats, a third man stood up. About Leona's age and height, with a growing pot belly, he wore a short sleeve collared blue shirt with a tan sweater vest. He spoke first. "I'm Inspector Brocker, Michael Brocker, with the Mountain View PD. And you are....?"

"My name is Leona Foxx. I'm a pastor in Chicago. I grew up with Kelly and Angie, her older sister, in Dearborn, Michigan. We've been lifelong friends. I'm so glad you're here, Inspector."

Next, a Japanese American woman stood up to say, "I'm Tina Matsuoka. I'm with the FBI, Pastor Foxx."

"Why's the FBI here?" questioned Leona.

Chris MacDonald interrupted. "We always involve the FBI when something comes up at NASA. It's a federal facility."

"Oh," said Leona, turning to Alex, who had finally freed himself from Angie's embrace. Leona stuck out her hand for a shake. Seeing the tears in his eyes, she moved her body close to his and gave him a comforting hug.

"Where are the children?" Leona asked Alex.

"My sister has them at her home right now. They're just fine."

After Angie and Leona had seated themselves and were served some decaffeinated coffee, it was time for a summary.

Inspector Brocker took the floor. "This is difficult to describe. Please tell me how much detail you think you'll be able to hear?"

"All of it. Every detail," said Leona. Then she looked sheepishly at Alex and Angie. They nodded agreement.

Brocker proceeded, looking at Angie. "Your sister's body was found in a Safeway dumpster. I regret to say that it was found in two locked suitcases. Her upper body had been severed from her lower extremities and stuffed separately into the two bags."

Both Angie and Leona winced. Alex turned his head and closed his eyes.

Brocker continued to describe the contents of the two suitcases, how and when they had been discovered, and what the coroner and forensics lab had determined. The estimated time of death was shortly after the NASA reception on Thursday evening. No one in the room could connect Kelly with the Safeway store. No one had seen Kelly returning to her NASA lab that evening. Everyone was stunned by the facts they were hearing.

"It's interesting," said Chris MacDonald. "We had two deaths that night. The other was Dr. Wu Phee Seng. He died in his sleep."

"Any connection?" asked Leona.

"Perhaps not," answered Tina Matsuoka. "Dr. Wu died of sleep apnea. He stopped breathing and suffocated. This is not uncommon for men with this condition. I would like to say that it's only a coincidence these two events took place at approximately the same time. But I can't disconnect them completely. You see, Kelly's car was found in the parking lot of the same hotel where Dr. Wu was found dead."

Mr. Compton gasped. Everyone looked startled. Nothing was said for a moment.

"The car keys?" asked Leona.

"Found in one of the suit cases," answered Tina.

"Let's get back to Kelly," requested Leona.

"I have photos of the suitcase contents and of the dismembered body parts," said Brocker. "If you wish to examine them....But you don't have to."

"No!" said Alex.

"No, I just can't," said Angie.

"Please let me look at them," said Leona, reaching across to take them. She studied them carefully as the conversation continued to buzz in the room.

"Mr. Brocker. You have pictures of Kelly's profile, from both the left and the right. Now, I see an earring on her right ear. But, no earring on her left ear. Did you locate the second earring?"

"You're very observant, Rev. Foxx," Brocker responded. "No. There was no sign of the second earring."

"By coincidence, I gave Kelly this very set of earrings. For her wedding." Leona bowed her head and leafed through the photos once again. She interrupted again. "What is this item? Here, in the corner of this suitcase?" Leona asked Brocker.

"Oh, that's a cell phone."

"Kelly's?"

"No. Kelly's phone was found underneath her body parts in the other suit case."

"So this is a second phone, right?"

"Right."

"Whose cell phone?"

"We've identified it as belonging to Doug Valentine."

MacDonald's face turned sheet white. "What? Doug Valentine! That can't be."

Matsuoka spoke. "We have a theory. Right now it's only a theory. I'm sorry to say this in front of Mrs. Compton's husband."

Alex nodded for her to continue.

"We conjecture that Mrs. Compton lied to Mr. Compton when she said she was going back to the lab to shut down a computer. Instead, we believe she met Mr. Valentine at some secluded location. It should be mentioned that the preliminary autopsy shows fresh semen in Mrs. Compton's vagina."

Alex turned his head again. Angie dropped her face into her hands.

Matsuoka continued. "It is possible that, following sex, the two had a falling out, perhaps an argument. At that time Mr. Valentine murdered Mrs. Compton. He then tried to dispose of the body in the manner you see here."

"My wife having an affair with Doug!" exclaimed Alex. "I find that just too hard to believe."

"I find it hard to believe too," added MacDonald.

"Right now," continued Matsuoka, "this is only a working hypothesis. We'll explore this until we meet a dead end."

"What about Doug?" asked MacDonald. "Have you talked to him?"

"As we speak," said Brocker, "he is being brought to headquarters for questioning. In fact, I need to get over there. Tina, are you coming along?"

After the good-byes were said, the two law officers took their leave. Leona asked permission to accompany them.

"You can ride with me," Brocker told Leona.

CHAPTER 48

MOUNTAIN VIEW

Doug Valentine was as bewildered as grieved over the disappearance and then the report of Kelly's death. To be questioned by police as a suspect elicited even more anxiety than the confusion had.

Leona along with Tina Matsuoka watched and listened to the questioning of Valentine from behind a one-way mirror. Michael Brocker led the interrogation in a small bare room in the Mountain View Police Department building.

Valentine was most cooperative, though distraught. He described in detail his close working relationship with Kelly Compton at NASA. He praised her abilities and lauded her zeal as a scientist. Yes, he had warm feelings for his lab rat colleague. No, he and Kelly had never flirted, let alone had an affair. Yes, he is happily married. No, he has never been involved in a violent crime.

"How did your cell phone get into the suitcase with Mrs. Compton's body?" Brocker asked the suspect.

"I have no idea," responded Valentine, shaking his head in dismay.

"When did you last see your phone?"

"On the night of the NASA and TTU reception. When I got home, I could not find it. I thought it would be in one of my pockets, but it wasn't."

"What time did you get home that evening?"

"About 10:00, if I recall correctly."

"Did you and your wife go home together?"

"Yes, of course."

"What time did you go to bed?"

"We were in bed by 11:00 pm. We were both scheduled to work the next day."

"Did you remain in bed all night? Can your wife vouch for you? Your alibi here could be important."

"I think so."

"What do you mean *you think so*? Either you were in bed with her all night or not. So?"

"We sleep in separate bedrooms."

"What?"

"Yes, separate bedrooms. I snore. I have sleep apnea. When I retire I put on a face mask. It's attached to an oxygen machine to insure that I don't suffocate. The machine is noisy and really disturbs her. So we sleep apart."

"This means, Mr. Valentine, that you could have snuck out of the house and returned without her having known you were gone. Is this right?"

"Well...." Valentine stumbled.

"That's enough," pronounced the inspector. The two sat in their respective chairs across a small table for minutes without speaking. Both were thinking. Then Brocker opened up a second line of questioning. He repeated many of his initial questions in slightly different words. The results were the same: Valentine could not account for his missing phone and he could not produce an alibi for his whereabouts at the time of the crime. Worry showed on both their faces.

"Let's take a break," said Brocker. "There's a water fountain in the hall. Don't go far."

Valentine stood and stretched. A uniformed policewoman guided him to the water fountain.

Michael Brocker walked around and joined the other two in the observation room. Each poured stale but hot coffee into a paper cup and begin to sip.

"Whatya think?" asked Brocker.

"It's pretty clear that Valentine had opportunity," said Matsuoka. "But we don't have a motive. Unless, of course, it's sex. Adultery and violence come shrink-wrapped together, even for otherwise nice people. I believe we should treat Valentine as guilty and see if we can prove it beyond a doubt."

"Rev. Foxx, do you have any opinions?" asked the inspector.

"Do you plan to run a DNA test to see if Valentine's semen matches what you found in Kelly?" asked Leona.

"Of course," answered Matsuoka.

"I may not be an infallible judge of character," Leona continued, "but Valentine just does not look like a killer to me. In fact, he doesn't even look like an adulterer. But the evidence so far is quite incriminating. I grant Tina that much."

The three sat and sipped.

Leona broke the brief silence. "I think we should press for more details on the missing phone. This appears to be so damning. Yet, it's the only material link between Valentine and the murder. It deserves further probing."

"I agree," said Brocker. Matsuoka shook her head with approval.

"With your permission, Inspector, I'd like to ask some questions," said Leona.

"Might as well," responded Brocker. "We need to break through this log jam." Turning to Matsuoka he added, "Would you like to join us in the interrogation room?"

She nodded and all three reconvened with Doug Valentine.

CHAPTER 49

MENLO PARK

"Doug, do you remember meeting me at the NASA-TTU reception? I'm Leona Foxx, a friend of Kelly's."

"Oh, yes," said Valentine. "Are you as overwhelmed by this as I am?" Doug's face was haggard and suffering with bewilderment.

"I'm devastated," said Leona. "Kelly's older sister Angie and I are BFF. I've known Kelly since she was a preschooler. I'm doubly sad because I feel her sister's sadness."

Valentine looked downward and shook his head in grief.

"On behalf of Inspector Brocker, I'd like to follow up on the matter of your cell phone," said Leona. "Now, you do realize how damning it is to have your phone appear in the suitcase, right?"

"Yes, I do. I do understand why the police need to interrogate me. I'd do the same. So please go ahead."

Leona looked Valentine in the face and established eye contact. "Doug, do you have Kelly on speed dial?"

"Yes."

"Why?"

"Kelly and I spoke frequently, sometimes even from the lab to the lunch room. We worked together on many projects and we explored our pet ideas with one another. We were very close colleagues, even friends. But there was never any adultery. She's happily married. So am I. That's..."

"Doug," interrupted Leona. "You have Kelly on speed dial." Leona removed Valentine's cell phone from the evidence baggie. "I can see it here when I look at your list of contacts. You include Kelly's photo, along with the photos of many other people in your contact list. Did Kelly have you on her speed dial?"

"Yes, of course."

"Did Kelly have your phone number memorized?"

"No. These days with speed dial I don't even have my own phone number memorized. Nobody does."

Leona turned to Brocker. "Do you have Kelly's phone handy?"

"Yes, it's in the next room."

"May I see it?"

"I'll go get it."

In a moment Brocker returned with Kelly's phone. Leona grabbed it and checked the contact list. She quickly located Doug Valentine's speed dial entry. Then, she went to the recent call record. She tapped some buttons.

"Look here," said Leona, drawing the attention of Brocker and Matsuoka. "Kelly has not one but two entries for Doug Valentine's number on her contact list. The older one has Doug's name and photo. The photo pops up whenever she receives a call from Doug or dials Doug as an existing contact. Now look. Here's a second contact entry. No photo. New name. Looks like 'KN.' This contact was added at 10:15 pm on Thursday."

"Mmmmmm," murmured Matsuoka.

"Here's the logic," continued Leona. "Kelly punched Doug's number into her phone at 10:15 not knowing it was Doug's number. She gave it the contact name, 'KN.' Then, at 11:16, she simply hit redial. She still did not know it was Doug's phone number. Perhaps it was dark or perhaps she simply hit redial and then quickly put the phone to her ear without seeing the number appear on her screen."

"Sure enough," mumbled Matsuoka. "Could 'KN' stand for Ken or Kent?"

"We don't know. But, if Kelly had not memorized Doug's number and wanted to phone him, she would have hit her own speed dial, her contact with the photo. Right? But she used the redialer for a number she'd punched in an hour earlier, not the existing contact. Could it be that Kelly mistakenly thought she was dialing somebody else, somebody other than Doug? Somebody who had Doug's phone but was not Doug?"

CHAPTER 50

MENLO PARK

KELLY LATHAM COMPTON's Memorial Service was held at the Menlo Park Presbyterian Church the following Tuesday. Closed casket. No cemetery ceremony.

The post-service reception was held in the parish hall. Leona carried her coffee and slice of cake to a table partially occupied. She found herself seated in the vicinity of Chris MacDonald, Buzz Kidd, and Alan Kurz, all dressed fittingly in suits and ties.

MacDonald and Kurz were already discussing the death of Wu Phee Seng and registering astonishment that the two deaths occurred so close to one another in time. They summarized the facts for Leona's benefit.

"And to think all this happened shortly after our NASA-TTU reception!" exclaimed Leona. "For the sake of Brewster, what do you think is the connection?"

"Dr. Wu died in his sleep," said MacDonald. "Most likely sleep apnea caused a stoppage of breathing. He suffocated. Just an accident. Just a coincidence that it occurred about the time Kelly was murdered."

"Still, it's curious," remarked Kurz.

"Now that Dr. Wu is out of the picture, how will this affect the satellite work that you two are planning?" asked Leona.

Kurz spoke. "Dr. Neshat has agreed to step in. He began work already, yesterday."

MacDonald followed. "Neshat will represent the TTU's IA project. I'll connect him with a counterpart at NASA and the two of them will program the satellite transmission system. Doctor Neshat has assumed responsibility for communications with implantees."

"Whom do you plan to appoint from NASA?"

"Don't know yet. No problem, though. We've got plenty at Moffat who can handle this," answered MacDonald. "Maybe with Neshat taking over, we might not need a NASA counterpart."

Leona turned her attention toward Kurz. "How did Kelly get along at TTU?"

"Oh, we all loved her," said Kurz. "Not only was she a sweet woman, she was as bright as a flash bulb and as sharp as a laser. She belonged to MENSA, like most of us at TTU. Here the brightest of the bright make profound breakthroughs. Only the greatest intelligence can create amplified intelligence."

"Did Kelly make any enemies?

"Oh no. As I said, we all loved Kelly. She made friends everywhere she went. I never witnessed any tension surrounding her."

"Was Kelly a card-carrying Transhumanist?" asked Leona.

"No. Actually, she wasn't. She was far more interested in dumb microbes than smart people. But that's okay. Not everyone has to think alike at TTU. Kelly enjoyed participating in our think-tank, and we benefited from her ideas."

"So, what're you doing with people's brains?" Leona said with a challenging tone to Kidd.

"We're making them better," responded Kidd with a note of pride. "We plan to augment the human memory and then, we hope, we can amplify intelligence itself. Once we get the ball rolling, amplified intelligence will further amplify itself and then on and on until we have made our entire solar system intelligent. It will be a posthuman intelligence, because it will eventually leave our physical bodies and become machine intelligence. We'll throw away our bodies and fill the cloud with our thoughts. Posthumanity will be so much more highly evolved than we *Homo sapiens* are."

"Let's stick for the moment to memory enhancement," said Leona. "How will you do this?"

"With a nanobiotech device that we implant in a person's brain," answered Kidd. "It will be connected by radio to Chris's satellite so we can pump in information in large quantities. The recipient's brain will have immediate access to this data."

"I'm not getting the picture," feigned Leona. "So, we've got this device implanted in a person's brain. Just how do you communicate with it?"

"The implanted microchip has an antenna," explained Kidd. "No, the antenna does not stick out of a person's head. It's totally embedded. Still, the antenna is designed to collect electromagnetic signals at a specified frequency and focus it to a point where the signal can be read in the brain. Our nano-antennas are fabricated from gold and placed directly on a silicon surface. Surface plasmons allow radio waves and even light waves to be converted to an electrical signal which the chip can read. We will pre-select the frequency, of course, so that only one transmission will be received and read."

"Sounds precarious to me," said Leona. "Virtually any computer can get hacked. If your satellite transmissions are like the internet, anything might pop up in my brain. If I had an implant, that is."

Kidd paused, his face reflecting the challenge. "Well, suppose instead of standard frequencies we used quantum key distribution. Each transmission would be unique. Unhackable. What do you think?"

"That would require practical application of entanglement," lectured the Chicago pastor. "Quantum entanglement means that two subatomic particles are generated or interact so that the quantum state of one cannot be described independently of the other. The two particles are always correlated according to spin, momentum, position, and polarization. The Einstein-Podolsky-Rosen Paradox was formulated in 1935. So have you found a practical way to create your own private quantum internet?"

Kidd and Kurz looked at one another with eyebrows furled quizically.

CHAPTER 51

MENLO PARK

"I AM TRYING to grasp what you smart guys are saying," Leona said. "Now, other than this memory gadget, your work is supposed to benefit some future species, right? It won't have any benefit for us poor backward human beings today. Am I getting you right?"

"*Au contraire, Mademoiselle.*" Kurz spoke impressively with the only French he likely knew. "The technology we develop to make possible the transition from the human to the posthuman will provide as yet unheard of improvements in our health and well being."

"How about an example?"

"It's complicated."

"I can handle it," said Leona with a smile. MacDonald added a laugh.

"Cybernetic immortality," Kurz began. "Here's how it works. First, you've got to begin with the information theory of mind I just mentioned. The brain and the mind are simply two sides of the same coin. Or, to use another analogy, your brain is the hardware and your mind is the software. Your mind consists of the information pattern provided by the synaptic circuitry of your brain. Follow?"

"Yes," mumbled Leona with a tinge of skepticism. "My brain is like my Dell PC. My mind is like Microsoft Word. Right?"

"Precisely," Kurz responded with a face full of glee. "And, as you know, you can remove your Word program from one hard drive and place it into another. Got it?"

"Yes," said Leona with a slight rolling of the eyes.

Kurz continued. "So, our first job will be to discern the information pattern in your brain that structures your mind. Once we have that, we can upload it into a computer. Listen carefully, now, Rev. Foxx. We can upload your very mind from the hardware that is your biological substrate and place it into a computer, a silicon substrate. After we do this, you'll be thinking from inside a computer. Even if your body dies and your brain is destroyed you—the conscious you—will continue to live on. As long as we keep the computer plugged in and make perpetual back-ups, you will live forever. That's why we call it *cybernetic immortality*." Kurz finished with a vocal swagger of triumph.

"Really?"

"Yes. Really. Of course we have a few bugs to work out before we actually do this to a human being. But this is one of the directions we're going at TTU. Oh, one more thing. Don't confuse cybernetic immortality with radical life extension, or RLE."

"Well, I am just the kind of person who might get confused. I don't know what RLE is," remarked Leona.

"RLE is simply extending physical life as we know it. CI means we extract mental intelligence from our physical body and place it into a machine. That's the difference."

"Got it," said Leona, shaking her head. "Do you guys believe?"

"What do you mean, believe?" asked Kidd.

"Do you believe in God? Is all your work guided by divine purpose?" asked Leona.

Kurz responded. "There is no god but nature, and evolution is its prophet. And survival of the fittest is nature's *Sharia*."

"Well, for the sake of Brisbane! If you deny the guidance of a transcendent deity, then what motivates you to devote such energy and resources into developing a posthuman species that will leave you on the trash heap of history?"

"Destiny," answered Kurz. "It is the destiny bequeathed to us by evolution."

CHAPTER 52

MENLO PARK

"What about consciousness?" interjected Leona.

Kidd paused before responding. "We have fed electroencephalographic or EEG recordings of brain activity into a sophisticated mathematical model. We've identified a neural signature of consciousness that is present in mentally healthy people. We also find this signature in brain-damaged patients who retain some awareness, but it is absent in those who are truly in a vegetative state. The signature is associated with sound and resides in the temporal cortex."

"You need more than this," said Leona.

"Yes, of course," broke in Kurz. "We work with an information theory of consciousness, as we just said. We make two assumptions. First, consciousness takes in information. Second, consciousness is unitary and integrated. The information we take in is immediately integrated. That is, we integrate our new perceptions with what we remember. We focus and connect and identify and categorize and utilize. Our plan is to provide additional information right within a person's consciousness that can be immediately integrated. At some point in the future we will extract the mental pattern from the brain, upload it into a computer, and discard the body. Then a person's consciousness can live virtually forever in the web cloud. This will be cybernetic immortality, as we just described. Are you getting it yet?"

"I don't like your theory of mind," Leona said sharply. "An information pattern? Internal to the brain? No way. I see two problems immediately. First, our mind is connected to our entire body, not just our brain. If I get a stone in my shoe, my mind responds with an 'ouch.' I cannot imagine a mind disconnected from a biological body. Second, our mind is extended, not confined. Writing with a pencil and paper is actually a thinking process, even though the pencil and paper are outside the brain, even outside the body. Teenagers with cell phones rely on their gadgets just to think about many things. They think *with* their texts, You Tube videos, and web propaganda. Once our mind sails off into the cloud, it'll lose these physical extensions. Am I too skeptical?"

"Well," said MacDonald, "I thought it was a pretty good theory until you got ahold of it."

Kurz chuckled.

Leona sat back and spoke again, "The word *Transhumanism* was coined by biologist Julian Huxley in 1967. He said then that *Transhumanism* refers to, and I quote, 'man remaining man, but transcending himself, by realizing new possibilities of and for his human nature.' So, if you are *trans*humanists, then you plan to transcend *Homo sapiens* with something posthuman, right? You will not make us *more* human, but rather make an entirely new posthuman species, right? This is where you depart from Huxley, right?"

Kurz and MacDonald both looked stunned. "What makes you so smart? How do you know about EPR or Huxley?" queried Kurz.

"I'm not smart. I just know facts."

"You have to be smart to know facts," interjected MacDonald.

"No, you don't," said Leona testily.

"Yes, you do," argued Kurz.

"No, you don't. What do you think intelligence really is?" challenged Leona.

"What do you think it is, Miss Smarty Pants?" counter-challenged Kurz with a grin.

"Insight."

"What?"

"Insight, I said. That's what distinguishes intelligence."

"OK. So what's insight?" Kurz pressed.

"When you get insight, you'll know it. It's a leap, a mental leap toward reality," she lectured. "Insight includes thinking counterfactually. It includes *pretend*. A three-year-old girl can dress and undress a doll, pretending it's her baby. A three-year-old boy can pretend he's driving a fire engine. This ability to pretend in a grown-up scientist is known as hypothesizing. No computational machine can hypothesize, can it?"

Kurz and MacDonald looked at each other. Then Kurz turned back toward Leona with a laugh. "How would you like to become a professor at TTU?"

Oops, thought Leona. *Maybe I went too far. I can't reveal that I've already got Kurz's chip. I'd better learn to hide it rather than...* Leona smiled innocently, accepting the compliment. "Gentlemen, before I leave, would you kindly give me your business cards? Just in case I decide to become a TTU professor, you know."

MacDonald and Kurz laughed. Kidd stared quizzically at this uncanny marvel from Chicago.

CHAPTER 53

DETROIT

THAT EVENING LEONA and Angie sat with shared melancholy in their double room at the Hilton Santa Clara. From their window they could see the Great America amusement park, if they cared to look. They didn't. The two Dearbornites rehearsed again and again the sequence of events leading up to the day's funeral. No insights penetrated the shroud of mystery. No words could adequately comfort them in their grief.

Angie stood up to go visit the toilet. Leona felt a sensation in her head. She did not recognize the feeling. Suddenly, in her mind she was watching a mental video. What she saw was herself firing a gun. She fired it at Graham. Graham fell over dead. Leona asked herself silently, *now, where did that thought come from?*

When Angie had returned and taken her seat, Leona spoke first. "I wish my mother could have been here."

"Oh, she wanted to come, Lee," responded Angie. "She just couldn't. The station is keeping her on a tight schedule. She called me, of course. I expect she'll call us sometime this evening. Have you checked your texts?"

Leona thumbed through her iPhone buttons. She found a text from her mother, "Watch 2nite!"

"Did you find something?"

"Yes. Mom wants us to watch her show tonight. I think we can get it on the internet. If it's 11:00 pm in Detroit, then that means 8:00 here, right?"

"Yes. We're coming up on eight right now," said Angie. "I'll see if I can get it on my computer. You see if you can find some wine and pour us each a glass. We deserve it."

As the *Karen Foxx Spotlight Show* opened, a dangling, almost dancing object filled the camera lens. It assaulted the television viewer's eyes, which had to strain to see just what was dancing. When viewers could finally focus, what they saw was a miniature replica of the "Spirit of Detroit." The original twenty-six-foot-tall "Spirit of Detroit" is a 1955 bronze statue created by Marshall Fredericks. It sits today in front the Coleman A. Young Municipal Center on Woodward Avenue. Centered by an idealized yet struggling human form with arms stretched in opposite directions, the monument draws the beholder's eyes in divisive tension toward the extremities. In the figure's left hand, a gilded sphere with sprouting rays reminds us of the sun. It symbolizes God. In the figure's right hand, a miniature family represents the relationships we individuals enjoy with one another and with all humanity. God and the human family in tension and in complement energize the Spirit of Detroit.

"You're looking at the right earring." The camera shifted to include both Karen Foxx and the earring she held in her right hand. "This is a special earring," she said with emphasis.

"Two years ago a special pair of fourteen-carat-gold "Spirit of Detroit" earrings was minted and given as an award to Miss Detroit. The judging criteria in the Miss Detroit competition included the usual: evening wear and swimsuit beauty, talent, interview composure, and lifestyle. Then we here in the Motor City added: do you plan to become a mother and raise a family here in the Detroit area?

Miss Susan Elliot answered emphatically, yes. The title *Miss Detroit* and the earrings were awarded to her."

Karen Foxx looked straight into the camera with angry and penetrating eyes. "Tonight I regret to announce that Susan Elliott, our Miss Detroit, is dead."

The screen shifted to an earlier TV news account of the discovery of the dismembered body of an at-first unidentified woman. Police cars with flashing lights. Medics rushing covered remains on a gurney into an ambulance. Cub reporters interviewing bystanders.

"Yes, I'm the one who called the police," said a thirtyish man with open shirt collar, glasses, and uncombed hair. "I was walking my dog. Off leash. He ran into that vacant building over there. He returned carrying something. At first I thought it was just a large stick. When I looked closer, I could hardly believe my eyes. It was the naked lower leg of a human person. I dialed 9-1-1 immediately."

The camera zoomed out so that the abandoned building filled the screen. Karen Foxx's voice took over the narration. "What you are looking at is Michigan Central Station. It was built in 1918. Just look at it. It is magnificent, a Beaux-Arts train station with office space above, eighteen floors of office space. The MCS was intended to establish a new center for Detroit on Michigan Avenue near the location of the former Tiger Stadium. It was intended to become a new hub around an imposing architectural celebration of the human spirit. It never happened. Increased use of the automobile decreased the use of the train. And the Great Depression paralyzed the growth of commerce. In 1988 the MSC was closed. Today its classic Corinthian columns are interspersed with broken windows. It is a monument to the failure of Detroit to keep up with civilization, let alone advance it."

The camera returned to a full facial of its hostess, Karen Foxx. "Today, the Michigan Central Station became the temporary cemetery of Susan Elliott. She was brutally raped and dismembered. Her separated body parts were found on the ground floor and on one of the office floors above. The horrific dimensions of this case astound us. Here to speak about this with us this evening is Detroit's mayor, Keith Steinke."

The camera zoomed out to encompass the guest and hostess.

"Welcome, Mister Mayor," said Foxx.

"It's always good to be here, Karen. That is, it's almost always good to be here."

"If the police department had patrolled the Michigan Central Station more thoroughly, do you think this murder might have been prevented?"

"Now, Karen, I didn't kill this unfortunate woman. Whenever I come on your show your accusations imply that I'm personally guilty of everything bad that happens in Detroit. You did not even allow me a moment to grieve with you and with our people."

Foxx was taken aback. She paused. "Yes, of course, Keith. She was not killed because of police neglect. And I know that you as mayor are just as shocked and just as concerned as any of us."

"That's right, Karen, and thank you. Today I visited Susan Elliott's parents. The devastation in that family is incomprehensible. The entire community that makes us one Detroit family is in grief. I've ordered the flags at City Hall to fly at half mast tomorrow."

"Let me ask you about the symbolism," said Foxx.

"I'm not an expert on symbols, Karen, but shoot."

"Why Miss Detroit? Why the Michigan Central Station? What's the connection? The MSC is a synecdoche for our entire city: the self-destruction of the auto capital of the world. And now, tonight, we mourn Miss Detroit, a symbol of Detroit's hope for the future. What does this mean, Keith?"

"It's so early in our police investigation of the crime. It was only a few hours ago that we were we able to discern the identity of the victim. We're still reeling from its impact. But I promise Detroiters that we will get to the bottom of this and we will bring the perpetrator to justice."

"That's the politician speaking now, Keith. It's what I expect." Foxx laughed. So did Steinke. "But I'm asking: why this place?"

"I don't know. Why this space?"

"I said place, not space. A place is a space with meaning. Let's pause for a moment. We in Detroit have a motto: *Speramus meliori, resurgit cineribus,* in Latin. It means that Detroit will "rise from the ashes: we hope for better things." This motto was given us by a Jesuit priest after the fire that nearly destroyed the entire city in 1805. I repeat it each evening to close my show. I want Detroiters today to keep that hope alive. I want us to embody that spirit of rising up from the ashes. But now, with the brutal murder of Miss Detroit, have our hopes been murdered as well? Would you say that?"

"I never give up hope, Karen."

"Nor do I," she said looking directly into the camera. Then, she turned back to the mayor. "One more thing, Keith." Foxx lifted up the earring, the miniature Spirit of Detroit.

"This earring was taken by the coroner off the victim's right ear. Is that correct?"

"Yes, that's correct."

"Where's the second one, the one that belongs in the left ear?"

Steinke shrugged his shoulders. "The investigators have not found it. As of now, it's missing."

Karen Foxx turned to her viewers. She paused. It became a long pause. Then she whispered audibly so her entire television audience could hear distinctly: "*Speramus meliori, resurgit cineribus.*"

CHAPTER 54

SANTA CLARA

"That poor girl!" whined Angie, shaking her head. "First, Kelly. Now, Miss Detroit. They had virtually the same thing happen to them. A vicious predator in California and another in Detroit. What kind of mind could conceive of such cruelty, let alone make it happen, Lee?"

Leona could not speak. She was thinking. Angie had long ago learned to wait for Leona. Time passed while each stared off into space.

"Are you thinking about evil, Lee?" asked Angie.

Leona looked up. "Yes." She paused. "I'm also asking myself whether these two—Kelly and Miss Detroit—could be connected. Both were raped. Both were dismembered. Both were found with one earring, not two."

"Mmmmmm. Might this be more than just a coincidence?"

"Probably not. I assume Miss Detroit had nothing to do with NASA or TTU or anything professional that would overlap with Kelly's situation. They weren't the same age. Still, I could ask Mom to look into Susan Elliot's background. Angie, do you think Kelly and Susan knew each other, by chance?"

"Oh, no. Kelly's been away from Michigan for a decade and a half. I can't imagine any Michigan connections still exist."

Leona picked up her iPhone and texted her mother, congratulating her on the show and asking for a little more background information on Miss Detroit. She put the phone down. The two women continued to sit, saying very little. Slowly the wine drained from their glasses.

"Would you mind if I took a long bath, Angie?" asked Leona. "In the warm water I'll think. And I'll pray. And I'll tell God just how pissed off I am for allowing such meaningless and cruel suffering."

"No, I don't mind. You can stay in the tub until the water evaporates, as far as I'm concerned. But if a pastor gets pissed off at God, then what should the rest of us do?"

Leona smiled.

Angie smiled and then spoke. "Lee, I remember how pissed off at God you were when you returned from that Iranian prison. You saw so much treachery, bloodshed, and death. You were so angry at the Almighty that you wanted to make God suffer. I began to fear for God's safety. Now, here you are again. Well, actually, here we both are. I'm just as angry. We've lost my precious sister." Angie began to cry. She pulled a tissue from a box on the table to pat her eyes.

Leona looked out the window, but she did not notice the lights of Great America. She noticed only the darkness within her own soul.

LATER, submerged in the bathtub, Leona opened her Bible. She started to read Psalm 27. "The LORD is my light and my salvation; whom shall I fear? The LORD is the stronghold of my life; of whom shall I be afraid?" She paused to meditate. *What I fear about the Lord is that he abandoned Kelly when she needed protection.* Then she addressed God directly in prayer. "God, I'm sad, grieved, confused, and pissed off."

Leona's body relaxed while her mind raced frantically from one entanglement of thoughts to another. Nothing would unravel. Though she strained to see a connection between the murders of Kelly and Miss Detroit, no link presented itself before her mental eye.

After smacking into one mental blind alley after another, the bathing pastor turned her anguish toward God. She entered into prayer again. "God," she began. "Here I am again, confounded by the goddamned theodicy problem. So, you created this fuck'n world out of love. Right? Well, bullshit." Time passed before the prayer continued. "Why? Why should the lovely Kelly, the warm-hearted mother, the wife, the sister, the scientist, the…why? Why? And Susan Elliot….why? Why? Who is the monster that did this? Why is there no chance for justice to be done? Why did you create human souls with such a potential for evil? I know you call me to have faith in the face of darkness; but, here I am again, wishing I had at least a flashlight to see my way. I believe, but I need you to help me in my unbelief. Amen."

The hotel bathroom door opened a crack. Through the slot came Angie's voice. "BFF?"

Leona smiled and raised a clenched fist with a wave of triumph. "Best Friends Forever! Damned right!"

CHAPTER 55

CHICAGO

Leona needed to wait only a few minutes at O'Hare's arrival curb before Graham pulled up in his CR-V. Leona immediately opened the passenger door, slid in, and in one continuous motion leaned over to place a kiss on Graham's lips. Graham put his left hand on the back of Leona's head to hold her close and lengthen the intimate greeting.

"It's really good to see you, Grammy," she said. "Thanks for all you do for me. I take none of it for granted, you know."

"Yes, I know," responded Graham.

"It's hotter here in the Windy City than it was in California," she said, buckling her seat belt. While pulling into traffic Graham proceeded to bring Leona up to date on parish activities. Leona then reported on the funeral, the dead-end investigation of Doug Valentine, and her mother's TV show. They scrutinized the facts and together weighed possible explanations.

MIDNIGHT WATCHED from her perch atop the living room sofa while Graham and Leona walked up the parsonage porch steps. She stood and stretched, which is about as much greeting as a human can expect from a feline. Buck was quite another matter. Upon opening the front door, this descendent of *canis lupus* whirled in tight circles with muffled yelps of joy. Leona did a deep knee bend so the two could rub noses.

Through the dining room arch Leona spotted a box and some papers on the table. Graham saw where her eyes were directed.

"You've received a few things," said Graham. "The box came via UPS. You've got a fax from your mother. The rest is an assortment of bills via snail mail."

Leona approached the box with curiosity written on her face. It was a box of Silver Oak Cabernet Sauvignon. Napa Valley. Not Alexander. Twelve bottles. "My gosh, this must have cost a couple thousand dollars!" she exclaimed. "Who's it from?"

Graham shrugged his shoulders. "I only sign for adult pick-ups. I don't investigate their source."

Leona opened the card and read the message. "Rev. Foxx: Dinner Friday? 7:00pm? Palmer House? Khalid." Leona let loose a wide angled smile, exuding a combination of surprise and dreamy contentment.

Graham coughed. It was a fake cough to regain attention. "I buy you Field Stone," he said. "Even the Staten Family Reserve."

"Oh, but that's only one bottle at a time," said Leona dismissively, with a tone of sarcasm. "Don't get me wrong, Grammy, your wine selections make for a pretty good second choice. But anyone who buys me Silver Oak is a king deserving homage. You do pretty well as a court jester."

Graham was livid. "I could never afford Silver Oak on a spy's salary, let alone on a clergyman's salary."

"Have you thought about getting an honest job?" Leona stepped up, putting her toes on the top of Graham's toes. She wrapped her arms around Graham's neck and pulled him down for a kiss. He resisted, arching his head backward.

"Now, we're not a tad jealous, are we, Grammy?"

Graham slowly put his arms around Leona and clasped them in the small of her back. He kissed her on the forehead, but he could not bring himself to express any affection beyond that.

"The fax is from your mother. Evidently, you wanted some background on Miss Detroit. This is a poop sheet."

"Is the coffee hot?" Leona asked Graham.

"No, but I'd be glad to warm up a cup for you. I'm ready for one too. It's Peet's, not Silver Oak. Will that be good enough?"

Leona waved her hand in approval, while lifting her cell phone to check text messages. One was from Angie. Angie reported that she'd heard from Tina Matsuoka that the semen DNA in Kelly did not match that of Doug Valentine. Valentine was no longer a suspect. "No match on the Valentine DNA," she hollered toward the kitchen.

"No surprise," Graham shouted back.

Leona then sat down on the La-Z-Boy to read her mother's fax about Susan Elliott. Midnight leaped into her lap, causing Leona to lift the paper in order to read it.

"Find anything?" asked Graham upon returning to the living room with two cups of coffee.

"Nothing much." Leona sipped with a slurping noise. "Hot," she murmured. "Susan went to Cody High School. She did two years at Wayne State and was planning to transfer in her junior year to Michigan State. Go Spartans! She was planning to study art and architecture. She had just begun a summer job at Nipendo, a computer peripherals factory on Detroit's west side. Nipendo has a Michigan Avenue address, actually. Mmmmmm. Well, that's all. I had hoped to find some sort of connection with Kelly. Anything. But nothing stands out here."

Graham nodded to indicate he was listening. "Did Kelly go to either Wayne State or MSU?"

"No. She's a U. of M. grad, a Wolverine. Even got her Ph.D. in Ann Arbor."

I thought you said Kelly had gone to that, whatever it is, that Transhumanist place near NASA."

"Yes, she did. But that was as a post-doc. She didn't get a degree from TTU."

"Gotcha." Graham coughed again.

Leona looked up with a coy smile. "Now, Grammy, what's on your mind?"

"Are you going to have that dinner with Khalid?" he asked.

CHAPTER 56

CHICAGO

Shortly before six o'clock on the following Friday, Graham walked up the steps of Leona's parsonage. He was sporting a blue blazer with an open-collar paisley short sleeve shirt. Leona, wearing a bright yellow sun dress with three-inch heels, was surprised to see him at the door.

"I'm here to walk you to the Metra," he said. "Actually, I'll ride to the Loop and walk you to the Palmer House."

"Thanks, Graham, but I'm old enough to go on a date without an escort."

"I'm not your escort. It's a coincidence. I got a message from Holthusen. He's in town. I'll meet him along with Hurley and another guy at the Berghof, only a block or so from the Palmer House. We'll eat schnitzel, sausage, sauerkraut, and spätzle."

"Come on, Mister Washington. It's not German cuisine that you're after. It's the beer and you know it."

Graham smiled as the two turned to walk out of the church parking lot and north on Burnham Avenue.

"Actually," Graham picked up the conversation, "Holthusen

wanted you to come to dinner with us. But I told him that the Rev. Dr. Leona Foxx has more important items on her schedule and could not be bothered dining with both of her bosses, both church and state."

"Why couldn't they pick another time?"

"Can you imagine the schedules that both Holthusen and Hurley must have? Imagine what they would have to cancel just to have high tea with the Queen. Holthusen's taking a late flight back to Washington tonight. It's either tonight or never, I think."

"It'll have to be never for me then," said Leona, chuckling.

Graham did not match her chuckle. He frowned.

WHILE WAITING for the Metra on the 79th Street / Cheltenham platform, Graham lightly touched Leona's left earring. It was a three-quarter-inch Latin cross. Silver. "Nice," he said.

"You should say that. You bought these earrings for me at Christmas. Remember?"

"Of course, I remember. I'm just saying they become you."

"I wear them on special occasions, such as going to a Cubs game. Or for this evening. I want to think of you."

"Come on, Lee. You forget about me completely when Hank Greer steps into the batters box."

"But only for a moment, Grammy."

GRAHAM SAID good-bye to Leona at the front door of the Palmer House. Then he continued to walk east on East Monroe. He crossed State Street and headed for the Berghof Restaurant. Soon he was seated with Gerhardt Holthusen, Director of the CIA, Justin Hurley, Presiding Bishop of the ELCA, and someone he was just meeting for the first time, Bernard Lee from Taipei. Once the beer was poured and the group ascertained that no one would hear the details of the conversation above the restaurant din, they tried to put some puzzle pieces together. Graham and the presiding bishop learned from Bernard Lee just what had happened when Leona was in Taipei and the value of the microchip they had secretly and successfully copied. Included in Lee's story was the mysterious death of the two Chinese women. The four men attempted to wrap their minds around the teachings of Transhumanism, but with each mug of German beer the subtleties of esoteric doctrine became increasingly illusive.

CHAPTER 57

CHICAGO

LEONA ASCENDED the Palmer House stairs and found herself gazing and gaping at the magnificent renaissance hall that some would call a 'lobby.' Built in Beaux-Arts style in 1925, the Palmer House was always an aesthetic treat for Leona's eyes.

Khalid approached with a welcoming smile. Dressed in an off-white linen suit with a light blue Alfani shirt and tasteful Escher tie, he gripped each of Leona's hands and placed a light kiss on each of her cheeks. With both of her hands in his grip, she was saved from the awkward ambiguity of deciding between offering a handshake, embrace, or kiss. She simply smiled and basked in Khalid's charm.

"Now, we could take our pre-dinner drinks here in one of the lounges," he said. "But I've got a lovely French Baroque suite upstairs. Much more private. And it's all ready for us. Won't you join me?"

"Oh, yes," responded Leona. "It sounds divine. And thank you for the Silver Oak. You shouldn't have..."

"Oh. 'Twas nothing."

The corner elevator required a special room key to operate, and it lifted the couple to numbered floors that did not appear among the public elevator choices. Soon Leona found herself entering the spacious drawing room of Khalid's suite. She noticed the bedroom and bathroom doors to the left of the fireplace. Centered between two love seats, she noticed a low coffee table already laden with single bite hors d'oeuvres: celery sailboats, smoked salmon on cucumber slices, crab salad in phyllo cups, stuffed mushrooms, and cheese blocks with crackers. A small bouquet of spring flowers stood at one end of the coffee table, and an ice bucket with champagne at the other. On the lamp table Leona noticed an unopened bottle of Silver Oak.

"With all of this I won't need any dinner," said the guest.

"But the lady doesn't need to consume all of it," responded her host. "Later we'll decide which restaurant to go to or, if we prefer, we could ask room service to send something up."

Leona smiled with gratitude.

Khalid poured champagne into each of two flutes and handed one to his guest, now seated across from him on one of the love seats. They toasted and drank and nibbled

"May I?" asked Khalid, holding up a pack of cigarettes.

Leona nodded.

Khalid lit up.

"You bolted out of the Hilton dining room the last time we were together," said Khalid with a hint of drama in his voice. "I'm certainly glad you didn't bolt out of my life."

"Oh, Khalid, I apologize for being so rude. I'd just received devastating news on my phone. After I left you I raced back to California, back to Mountain View, actually." Leona then provided a brief recounting of the finding of Kelly's body and Leona's investigation.

"I'm so sorry to hear of this. I believe I met the woman....Kelly, is it?....at the NASA reception. Delightful person. This is tragic."

Small talk was interspersed with serious matters. Khalid posed questions and sustained an interest in Leona's answers. She in turn asked him about his professional interests and, of course, about Transhumanism.

"Will the posthuman have a soul?" asked Leona, leaning forward with her champagne glass near her lips.

"I don't know what a soul is, Lee. I tend to doubt that there is such a thing as a human soul. If *we* don't have souls, neither will our cyborg descendants."

"But Khalid, I thought you were a Muslim, a Shiite Muslim. Certainly you should know what a soul is."

"I grew up in a Shia family and culture. But I've had a secular education. I've learned to look at the world materialistically. No need for souls if it's all just mass and energy, you know." Khalid looked straight into Leona's eyes. He puffed his cigarette and deliberately blew the exhaled smoke over his right shoulder. "So, my dear pastor, why would I need to have a soul?"

Leona stared straight back and spoke with intensity. "You need to have a soul to have an essence. Your soul is who you truly are."

"Why bother with essence? Why not just be a body with epiphenomenal consciousness? That's good enough for me."

"No, it's not, Khalid. For the sake of Bristol, there's much more. I believe your soul—like my soul—is like a castle. It's surrounded by a high stone wall with an open gate. It's filled with courtyards and gardens where your inner beauty flowers. There are many rooms within your soul, each dedicated to one or another of your favorite hopes and dreams and activities. Then, right in the center of this castle is a special chamber, a private and almost secret chamber. In this innermost chamber is where you and God share the deepest intimacy. It is here that God enjoys the treasure of the true Khalid, the true you."

Khalid looked away. Then he turned back to make eye contact again. He smirked slightly. "I think I'll keep my gate closed. God can stay outside, as far as I'm concerned."

Leona leaned back on the couch, keeping eye contact. She relaxed her arms but her face continued to show intensity. "A closed gate, huh? That's like having a winning lottery ticket and tossing it into the trash without matching the numbers."

CHAPTER 58

CHICAGO

GRAHAM HAD ORDERED sauerbraten with spätzle. He was unsure whether it was the beer that made the spätzle taste good or the spätzle that made the beer taste good. Regardless, being a spy has its delightful moments.

Bernard Lee led the meeting. His basic task was to sound an alert, to ask his colleagues to keep their eyes peeled for connections. He walked his two confreres through the list of names of those meeting at TaiCom while speculating on what the future might bring. Each name was accompanied by a brief biographical sketch. Lionel Chang and Buzz Kidd were given the bulk of the attention.

When Lee came to the name Khalid Neshat, Graham invested an extra measure of attention. "Tell me more about this guy, Neshat."

"Persian," said Lee. "Physicist. Comes from a royal family. Way back. Sort of an international playboy. Runs his own business: *Tehran Technologies Incorporated.* He's been linked to Iranian government espionage, though he doesn't work for anybody now. He's independently wealthy. Pays his own bills. He's death on Mossad. Death on Israel. Death on Saudi Arabia. Death on all enemies of Iran. Fanatic, actually. Even though he's given up the faith, he's death on anyone who is not a Muslim, especially someone who is not a Shia Muslim. He oversaw the imprisonment and torture of Bahais, even though Bahai is indigenous to Iran. Rumor has it that he raped and murdered Bahai women, all in the name of government service."

"Given up the faith? Still Muslim?" asked Hurley.

"Allah is the one and only! Even if you're an atheist Muslim, I guess," said Lee. "So, he believes everyone who doesn't believe Allah is One is either an atheist or polytheist. And both atheists and polytheists are infidels. Now, to pile on a crazy additional tenet in his confused belief system, Neshat holds that non-Muslims have no souls. This means he can murder non-Muslims without qualms. He's an Iranian nationalist in the dress of a religious fanatic."

"Does he treat himself like an infidel?" asked Hurley.

Both Lee and Holthusen laughed.

"Sounds like a mean son-of-a-bitch," commented the bishop, somewhat out of character.

"Yep, mean and dangerous," Holthusen said. "He's on everyone's watch list. Even so, I don't see how he could pledge loyalty to whatever TaiCom is planning. I bet he's out to get whatever he can get for his own purposes. Just my hunch."

"So, he was at the TaiCom meeting in Taipei, right?" asked Graham.

"Right."

"Where else have you tracked him? Did he show up at that NASA meeting with TTU?"

"Yep."

Graham seemed to turn his attention back to the sauerbraten. But he did not exactly pick up a bite to eat. The gears in his brain seemed to be winding and spinning. When Hurley and Lee and Holthusen started a new conversation, Graham seemed to make a judgment. "Gentlemen, please excuse me!" He leaped up and headed for the exit.

CHAPTER 59

CHICAGO

AFTER A LONG SLOW exhale creating a cloud of cigarette smoke above him, Khalid broke the temporary silence. "I don't have to believe in God to hate Israel."

"The God of Israel, Mister Neshat, is a God of love, not hatred," said the pastor firmly.

"We're not talking about God any more. We're talking about Israel."

"Oh, for the sake of Bat Yam, why Israel?"

"Because if it were not for the protection of your White House, Israel would bomb Iran back to the stone age. The only reason Washington puts reigns on Israel is out of fear that Iran might make a dirty bomb. Iran needs to play the nuclear weapon card in order to persuade the US to persuade Israel to leave us in peace. We don't want to give up that trump card easily."

"If Iran wants peace, why do you fund terrorists in Iraq and Syria?"

"That's simple," said Khalid between cigarette puffs and champagne swallows. "You must understand what underlies the turmoil in my part of the world. What literally underlies the struggle is the South Pars/North Dome Condensate Gas Field. This is the world's largest gas field. It underlies two countries, Qatar and Iran. Back in 2000 Qatar, along with its allies, the United States and Saudi Arabia, came up with a plan to exploit this resource. Qatar would build a pipeline running through Saudi Arabia, Jordan, Syria, and Turkey so that it could directly reach European markets. This would make the Sunni Muslims of Qatar very rich while the Americans would get to keep their massive military bases on the peninsula."

Leona leaned forward to listen.

"As you know, I'm a Shia. So is almost everybody in Iran. We in Iran have decided to drill for the same gas, put it in our own pipeline, and send it through Iraq and Syria to a Mediterranean port. Then, on to Europe. Why should Sunni Qatar profit from what rightly belongs to us Iranian Shiites?"

"Why not two pipelines?"

"Are you really naive or just pretending?"

Leona said nothing.

"The ruling family in Damascus is Alawite Muslim, a close ally to us Shiites. So, Damascus prefers our Islamic Pipeline running through Syria, not the Qatari pipeline. This prompted the United States and Saudi Arabia to instigate a Sunni uprising in Syria to foment a regime change, to get a government in Damascus favorable to the Qatari plan. We in Iran gotta defend our market share, ya know. So we fund anybody who'll side with the Shiites. Oh, and Russia sides with Iran too. Did I mention this?"

Leona leaned back and took a sip from her flute. "So, how does Israel fit into this?"

"We fear that Israel will sabotage—if not bomb—our pipeline."

"Got any evidence?"

"Circumstantial."

"Circumstantial evidence is not good enough. Any intelligence?"

"Doesn't matter. We've got to protect our interests from Israel."

"Could you be paranoid, Khalid? Why would Israel care one way or the other?"

"Israel will do anything to cripple Iran."

Leona nodded and sipped.

"I can't figure you out, Leona. For a pastor, or whatever you call yourself, you seem both naive and, well, knowledgeable. I'm finding it hard to peg you."

Leona only smiled.

CHAPTER 60

CHICAGO

KHALID'S CELL PHONE SOUNDED. He looked at his screen and recognized the caller. "I must take this call," he said. "Dreadfully sorry."

"Of course," responded Leona, nodding.

Neshat disappeared into the bedroom holding the phone to his ear. He slammed the door to emphasize his privacy demand. Leona stood and ambled around the living room, giving it a curious tourist's inspection. She sniffed the fresh flowers. She leaned down to see whether the wood in the fireplace was genuine or fake. She refilled her champagne flute. She glanced at her wristwatch.

On the desk she found Neshat's open laptop and assorted note pads, pens, and paper clips. A leather jewelry box caught her eye. Out of curiosity she opened it to see a red felt lining holding what she at first thought might be a collection of cuff links. Upon closer inspection, she was astounded to see an array of earrings, women's earrings. She fingered them. *It seems that none are in pairs. They're all singles. Odd.*

One was particularly striking: a jade earring with a yin-yang symbol. Then her fingers touched an item so very familiar: a cubic zirconium double stone. *Kelly?* She paused. *Oh my God!*

She tried to think. She put Kelly's earring in her clutch purse. She searched through the jewelry box again until she found something else recognizable. She picked up the Spirit of Detroit. Leona had seen this one before. She had seen it between her mother's fingers displayed on a monitor. It belonged to another murdered young woman. She threw the Spirit of Detroit back into the jewelry box but did not close the lid. She grasped her purse tightly, opened the door to the hallway, and ran for the elevator.

She was stymied. To make the elevator work, Leona would need an electronic key. She turned abruptly and followed the exit signs to a stairwell and began her descent on foot. She threw off her heels and leaped downward, three to four steps per bound.

When Khalid returned to the fireplace parlor and saw the open box plus the absence of his guest, he raced out into the hallway and looked both directions. He thought he could see the stairway door closing. He withdrew a Glock 17 from his belt and sped toward the stairwell in pursuit.

Not remembering how many stories she would need to descend, Leona's heart raced as fast as her legs. Her ears picked up the sound of other feet on the steps. *He's chasing me!* Could she move any faster? *Are those footsteps sounding louder or softer?* She could not be sure. She would need a diversionary move. What could that be?

Have I descended far enough to make it past the locked floors? Through a door Leona raced, finding herself on the twentieth floor. She ran down the hall to the elevators, pushing a down button. She waited. She waited some more, pushing and tapping and slamming the button. *Did he see where I went?* Finally, after a bell rang, Leona was in the elevator pushing the button to the basement. *I hope this is an express. I hope no one tries to stop me.*

When Leona's elevator door finally opened, she leaped out onto the floor beneath the Palmer House lobby. She passed quickly from the elevator well and into a shopping promenade. She turned right and walked rapidly past the boutiques in the direction of Wabash Avenue. She heard a second elevator door ring. *Could that be him?* She began to run, weaving between sauntering window shoppers and commuters.

Suddenly she heard a loud voice—"Leona! Down!"

Dumfounded, she looked ahead toward the Wabash opening and saw a human form. It was a man. Legs spread for stability. In his hand he seemed to be holding a gun, aiming a gun. *Could it be Graham?!* She dove onto the floor like Hank Greer making a head-first slide into second base. She could hear the blast of a gunshot. And she thought she heard the bullet whizzing past her right where her head had just been. *Did Graham fire his weapon?*

The other pedestrians in the shopping promenade either flattened themselves to the walls or ducked down to near floor level. As soon as all was quiet, they resumed their normal posture while keeping a wary eye on Graham. "What was that all about?" shouted a rather indignant man.

Graham ignored the remark, racing to where Leona lay and kneeling down. He directed his eyes not at Leona but at the elevator well. "Don't move, Lee." Then Graham shouted, "Everyone! Take cover! Stay down!" Everyone froze. Graham slowly stood and walked gingerly to the elevator well. When he saw no one he turned to the frightened crowd to announce, "All clear. You may return safely to what you were doing!" Soon everyone was milling about and murmuring about the excitement. More than one was dialing 9-1-1.

"Let's go, Lee!" ordered Graham, while helping Leona to her feet. She complied without saying anything. In moments they made it through throngs of pedestrians to the Metra station without stopping to engage any arriving police.

CHAPTER 61

CHICAGO

ONCE ON THE TRAIN, Graham and Leona found a bench seat below a large poster of Sugar Daley, Mayor of Chicago. The feminine but firm face of Mayor Daley looked straight into the eye of the poster viewer to say, "Proud to be Hog Butcher, Tool Maker, Stacker of Wheat, Player with Railroads and Freight Handler to the Nation."

After taking a deep breath, and despite the stern ambiance, the two could finally talk to one another.

"Whom did you shoot at, Graham?" asked Leona.

"Neshat," he responded.

"What? Why? How did…?"

"While talking with Holthusen and Lee and Hurley, I kinda put two and two together. Actually, I didn't get four. But what I got was just a bad number. I raced over to the Palmer House to find you. I felt I needed to prevent something happening to you like what happened to Kelly. I just didn't like that guy, Neshat."

"Did you see Neshat with a gun?"

"Yes. He was aiming at your back while you ran toward me."

"Oh, Grammy! I'm so grateful to you!" Leona gave Graham a hug and a cheek kiss. "You were right, Grammy. Look at this." She extracted and displayed Kelly's earring. "This is evidence that Khalid's responsible for Kelly's murder. And the murder of that poor young Miss Detroit. And perhaps many others as well. He's some kind of maniac."

The two watched the telephone poles pass by through the train windows.

"Lee, are you attracted to Khalid?" asked Graham in a barely audible voice.

"No, Graham, of course not."

"He's intelligent. Rich. Cosmopolitan. Exotic."

"He's evil, Graham. What is evil is ugly. I'm attracted to what is good, and so are you."

"But some women kinda like the bad boy. Maybe there's just a part of you, just a little part of you, that's still attracted to Khalid the bad boy."

"The bad boy lovers are giggly airheads in their twenties. In case you haven't noticed, that's not me. And furthermore, bad boy doesn't really fit Neshat. Not only is he a rapist and serial killer, his delusions of grandeur are leading him to play a game of geopolitical extortion that risks a thermonuclear disaster of hellish proportions. He borders on candidacy for the Anti-Christ."

"Even so, doesn't he elicit just a little titillation in you?"

Leona took time in answering. "Remember Leona's Law of Evil: you know it's the voice of Satan when you hear the call to shed innocent blood. Khalid Neshat has shed innocent blood. I don't like Satan, Grammy. I like you." She nestled her head in Graham's lap. He wrapped his left arm around Leona. Leona ran the fingers of her left hand across Graham's scalp. "Grammy?"

"Yes."

"I'm not shopping for a boyfriend. If I were, I certainly would not give a guy like Khalid a second look."

"Despite the fact that he can afford Silver Oak?"

"Silver Oak a boyfriend does not make. Anyhow, Grammy, I simply do not have a need for a boyfriend as long as I have you!"

Graham winced. Both laughed.

CHAPTER 62

THE CLOUD

"John Blair here."

Each member of the TaiCom group watched Blair on video screen while hearing his voice on their respective cell phones. Abnu Sharma in Mumbai. Buzz Kidd and Olga Louchakova in Mountain View. Lionel Chang in Taipei. Geraldine Bourne in Toronto.

"Glad you're with us, John," said Chang, who was chairing the conference call. "Let me continue. I have two items of good news. Our satellite is up, in orbit, and connected."

The group applauded, showing their clapping hands to their respective cameras.

Chang continued. "The second item of good news is that we at TaiCom have our first paying customer: HaMossad leModiʻin ule Tafkidim Meyuhadim, that is, the national intelligence agency of Israel. Just this past week Geraldine flew to a secret location and implanted two chips in Mossad assets. Mossad paid well and was quite willing to buy in even though we are only at the clinical trial stage. We did not need to make any guarantees."

"Probably got the cash from the US," offered Kidd.

"Doesn't matter to us now, does it?" said Chang.

"Just how does Israel plan to use our device?" quizzed Kidd.

"I will answer your question, but first I must lower the curtain of confidentiality. That is, this is the equivalent of top secret. All agreed?"

Affirmations were heard from all parties. Chang continued. "Here is the larger picture. Israel has an opportunity to develop a positive alliance with Sunni Muslim countries, because these Arab states cower in fear at the growing influence of Shia Iran. If Israel can demonstrate a capacity to protect Sunnis from Shiites, it will be in a strong negotiating position. Israel is ramping up its intelligence gathering and espionage. TaiCom and Mossad agreed to conduct an experiment, a trial run. Israel wanted to sabotage a construction project. They wanted to disable the Islamic gas pipeline running from Iran through Syria to the Mediterranean. We asked our partner, Doctor Neshat, to provide satellite transmissions to our implantees with all the intelligence—logistics, onsite activity, and everything else—they need to carry out a clandestine bombing operation. If successful, this would add to our proof of concept. It would persuade Israel to become a regular customer."

"How successful were we?" asked Sharma.

"Well," drawled Chang, "this is the bad news. The bombing operation went off at just the right time. However, what was bombed was not the Islamic pipeline. Rather, what was bombed successfully was the Qatari pipeline. The United States and Saudi Arabia are building a pipeline stretching from Qatar through Iraq, Syria, and Turkey to Europe. That's the one bombed. Mossad disabled the wrong pipeline!"

"Will Mossad come to disable *us* now?" asked Kidd.

"There's no place to hide," added Sharma.

"Time to learn to speak Hebrew, and fast!" exclaimed Bourne.

After a brief period of interchange with nearly everyone in the group speaking at the same time, Lionel Chang raised his voice authoritatively. "Perhaps you know now why one member of our group has not been included in this call."

"Do you mean Khalid?" asked Olga.

"Precisely!" responded Chang. "I need to tell you frankly that I'm a bit worried. Suspicious, actually."

"Do you think Khalid would object to our selling to Israel?" asked Sharma. "Do you think Khalid deliberately provided disinformation to those two Mossad agents?"

"Maybe," responded Chang. "Maybe he would do more than merely object to doing business with Israel. He might even go rogue."

"What do you mean?" asked Buzz.

"Let me be very frank," continued Chang. "I do not believe Phee Seng died of natural causes. I have spoken at length with his wife. Yes, Phee Seng had sleep apnea. But, he also carried a portable CPAP when he traveled. The police report does not indicate Phee Seng was wearing it at the time of his death. This suggests that he died before he could put it on. In short, I believe he may have been murdered."

The group gasped.

"We know that Phee Seng's death put Khalid in sole control of our satellite operations," interjected Blair. "Khalid is a physicist and quite capable of handling the quantum key. Might there be a connection between Phee Seng's death and the Qatari pipeline?"

"I have thought of this," answered Chang. "I am now considering a plan to remove Dr. Neshat from his responsibilities and to replace him. I have not acted because I cannot yet be sure about these things. I'm asking you to assist in my decision."

"If Khalid has taken full control of satellite transmissions, then he could have determined what gets downloaded into the Mossad chips," exclaimed Bourne, "and every other chip we eventually implant."

"Yes," said Chang with a pause. "I fear this is the case."

CHAPTER 63

CHICAGO

LEONA PULLED out the business cards she'd gathered on her recent trips. She laid them on her desk and brought up her Skype. She put in the Skype address of Chris MacDonald and requested contact. It was relatively early morning in Chicago, so MacDonald in Mountain View might not see the request for another hour or more.

Next she clicked on the name of Hayim Levy. In moments a video connection was established. "Hi, Hi. How's my favorite rabbi?" asked Leona in a singsong rhythm, as was her routine.

"Your favorite rabbi is suffering from jet lag," said Hayim Levy. "Nancy and I just got back last evening from Israel. Got some jet lag to sleep off. How's my favorite Lutheran? Got grace?"

"Was it hot in Israel?"

"Hotter'n hell! But Chicago's not much better this time of year."

"Apart from the heat, is the Holy Land still holy?"

"We had some excitement before we left. Everyone was abuzz about a terrorist bombing. That giant gas line—you know the one from Qatar through Syria that the US and Saudi Arabia are building —it got bombed. Big explosion. I mean big! It won't be sending any gas to Europe anytime soon. Nobody knows who did it. Maybe the Iranians. But everybody was talking about it. Did it make the news here?"

"Oh, no. Our news still pretends it's a religious war going on there."

After more small talk, the rabbi invited Leona, "Gonna come by as part of another long jog?"

"Not gonna run that far today. Anyway, your bagels are fattening. Gotta keep my figure."

"Why? Nobody can see your figure beneath that tent sized white alb you wear."

A Skype tune interrupted Leona so she signed off with Hayim. In a moment she was face to face with Chris MacDonald.

"Why are you up so early, Chris? Californians should still be in bed at this hour," jabbed Leona.

"I get to the lab early every day," said Chris, not acknowledging Leona's humor. "I work best in the morning. Why am I getting a call from the Chicago clergy?"

"To get to the point, Chris, tell me what's happening with the NASA satellite? I know it's up. Who's in charge of the TaiCom transmissions? You?"

"Nope. We turned everything over to Doctor Neshat. I may have mentioned this at Kelly's funeral. Neshat runs around with a special laptop that Kurz and I put together. It's got the power and the range to maintain satellite communications wherever he goes. No need for a NASA location as long as Neshat's got his computer with him."

CHAPTER 64

CHICAGO

Leona stepped out her front door and stood for a moment on the porch. She reminded herself of the weather report. The thermometer would spout above the century mark by midday. It would be a day of sun without clouds and enough humidity to still all but the most essential movements of every living creature. Such a portent had no affect on Leona's disposition. Whether due to a good night's sleep or the refreshing oxygen of the early morning air or a sanctified spirit, Leona was feeling no stress or even the threat of stress. She took a deep breath while appreciating the roses and lilacs. By the time she was out of the parking lot, her jog was full pace. She headed north on Burnham and east on 79th toward Lake Michigan.

Although she'd seen this Great Lake almost daily for a couple of years, each encounter refreshed her anew. The sun spoke and the water responded with dancing sparkles, with white mirages gliding and jerking atop the undulating blue green surface. Leona didn't merely see Lake Michigan. Her skin celebrated the fresh breeze. Her ears tended to the subtle lapping of the waves punctuated by robins singing. Her nose inhaled the symphony of scents wafting from the grass, the flowers, the trees, and the shore. Somehow Leona could feel the depth of this unfathomable sea welling up and taking its rightful place within her soul.

Three miles north. Three miles back. There was no one Leona envied. Nothing she wanted to possess. What evils she had suffered she had forgotten, at least temporarily. *How does that poem by Czeslaw Milosz go?* she asked herself. *Was it called "Gift"?* The implanted chip answered: "a day so happy."

Her happiness was interrupted by something else taking place within her head. Some sort of sensation. Some sort of activity. Her mind's eye began watching a mental You Tube video. What she saw was startling. She saw herself with a handgun, firing bullets. At whom? At Graham. Graham's dead body fell to the ground. Then Leona walked away from Graham's corpse.

All this took place within Leona's mind. Leona stopped for a moment to assess what was going on. Then she resumed her jog.

CHAPTER 65

CHICAGO

Leona slowed her jog as she turned into the church parking lot. She opened her awareness to allow the stultifying alliance of heat and humidity to encroach on her previous sense of wellbeing. *How can I turn this sow's ear into a silk purse?* she asked herself. *Suppose I wash the car. Yes, that's it. I'll wash the car.*

By midday she was wearing her two-piece Speedo. The car had been pulled up to the parsonage front walk near the church's rear door. A bucket with soap and a sponge sat by the left rear tire. She glanced up at the sun through her Ray-Bans and then reached for the spring loaded hose nozzle. She heard a faint voice.

"Good morning, Pastor Lee." It was the voice of Cupid, the six-year-old African American girl who had become Leona's best little friend. "It's hot," she exclaimed, hopping from one foot to another on the parking lot asphalt.

"Where are your shoes?" asked Leona.

"Home."

"Step on the grass, quickly."

Once on the grass, Cupid relaxed. Leona bent down for an eye-level conversation. "Would you like a fudgesickle?"

Cupid's head nodded up and down vigorously. Leona thought for a moment. "Cupid, would you go down into the church basement and find a child's chair for me? Then bring it up and put it in the parking lot behind the car. Okay?"

"Okay."

Soon the chair was in the parking lot and Leona had returned with a fudgesickle. Leona's eyes scanned what she could see of the neighborhood. Nothing appeared to be moving. Buck lay in the grass with his tongue drooping from an open mouth. Midnight watched everything through the picture window within the air conditioned house. Leona concluded that a sufficient level of privacy prevailed.

"Take off your t-shirt," she said to Cupid. Cupid removed her shirt, leaving her in her shorts and bare feet. Leona directed her to sit in the small chair and handed her the fudgesickle. With the concentration of a pilot landing a plane, the little girl began a systematic licking of her cold treat. The sun beat down and melted the fudgesickle faster than she could eat. Chocolate dripped and ran like rivers down her cheeks, shoulders, and tummy.

Cupid followed some of the chocolate rivers with her fingers, licking the retrieved taste. One finger made its home in her navel. She looked down. "Why do I have a belly button, Pastor Lee?"

"Cupid, when God was making you he gave you a belly button so that you'd have a place to put the salt when you eat celery in bed."

Cupid looked up at Leona with a puzzled expression. "I don't like celery. I like fudgesickles."

"Well, Cupid, when we grow up our tastes change. Maybe someday you'll like to eat celery in bed. Then, you'll be ready."

"Oh."

With the chocolate treat nearly gone, Leona picked up the hose and removed the nozzle. She took the fudgesickle stick and then squirted Cupid. The little one sat in the chair, welcoming the shower, wiggling at the combination of hot sun and cool water. She stood up when Leona motioned to her and went through the de-fudging with a giggle. Leona's smile of inner joy and outer satisfaction was a perfect testament to her sense of full presence to the moment.

What neither Leona nor Cupid knew, and what even Buck was unaware of, was that they in fact were not alone. An almost silent drone hovering above was signaling a computer screen two blocks away. Its camera monitored every movement of Leona, Buck, Midnight, and, of course, Cupid. Watching that computer screen: Khalid Neshat.

CHAPTER 66

CHICAGO

LEONA'S EARS picked up the noise of activity coming from the concrete stairwell at the rear of the church. Soon Hillar emerged along with Owl, the African American teenage girl who spent nearly as much time around the parsonage as Cupid. The two teenagers were carrying a ping-pong table. Buck was following. After a couple of trips, the green table was set up in the parking lot, complete with net. Both the boy and the girl wore only bathing suits and flip flops.

"We're gonna sweat and then squirt," proclaimed Hillar as he waved his ping-pong paddle. Owl took her place at the street end of the table, just waiting for Hillar to begin. In minutes the ball was clacking back and forth over the net.

Leona picked up the hose. "Should I squirt now?"

"No," bellowed Hillar. Wait until after the rubber game."

LEONA HAD JUST FINISHED WASHING the car when she heard a cuss word. She turned just in time to see Hillar pick up the ball and serve.

The ball bounced on Hillar's side but then crashed into the net. "Shit!" hollered Hillar.

The tattooed teenager with the spiked hair tossed the ball again and then swung the paddle level with the ground. His serve clipped the net and bounced off onto the asphalt. "Shit!" he said, while slamming the paddle edge on the table top. Buck raced to retrieve the ball.

Leona stopped to watch. Once the ball was retrieved from Buck's mouth and Hillar had hit the net for the third time in a row, he yowled, "Goddamit!" This time he slammed the paddle on the table top so hard it splintered and broke. Owl looked at Hillar with a relaxed stare, as if to tell him, "I'm waiting."

"Do you need a new paddle, Quazzie, dear?" said Leona in a singsong voice.

With a growl Hillar disappeared into the church basement and returned with a new paddle.

Soon the click and clack of the ball on the tabletop resumed. Leona began spraying Cupid with the hose while she twirled and giggled.

Then the pastor heard a string of cussing that shocked even her experienced ears: "God damned son-of-a-bitching fuck'n shit!" It came from Hillar's mouth. The pastor marched over and yanked the paddle from the angry teenager's hand.

"For the sake of Belgrade, Quaz, you're turning the air blue. "Why don't you just stop it?"

"I can't."

"What do you mean, you can't?"

"Those words just come firing up like sky rockets from my gut. I can't help it."

"That's not true, Hillar. When cuss words come up from, I don't know where, just stop 'm. Hammer 'm back down to where they came from. You don't need to cuss if you don't want to."

"Yes, I do."

Leona just stared affectionately at the teenager unable to control himself. She rested her left hand on his right shoulder. Owl walked around the table and added her hand to the other shoulder.

"Pastor Lee, it feels like a force coming up like a jack-in-the-box; and I can't slam the lid down on it."

"Take a deep breath, Quaz." Hillar complied. She continued. "Now, you've got all the oxygen in your brain that it needs. Ask yourself, 'do I want to cuss like this?'"

"No."

"Then put a stop to it right now. Are you ready to play again?"

"I think so."

In no time ball clacking and teenaged laughing ensued.

CHAPTER 67

THE CLOUD

"Choong Lo will join us for today's conference call," announced Lionel Chang once the TaiCom syndicate had assembled at their respective computer sites. "Now that the iron curtain of secrecy has been dropped—I assure you that the encryption of this conversation is secure from hacking—I would like to report current progress." Mumbles of greeting and gratitude followed.

Khalid Neshat smiled. He was looking at his laptop screen, listening on his ear buds through Choong Lo's implant.

Chang continued. "It appears that our two Mossad spies have been interviewed and disciplined by their superiors. The two reported that the intelligence they received from their implants led them to execute the bombing plot against the Qatari pipeline, not the Islamic pipeline. This was no accident. They received disinformation from our satellite. They were already disposed to carry out this act of sabotage, to be sure; but the satellite intelligence led to this colossally counterproductive execution. It appears that we at TaiCom have a mole. Or, more accurately, we have in our midst not just a mole, but an excavator."

Khalid Neshat's name was verbalized repeatedly.

"This places us in more than merely an awkward position," said John Blair. "First, TaiCom will no longer be trusted by Mossad. And when other security agencies hear the facts, they will be more than a little reluctant to enter our clinical trial, let alone order our product once it is proven. Second, in spy circles this will give Transhumanism a bad name. The Transhumanist movement might become associated with malfunction, if not treachery."

"I can't wait to see how Saturday Night Live will handle this, if the news ever gets out," said Buzz Kidd.

"As you can imagine," Chang said while regaining leadership of the interchange, "I have expressed my apologies to our Mossad contact and promised to rectify our communications network. This means that we at TaiCom must find Doctor Neshat quickly and persuade him to cease his perfidious activities."

"If Doctor Neshat is both a murderer and a traitor, perhaps you might try a permanent mode of persuasion, Lionel," added Abnu Sharma.

"May I ask Mister Lo a question," posed Geraldine Bourne.

"Yes, of course," answered Choong Lo. "Anything."

"What is your experience with the chip I implanted in your brain. Any pain? Unusual sensations? Problems with access?"

"No problems at all, Doctor Bourne. Sometimes I feel a sensation when it is activated by a transmission, which only comes to alert me to pay attention. Otherwise it's benign."

"Do you feel you can control the memory chip? Or, do you feel it controls you?"

"Thank you for asking. Actually, I don't know. I am told by others that sometimes I appear to them as a completely different person. I don't remember these incidents. It seems that I just black out. Suddenly I return to consciousness and I notice that time has elapsed. If it's true what others tell me, then it must be the case that the chip takes over, I black out, and I don't relate to what the chip does to me."

"Are you comfortable with this, Mister Lo?"

"Absolutely not. No one likes to lose self-control. As soon as this experiment is complete, I will request that the chip be removed. Will you do that for me, Doctor Bourne."

"Of course, Mister Lo. Thank you for your frankness."

CHAPTER 68

THE CLOUD

"WE HAVE two more items of business," interposed Chang. "Doctor Bourne will report on our clinic location plans."

"Yes," said Bourne. "During the period of clinical trials, we want zero exposure to the public. We want zero supervision by medical authorities. We may even wish to keep our operations secret during the first period of sales if it turns out our principal customers come from intelligence-gathering agencies. With this in mind, I have hired a staff, including nursing personnel, who will be paid well both to support me and to maintain secrecy. Each one is a committed Transhumanist. We will set everything up in an ordinary house in the Dalmatian Islands just off the coast of Croatia. The precise location will remain known only to those of us who come and go. We are ready for our next customer. I mean, we are ready for our next clinical trial."

"How skilled will your assistants be?" asked Olga Louchakova. "Will they be able to perform the implantation procedure in your absence? Must you be on site?"

"No, I don't have to be on site. I will guide the surgical procedure from my home in Canada via video screen. This has become common practice in today's medicine. My Dalmatian surgical nurse has the professional prerequisites. I have the expertise. At some point I might even transfer my expertise to a satellite transmission directly into the brain of a nurse with one of our deep brain implants." Bourne laughed.

"Before we sign off," interrupted Chang. "Buzz, would you report on a new branch of research that we're planning?"

"Yes. Thanks. Now that we have virtual proof of concept, we'd like to begin experimenting on children. If a school child attends class with one of our brain implants, will classroom interaction lead to increased intelligence? An active and intelligent brain relies on strong neurocircuits, and neurocircuitry is partially established by repetitive thinking. Thinking actually structures the brain for more thinking. It's kinda like exercising to make stronger muscles. Our theory is that if a child thinks frequently about complex data—and we provide data in complex figurations in the implant—then the resulting buildup of circuitry in the brain will prompt the leap in intelligence we're hoping for. What we want in the next stage of our clinical trial is to experiment on school children."

"Would you like to have some implants in place before school opens in September?" asked Louchakova.

"That would be rushing it," said Kidd. "But in the best case scenario, yes. The problem, of course, is that no set of parents would approve of sending their child offshore for surgery even for a clinical trial. We've got work to do on our human subjects protocol."

Chang took over. "We think that the education market will be so much larger than the espionage market, that we should be looking ahead. If the Transhumanist idealists among us are going to buy into TaiCom's product leadership, then implants for the education market would best fit both the H+ vision and our bank accounts."

CHAPTER 69

CHICAGO

"IN THE NAME OF GOD, the Most Compassionate, the Most Merciful." It was Muzaffar Haq. Leona responded to Muzaffar's visage on her Skype screen: "In the name of God, the Most Compassionate, the Most Merciful."

Professor Haq was dressed in a brown suit, white shirt, and brown tie. "I see you're dressed up for something important, Muzaffar. Aren't you going to sweat in that hot LaHore sun?"

"My office is air-conditioned," responded the Pakistani biology professor. "I've got to go to a departmental meeting later today. That'll be air-conditioned too. Can't think clearly without AC. Now, how is my favorite Lutheran shepherd and her flock this day?"

"Just fine, Muzaffar. Got a question for you. It's a Muslim question. Is it possible for a Muslim to become a non-believer or even an atheist and still be a Muslim? Many Jews do it. But can a Muslim?"

"Oh, that hurts, Leona. But as you can imagine, there are various levels of personal commitment in Islam just as there are in your Christian churches. What we teach and what we personally hold in our hearts and minds could differ. I dare say that most devout individuals don't understand, let alone accept everything in either the Qu'ran or the Bible. Wouldn't you say?"

"Yes, of course. But let me be more specific. Could a Shi'ite cease to believe, yet still behave like a religious fanatic?"

"I bet you have a particular individual in mind."

"Yes, of course. But you don't know him. I'm just trying to do some profiling," she said.

"Both you and I believe that the one God is a God of mercy. We've talked about this many times before, Lee. So I should think your Shi'ite friend could rely upon the most merciful One to forgive him. You did say it was a 'him,' I think. God can forgive us for finding belief difficult. Putting our faith in God is quite difficult for most of us in this postmodern world of ours."

"Yes, it's a him in this case," said Leona. "You're not exactly answering my question, Muzaffar. Knowing that God forgives us in our unbelief is comforting, but my concern lies elsewhere. I guess I'm asking something like this: can you produce religious fanaticism without religion?"

"Well, Leona," said Muzaffar, "can you produce smoke without fire, or at least something hot? Can you produce wool without sheep? Can you produce wetness without water?"

"What are you saying, Muzaffar?"

"If you see fanaticism, you see religion. It just might not be a religion with a name on it. If the name on it is *Christianity*, the real religion might be American patriotism. If the name on it is *Judaism*, the real religion might be Israel. If the name on it is *Islam*, the real religion might be the tribe or sect or something like that. Some people are fanatical about the Chicago Cubs, and baseball itself becomes a kind of religion for Cubs fans."

"As you well know, Muzaffar, I sometimes find myself worshipping at Wrigley Field," said Leona. "This raises the problem of evil. The Cubbies have won only one World Series in a century. This means those of us who believe in the Cubs have to endure a hundred lean years just to get one fat year. Cub fans suffer for their faith."

After pausing to chuckle, Muzaffar continued pensively. "I have another thought, Lee. Sometimes I wonder if fanaticism can itself become its own religion. Fanatics, when together in a group, feed off their shared sense of outrage. Just a thought."

"You may have the right thought, Muzaffar, even though it explains the group but not the loner," said Leona. "Be that as it may, I need to go now. May God be with you."

"And with you too."

CHAPTER 70

CHICAGO

"I've been visiting Transhumanist websites, Pastor Lee." It was Hillar talking to Leona in the parsonage living room. Midnight sat on the sofa top watching the action from her imaginary throne. Buck sat at the feet of Owl, who was stroking his ears. Hillar exclaimed, "Look here!"

Leona positioned herself to see over Hillar's shoulder while he punched computer keys on his laptop, even though the projector lit up the entire west wall of the parsonage living room with the computer's image. "See! The Transhumanists wanna take control of matter at the atomic level so they can improve humanity through technological innovation. This is great! Look: cybernetics; genetic interference; space colonization; autonomous self-replicating robots; uploading minds into computers; and overcoming death through cryonics and radical life extension. This is just like *The Matrix* movie, but it's real."

"Is it really real?" challenged Leona.

"Of course, Pastor Lee. Look. I bet I could show some movies tonight on our wall here. Wanna see *Transcendence* or *Her* or *Robocop* again?"

The front door opened with a startling sound. Graham leaned in to say, "Lee, you'd better come quickly. We've got a problem. Cupid did not come home for supper. She seems to be missing."

Leona and Buck both leapt up and followed Graham out the parsonage door, into the parking lot, and north on Burnham Avenue three doors to Cupid's home. Entering through the front door, Graham and Leona along with Buck found Cupid's mother, Victoria Walker, seated on the living room couch with Cupid's baby sister in her arms. Victoria's puffy eyes told the story.

Cupid played in the neighborhood much of the day, spending considerable time in or around Trinity Church. Leona had seen Cupid, but that was midday. Leona had no knowledge of Cupid's whereabouts during the late afternoon or early evening. Cupid did not return home for lunch or dinner. Mrs. Walker was more than a little worried.

A squad car rolled up, and two policemen walked up the front steps to the house. Graham ushered them into the living room where Victoria told her story one more time. One officer took notes. He asked everyone in the room about what they knew or didn't know.

"We see children miss a meal every day, Mrs. Walker," said the officer with the name "Ward" written on his uniform breast pocket. "Then they come wandering home wondering what all the fuss is about."

"For the sake of Brasilia, Officer," interposed Leona. "That doesn't offer any comfort at this moment. We need action. We need a search. We need to know what's happened."

"Now calm down, Pastor Lee," said Officer Ward. "We will do everything we can to find Cupid. By the way, Pastor, you are widely respected at the Police Department for your work in this neighborhood. It's nice to finally meet you."

CHAPTER 71

CHICAGO

DAYS PASSED without any word of Cupid's whereabouts. Morning and evening Leona or Graham or both would visit Victoria Walker. Every two hours Leona would telephone one or another of her friends at the Chicago PD for an update on the investigation. Runaway? Kidnapping? Child molester? Professional hit?

Leona kept Hillar at the computer. "Look for anything that connects Transhumanism with Intelligence Amplification with deep brain implantation with NASA with TTU with TaiCom with children with Khalid Neshat. Hack, Hillar, hack!"

Leona prodded Graham to connect with colleagues at the CIA. Graham even called Director Gerhard Holthusen. Leona called Bernard Lee. Neither CIA officials could connect Cupid's disappearance with what they knew about TaiCom.

Gerhard Holthusen found that Neshat had left the US, but he could not identify Neshat's destination. Bernard Lee said he would attempt to hack into TaiCom internal memos. Although he found no links to Cupid or to Chicago or even to Leona in TaiCom's computer storage, he did find a mention of children in communiqués involving

Buzz Kidd. He also found reference to the Dalmatian Islands. But to Lee, nothing stood out as helpful. Nevertheless, Bernard reported all of this to Graham and Leona.

"Bernie," Leona ordered sternly over the phone, "please go back to your computer and trace down everything you and the CIA know about the TaiCom people. Background this time. Send me what you get."

"Hey, Lee, I thought you worked for me. Not the other way around."

"Get used to it, Lee. Now the other Lee works for Lee. And by the way, thanks Bernie."

"You're welcome."

"GRAMMY AND GERHARD," Leona pressed in a three-way Skype call, "can you track the traveling of the TaiCom syndicate members? I want to know where they've gone in the last six months. Who did they talk to? Have any of them been to Chicago? Anything?"

"Graham," said Gerhard, "are you sure I should leave you unprotected there in Chicago?"

"Cut the crap, you guys," said Leona. "I'll be nice to you when this is over."

"Hillar, can you trace H+ internet communications to place of origin? Can you look for anything that connects anything we know to Croatia? To the Dalmatian Islands?" The pastor pressed Hillar to keep working like a slave ship drummer beats out the rowing speed. She softened her ruthlessness with cups of hot chocolate and cold smoothies.

In time, Bernard Lee provided Leona with some scholarly papers written by both John Blair and a counterpart in Heidelberg, Germany, named Hans-Georg Welker. "I don't know if this'll help, but here it is."

It was a collection of pieces regarding a theoretical debate over the nature of intelligence. Blair was arguing that intelligence is a short quantitative step beyond computation. To be intelligent is to compute more information faster. Welker, in contrast, held that no amount of computation would lead to intelligence. To be intelligent, insisted Welker in his writings, requires a qualitative leap to insight. Leaps to insight are traits of human intelligence, but such leaps would be impossible for computers. "Artificial Intelligence simply isn't," said Welker.

Lee told Leona in an email that this public dispute between scientists could indirectly harm TaiCom's bottom line. Unless the public believes in both AI and IA, customers would be no more interested in buying expensive TaiCom products than buying cheap adding machines.

Leona thought she'd bet on Welker to win this debate. But to Blair's credit, she would take advantage of the encyclopedia now attached to her brain to prove Welker right. To Welker's credit, nothing could happen without a leap to insight. She'd believed in insight all along. But for an insight to matter, it would have to employ data, facts, knowledge, and even connections between data, facts, and knowledge. Could she think her way toward the next step in chasing down Cupid's whereabouts?

CHAPTER 72

CHICAGO

"Justin Hurley here," said the Presiding Bishop of the Evangelical Lutheran Church of America. His secretary told him that Leona Foxx was calling, and the bishop granted access.

"You could've used my cell phone, Lee."

"This is official business, good Bishop. Thanks to you, I now serve both God and mammon. Mammon—that's the CIA, as you know—is sorta calling me to get back on the road. At some point I want Graham to meet me on the road. Could you by chance send a supply pastor out to Trinity for the next two Sundays? Some preacher who's never had pastoral care, so he or she won't ask too many questions."

"That's the job of your synod bishop, Gerald Botwright, not me," said Hurley.

"Didja hear me? I want a supply preacher who is carefully chosen."

"Oh, I get you. Yes, I'll get a seminarian. Someone very green."

"Thanks, Justin," said Leona, hanging up.

After clicking off the phone, Leona turned her head slightly because she felt something. Some kind of activity seemed to be taking place within her brain. Before her mind's eye there appeared a drama. Like a play on stage, Leona saw herself with a gun, shooting and killing Graham. *Is this what I'm being told to do?* she quizzed herself. Then she smiled.

CHAPTER 73

CHICAGO

"Do you miss Pastor Lee?" Hillar asked Graham. "I guess she won't be back before Sunday. You'll have to preach again."

Graham grunted. "Actually, I won't have to preach this Sunday. We've got a guest preacher. Somebody from the seminary in Hyde Park."

Hillar and Graham were sitting on the parsonage front steps, Graham with his PC and Hillar with his iPod. Hillar was concentrating. His right hand was moving as though glued to the screen. With his left hand he was waving. He slapped his own forehead. He could be heard repeating, "Fuck off! Fuck off!" He was commanding mosquitoes to leave him alone or die.

"Hillar!" said Graham in a judgmental tone. The teenage boy did not look up. He ignored Graham's voice.

Graham continued talking with the dubious assumption that Hillar would be listening. "Look, Hillar, you don't need to be so violent. Simply wave your left hand deftly and say, 'Shoo! Shoo!' See how the mosquitoes fuck off?"

Not being certain of what he was hearing, Hillar interrupted his game to look Graham in the eye. But Graham was by then focused on his computer screen.

Both Hillar and Graham then heard a voice. "Hey there!" It was Trudy Lincoln standing at the parsonage gate. She was wearing a tank top, denim shorts, and high heels.

"Come right on in," said Graham.

"Pastor Gee, I cannot reject your invitation." Trudy opened and closed the gate. She sauntered up onto the porch and took a seat between the two.

"Trudy, you know Hillar, don't you?" Graham said.

"I'm Trudy Lincoln," she said, turning to Hillar.

"Oh, Oh. I'm sitting with two famous presidents," said Hillar grinning. "Washington and Lincoln."

Trudy offered a laugh of courtesy.

"So what brings you to church, Miss Trudy?" quizzed Graham.

"Well, I didn't know I'd be in church, Pastor Gee," she said in her singsong voice. "I just thought a little visit might be in order. It's been what, two weeks, since you called on me, Pastor Gee?"

Graham grunted. Later in the otherwise boring conversation, Graham's ears picked up when Trudy mentioned something about strange people in the neighborhood. "Here in South Shore we've got white people like Hillar here. And we've got black people like you and me. But have you noticed that in the past few days some Asian looking men wandering around? I sometimes see them on Burnham. Sometimes in the alley."

"What do you mean, Asian?"

"Chinese maybe. But not exactly Chinese. I see Chinese people every day in the Loop, but never down here on the South Side."

"Did you get a close look?" asked Graham.

"I walked up and introduced myself."

"That doesn't surprise me. What did you notice?"

"None of them would talk to me. I wondered if they knew English. They just waved me away. Then I noticed something interesting."

"What?"

"On their left hands they had an identical tattoo. It was a dragon with a tail as long as a snake. The tail pointed down towards their wrists. Under the dragon was something in Chinese. What do you think it means, Pastor Gee?"

CHAPTER 74

As soon as the gate closed behind Trudy, Graham went straight to his laptop. Graham opened his email. He'd love to connect with Leona, *but how?*

Perhaps checking his inbox would be a useless effort. Whoever was tagging him would be randomly, if not systematically monitoring his emails, looking for signs of communication with Leona. This means whatever Leona selected as a disguise might fool Graham as well.

He glanced at the return addresses. None were obviously from Leona. His eyes fixed momentarily on one curious item: spamfilter-inc. *Now,* he thought, *why didn't my spam filter filter it out?* With his finger on the delete button, he paused. *Would someone sending spam use the word 'spam'?* He clicked. On his screen appeared an email. No greeting. Just a series of phrases.

Miss you.
   Find Croatia on the map
   Šibenik
   Ferry to Prvić Luka (pronounced per-vich-looka)

> Overnight at Maestral Hotel
> Wednesday, August 18
> By 7:00pm make dinner reservation at Stara Makina for 8:30pm
> Order *ispod peke* with octopus for two to be served at 9:00pm
> Arrive at 8:30pm
> Order a bottle of Graševina with three glasses
> I will meet you there
> Miss you

Graham sat back and paused, repeating to himself "miss you." *Twice?* He looked again. *Yes, twice!* Graham was unaware of the smile decorating his face. Moments passed before he refocused his attention on the email contents. Then he went into the house to make a hardcopy.

Graham quizzed himself. *Might the spies have spotted this? Might they have intercepted it? Might they have disregarded it as spam? Or might it be from someone other than Leona, someone setting a trap? No mention of Cyrus Twelve. No secret password or private indicator that could assure me that it was from Leona and not an imposter. If only Leona and I had a secret life, then she'd know just how to tip me off. Hmmm. What shall I do?*

CHAPTER 75

CROATIA

His plane touched down at the Split Airport, north of Dubrovnik yet south of Zagreb. Croatia is an ancient country, recently separated from its neighbors in the former Yugoslavia. Graham took a harrowing hour-long taxi ride around hairpin turns up a mountainside. On one side before him lay the sun crested splendor of the Adriatic Sea with its twelve-hundred-island archipelago. On the other side he could see strata of rock outcroppings, stone ribs holding up scrub bushes and dwarf trees. During the miles crossing the apparently waterless plateau he noted how the bowling ball sized rocks had been carefully arranged into waist high fences, protecting acre sized squares for...what? He could see no farming. No goats. Nothing but sand and brush and, of course, more rocks. On the descent to Šibenik he spotted vineyards, olive trees, fig trees, and signs of human habitation once again.

King Petar Krešimir IV's memoirs of 1066 AD mention Šibenik. He's regarded as the city's founder. This small Adriatic town had missed the influence of the Greeks and Romans in antiquity. But later Venetian and then Ottoman rule left a lasting imprint. In Šibenik Graham found a ferry departing at 3:30pm that would take him to the island of Prvić Luka, about a forty-five minute boat ride, he was told.

His ferry, the Tijat, operated by the Jadrolinija company, carried fifty passengers along with Graham westward between some of the Dalmatian islands. Graham could remember what Dalmatian dogs looked like: a white coat with black spots. *Could there be one spot for each of the twelve hundred Dalmatian islands? Maybe?*

He didn't need to be told the temperature was thirty-six degrees Celsius to know it was hot enough for him to remove his safari jacket and roll up his shirt sleeves. Despite clusters of conversation, Graham's ears picked up no English. The guttural sounds of what to Graham were unpronounceable syllables gave him that linguistically orphaned feeling. So many Croatian words looked like they consisted of all consonants. *Where are the vowels? Did the Scandinavian theologians steal Croatia's vowels? Dane Søren Kierkegaard could certainly send them an extra 'a'. So could the Finn, Tuomo Manermaa.*

One out of every three men reminded Graham of Serbian president and war criminal Slobodan Milošević: dark short cropped hair with patches of gray. This made Graham wonder how large the Croatian gene pool might be. It appeared that both men and women bore the same mesomorphic, even ursine physique. The smokers' quarter near the bow hosted four women, three with cigarettes and one puffing on a cigar.

The second stop would be Prvić Luka. The ferry dock was located on the east side of a narrow harbor, where the crystal clear water was calm and nearly waveless. As the Tijat approached the concrete pier jutting a football field's length out from shore, Graham saw it peopled with teenagers lounging in their swimsuits. The bikinis on the full-figured young women especially caught his attention. What he didn't notice at first was the glint in the teenage boys' eyes.

After coughing up the arriving passengers and drinking in the departers, the Tijat began to pull away from the pier. By then Graham could see that the mischievous boys had tied ropes at various places on the ferry. As the boat's engine roared and it began its journey to the open sea, the boys clung to the ropes for a free speed ride in the water. The ship's staff harangued the youngsters and severed the ropes. The interaction of sun, water, and mischief was met with considerable teenage glee.

Graham pulled his wheeled Briggs and Riley across the miniscule town square and between scampering dogs to the Maestral Hotel. He showered and put on shorts and a t-shirt. Then the new visitor took to walking about the tiny fishing village. No automobiles were allowed in this seaside town. Bare feet were augmented only by sandals and a few bicycles. Due to the heat, people were scantily clad. Many men were shirtless. Women wore no bras. Graham could not help but notice sagging breasts beneath tank tops, succumbing to age and gravity. Both genders carried years of fine food and cold beer in beach balls of fat right behind their navels. *Should I walk back to the pier and its bikinis?*

The bell on the four-century-old Roman Catholic church rang on the hour and the half hour. Houses were square with walls of stone. Roofs were sandy red tile. Fig trees adorned the walkways. A rooster, apparently unable to distinguish evening from morning, crowed.

The crisp Adriatic waters were met not by a beach but by a stone wall. The soft lapping stopped only a foot or so below the rim of the paved embarcadero and its foot traffic. Occasionally someone would dive between the moored sail boats into the very inviting clear water with its rock seabed visible eight feet underneath the surface.

Graham found the Stara Makina and dutifully made the reservation. He noticed how the outdoor kitchen included a large grill fueled by logs. The *ispod peke* would sit in its brick cast iron oven with coals piled on its top for two hours later that evening. *No wonder Lee told me to make advanced reservations. But where is she?* Graham allowed himself to think for a moment that the life of a spy could not be all that bad.

By 8:30 Graham was seated on a wooden chair adjacent to an olive press table within ten feet of the point where the water lapped the stone wall. The sun had just set, but the afterglow was sufficient to see the surroundings as if in daylight. As instructed, he asked for three wine glasses. He poured himself a glass of Graševina, the celebrated local white wine. *Reminds me of Pino Grigio,* he said to himself. *Nice.* He sipped and wondered. *How the hell is Leona going to arrive here? Will she be on time? Who is the third person? What is this all about? Am I a fool to read an unsigned email and then travel a third of the way around the globe just to eat octopus?*

Graham looked around, trying to find something to occupy his mind while waiting. He noticed a head a hundred feet out from shore. *Must be a swimmer.* Once the head was close enough, it spoke to a Croat friend standing on the stone wall. Again, Graham could understand nothing of the guttural grunts.

"May I have a glass of vine? Yes?" said a strange voice in a thick accent. Graham turned to see that across from him a woman was sitting, someone he'd never seen before. She was holding up her wine glass, one of the three he'd put on the tabletop. Her darkish blond hair was pulled back in a French twist. Her white tank top loosely covered nothing that was sagging; rather it uncovered a cleavage magnetic to Graham's eyes. Before he could decide whether she would be in her thirties or her forties, he was hastily pouring Graševina into her glass.

"You must be Graham Vashington, yes?" she continued in a deep but sexy smoker's voice. She sipped her wine. Her eyes turned momentarily toward the glass to register satisfaction. Watching the show, Graham muttered, "Yes, of course. And you?"

"Katarina Louchakova. My friends call me Katya."

"I have heard the name Louchakova before. But should I know you?"

"No. But you might know this...Cyrus Twelve."

"Yes, I know Cyrus. He's twelve."

She simply looked at him, waiting for Graham to say something that she would understand. Graham laughed at his own joke and added a bit more wine to his half empty glass.

CHAPTER 76

PRVIĆ LUKA

"I HAVE FOR YOU A NOTE. This is information for Leona Foxx. Can I trust you to make certain she receives it?"

"Yes, of course. I believe that is why I am here. I am Ms. Foxx's associate, her partner."

Graham's mysterious female guest twisted slightly, crossed her legs, and lit a filtered cigarette. She held the cigarette between her middle fingers and drew the wine to her succulent lips. While sipping she looked up at Graham and made eye contact. Although calm on the outside, Graham felt himself twitch on the inside. With her nonsmoking and nondrinking hand, she slid a small piece of paper across the table. Graham retrieved it and placed it in his t-shirt pocket. It disappeared from visibility.

She placed her wine glass on the table and took a long draught of cigarette smoke. She exhaled it slowly off to one side through her puckered lips. Her next glance at Graham told him she recognized his curiosity.

"You vant to know about me?"

"Yes, I certainly do."

"You can ask Leona. She tell you everything. She has told me everything about you. You are quite a man, Mr. Vashington!" She repeated the cycle of a drink of wine and a puff of the cigarette.

"Well, if you know so much about me and I know nothing about you, perhaps it's your turn to talk."

"I live up the hill. The green house with the flamingo shutters. Built by two lesbians. You must know it. It's a safe house for the Russian Mafia."

"Russian Mafia? I thought you people worked in secret. Why should I know anything about this?"

"Everybody knows this. What people do not know..." Katarina leaned toward Graham, inviting him to come closer. He leaned in her direction. "What people do not know is just who is Mafia, who is an agent, and who is a double agent. We all share the same house."

"Which one are you?"

Katarina smiled, sipped, and smoked.

Graham realized that this was the end of the conversation. His eyes drifted. Once again he saw a head bobbing in the water. He turned back toward Katya and poured more wine, asking the waiter in a black and white striped shirt for a second bottle. He asked the waiter for the meaning of the Korean symbols tattooed on his neck. "Happiness. Peace. And Love. I like these," said the waiter. When Graham's eyes turned once again to the harbor, to his astonishment he recognized the swimmer.

Leona paused to dunk her head and let the water comb her hair backward. In her deep blue bikini, she climbed up a ladder to the rock wall top and walked toward the table. Katarina leaped from her chair and ran to hug the dripping swimmer. The two women exchanged greetings in a tongue Graham did not know. Finally, Leona approached Graham and asked, "Do you want to hug a wet girl?"

"Of course. If Katya can do it, so can I." She embraced him, wetting his clothes as she had Katarina's. They seated themselves. Leona received her glass of wine and the waiter showed up with the *ispod peke*. Once the lid was removed and the vegetables with octopus were on two plates, Graham noticed that Katarina was nowhere to be seen. She was gone.

"Did Katya leave anything for me?" Leona asked Graham. This led Graham to scowl.

"Hi, Ms. Foxx. I'm Graham Washington. Nice to meet you. Ever heard of me? Why is your first question about the mysterious Russian vamp?"

"Grammy?" Leona looked a tad startled, giving him a punishing frown.

"Goddamit," Graham ranted. "Why the hell am I here on an island that doesn't even rate a fly turd on the map? Why am I watching you rise up from the water like Venus out of a clam shell? Where did you swim from, New York? Who was your Muscovite girlfriend who knows 'all about' me? I don't like to cuss, but what the fuck is going on?!" Graham's right hand pounded the tabletop.

Leona stared at Graham, saying nothing. She spoke after Graham appeared to have calmed enough to allow her to seize the agenda. "Did Katya give you a note or anything?"

Graham fingered his pocket. He handed the folded paper to Leona without reading it. Leona placed it in front of her, next to the candle now lighting the table as darkness was falling. She sipped her Graševina and registered satisfaction with her eyes. After reading the note she turned it around and slid it over for Graham's reading.

Šibenik
Svetiste Square
Medicinska Masaža
Top floor

"Here's what I want you to do, Graham. I suggest you take notes. Write on this paper if you need to."

Graham dutifully pulled a pen from his cargo shorts and readied himself to write.

"Tomorrow morning take the 6:45am ferry back to Šibenik. First, rent a motorcycle. Make it a Vespa, just right for two riders. Then arrange for a speed boat, a hydroplane with pilot if necessary. Gas it up for a trip to Split."

"That's going to be costly."

"You've got a CIA budget, Graham. Don't be stingy when it's a matter of life and death."

"Since when do we care about death?" Graham was wearing the kind of smile that indicated he knew his joke would not be funny.

Leona granted him respect for his attempt at humor. "Well, then, call it national security. But spend the damned money."

Graham nodded and then raised his pen above the paper. "OK, I'll write 'spend money,' exclamation point."

"Here's what you write: 'Ulica Sv. Nikole Tavelica sign'."

"What?"

Leona repeated and spelled the words. "Find the square in Šibenik in front of the church of St. Nikolas—yes, Santa Claus. It's a small square. On the far side you'll find a narrow alley, only wide enough for a single small car. On the building's corner is a sign, 'Ulica Sv. Nikole Tavelica'. At 1:30am tomorrow night—that's Friday morning—park the Vespa under that sign. Leave the keys in it, so all I have to do is turn on the engine and fly. Can you handle this?"

Graham pretended to be taking dictation. "Can you handle this..." He placed the pen point on his lower lip. Leona let out the first chuckle of the interchange.

"Next, boss," said Graham.

Leona continued. "Have the pilot and the speed boat quietly sitting just a few feet off the ferry landing in Šibenik. Not moored. Free. But close to the concrete pier. Be ready to peel off at full throttle."

"When?"

"Please be ready by 2:05am. More than likely I'll be a few minutes later than that. But don't flag in zeal."

"What happens then?"

"Just wait and see."

CHAPTER 77

PRVIĆ LUKA

It was not hard for Leona to turn on her feminine charm and reshape the evening's mood. Two 'X' chromosomes trump an 'XY' combo whenever subtle cards are being played.

After paying the bill and rising from the table, the two Americans walked a few steps to the water's edge. The full moon's pearly white glow spangled the open sea with a glittering pathway leading from earth to heaven. Graham's right arm reached around to clasp Leona's right hip. She complemented the gesture by placing her left arm and hand on his back. She laid her head on his right shoulder. They stood for a moment, silent and immobile. Graham turned his gaze toward her forehead. She looked up. Their eyes met. Then, she closed hers and stood quietly in wait.

They were interrupted by a loud noise. A bang. Then two more.

"Were those gun shots?" queried Graham.

"I think so."

Graham took off running in the direction of the shots. He moved quickly along the escalade in his sandals. Leona, still with bare swimmer's feet, followed, but more slowly. Around the hotel and across the square they could see activity on the steps below the post office. Graham arrived to find three onlookers surrounding a body. Down on one knee he picked up the hand of the woman in the white tank top. He felt the pulse of her lifeless wrist and realized it was over for the victim. Blood was flowing from the center of her chest, flooding both the clothing and her open skin. Graham tenderly reached up and closed the eyes of Katarina Louchakova.

Leona stood among the onlookers. Graham rose to his feet and placed his arms around Leona. "Is it Katya?" she asked.

"Yes. I am afraid it is. She's dead. No hope. Two, maybe three bullets in her chest. I'm so sorry, Lee."

Lee placed her head on Graham's chest, but only momentarily. Within the cacophony of voices Leona could hear someone exclaiming that the police had been called and were now on the way. Leona looked out toward the harbor and could see the police boat racing toward the pier. She grabbed Graham by the hand and pulled him away from the hubbub toward the hotel and the shore line.

"This is awful, Graham. Just awful," she whined. They hugged again.

"Now, Graham, are you clear on my instructions?"

Graham looked surprised. He paused. "Yes, of course."

"You're on your own until I see you at the speed boat in the middle of tomorrow night."

"What the fuck?!"

Leona kissed him sweetly but briefly. She turned quickly and took a run toward the water. She sprang with outstretched arms that came together in prayer just before slicing the water's surface. With hardly a splash she disappeared from Graham's sight. He thought he saw her head surface a hundred feet further out; but then she disappeared again into the night.

CHAPTER 78

CROATIA

It was 1:30am. Although the moon was again bright, the narrow streets and alleys of Šibenik were relatively dark. All was quiet. Leona stood silently on top of the bell tower of St. Lawrence's Monastery. She surveyed the buildings below her while she raised a wet finger to feel the speed of the air currents. Like a swimmer diving, she threw herself off the bell tower into the surrounding empty space.

After a ten-foot plunge, the wings of her wingsuit took hold and she began to sail. She swirled. She kept her eyes on her target. After another descending pirouette she readied herself for landing. Most roofs were steep and covered with round tiles. Leona's target was a flat roof patio with laundry drying on a clothes line atop a two-plus-story green row house. She landed with less noise than a rabbit pawing straw.

She divested herself of the wingsuit and felt for her Kimber Mach II and her rope. The Kimber was holstered on her right side, while a coiled wire hung from her left. She walked to the balcony's edge and looked down. Parked in the alley below was a Vespa. *Could that be Graham's Vespa? I guess I'm betting human lives that it is.*

CHAPTER 79

CROATIA

Leona crept through the entrance door and down a half flight of stairs to the second story landing. The dormer room was filled with sleepers, three close by and one over against the far wall. After pausing to adjust her eyes to the dim light, she believed she could see that the sleeper at the far wall was Cupid. Those on the near side must be the hostage holders. Deftly she made her way between the beds to the far side of the room. Leaning down she put her mouth to Cupid's ear.

"Don't make a sound, Cupid," she whispered.

Cupid awoke but could not help a breathy, "Pastor Lee!" The child clasped her arms around Leona's neck, and cheek rubbed cheek.

"Shhh," whispered the pastor. But Cupid did not let go of the desperate hug. Nearly a minute passed. Leona's mind was working. *Should I try to sneak out noiselessly? Or should I wake everyone and... and...and...then what?* No one seemed to be disturbed.

The rescuer's hands directed Cupid to turn her legs to the bed's side and stand up. No sound was made. Fragments of moonlight showed through the front window, but only shadows could be seen by anyone within the room who might be looking.

Leona sought for and found a secure place to tie the rope, the elbow of a water pipe. She knotted her metal reinforced twine. At the other end she formed a harness and directed Cupid to step into it. Through the open front window she slowly lowered the little girl, having instructed her to wait on the road below. Once Cupid was safe at the bottom, Leona threw the rest of the rope out and then began her own repel descent. Her foot slammed against the building wall loud enough for one of the sleepers to ask the others, "What was that?" In seconds the three Mongolian thugs realized their captive was missing and darted to the open window. They could hear the motorcycle engine turn over and saw Cupid holding on to a strange Vespa driver whizzing across the church square. They screamed for reinforcements and dialed their cell phones to sound the alert.

"Hold on tightly," Leona told her rider. Cupid's hands clasped each other just below the driver's windpipe. The Vespa buzzed and whined through the narrow streets, down two-step stairs and on occasion full staircases. Sharp corners caused slowing, then speeding. By the time they turned on to Obala Franje Tuđmana, two pursuers in a Renault were following them. The passenger reached through the window and fired two wild shots at the racing cycle.

The cycle's driver pressed forward with her eyes set on the pier and the moored boats. To her right Leona thought she could make out the parked hydroplane. It was puttering just off the end of the Šibenik pier. She turned the Vespa sharply to the right, providing a better target for the pursuing Renault. Even so, the bullets missed the two escapees. Leona accelerated. The Renault turned to follow. Now both vehicles were on the pier, heading straight for the open water. Leona continued to accelerate. Soon the Vespa was airborne. Off the end of the pier it flew. The Renault screeched to a halt.

With the splash Graham knew exactly where to find the cyclists. Without turning on lights, the hydroplane drifted close enough for Graham to throw a donut life preserver. Leona was swimming toward the boat, paddling with her left arm while her right held Cupid's chin with her nose well above water. In moments both were in the boat.

"Give it all you've got!" Graham told the pilot. Within seconds the roar of the engines and the new wake signaled that they had begun their trip to the south at nearly sixty miles per hour.

CHAPTER 80

CROATIA

Leona and Cupid held hands at the Split International Airport. Graham carried two light suitcases, ready for checking.

"Grammy will take you to Chicago and back to see your mommy, Cupid. Your mommy will be so glad to have you home! Get ready for tons and tons of hugs," promised Leona.

"I want you to come home too, Pastor Lee," pined Cupid.

"Grammy will take good care of you. But I'll be back home before you go to school." The two hugged.

"Cupid asks the right question, Lee. Why the hell aren't you coming home with us?"

"For the sake of Brostock, Grammy!"

"I'm sorry. There is no place called Brostock! Only Rostock. Rostock is on the Baltic Sea. Get your cities right!"

"Okay, then. For the sake of Rostock!"

Before the conversation could continue, it was time for Cupid's retinue to check in.

"How did you know, Lee?" asked Graham while en route to the security line.

"Katya was an old friend I made in my CIA days. She was a Russian Mafia informant. Double agent, so to speak. As it turns out, her older sister is Olga Louchakova, the computer hacker in the TaiCom Syndicate. Olga and Geraldine Bourne, the Canadian neurosurgeon, made a deal through Katya to place their so-called clinic in Prvić Luka. The Mafia would insure privacy and conduct patient traffic in and out. Even though Katya wanted to protect her sister, she was willing to work with me on a plan to extricate Cupid."

"Why would anybody want to bring Cupid here?"

"I think a TaiCom rogue wanted to get proof of concept on making children more intelligent. Once such a chip were to be patented, just think of the number of parents who could be hoodwinked into purchasing the implantation device. They'd take out second mortgages just to advance their kid. The sales would be enormous worldwide. I think we are seeing a race to patent going on here. Whoever is behind this plot probably thought the Russian Mafia could strong-arm the clinic to rush the clinical trials. Most likely, Cupid would have been a guinea pig."

"But why Cupid? You can get a kid from anywhere."

"Because of me. I think the kidnapping might've been done to spite me," said Leona pondering.

"All this points to Khalid Neshat, Lee. Your boyfriend is a bad boy."

CHAPTER 81

CHICAGO

GRAHAM LOOKED INTENTLY at his computer screen. He knew this email had come from Leona.

Dear G:

Still need to stay out of sight.

Next rendezvous: Heidelberg on the 24th.

At 10:00am purchase two coffees at a Conditeri near Marktplatz. I would like a vanilla snowball. This is a round baked cookie called a Schneeball. You'll find chairs and tables surrounding the fountain. Sit. Sip your coffee and read a copy of the *Frankfurter Allgemeinezeitung*. I'll contact you.

If it rains, I'll meet you inside the *Heiliggeistkirche*.

Miss you.

L

"I think I've got to pack my suitcase again," Graham muttered to himself. "Right after I call Hurley."

CHAPTER 82

OXFORD

AFTER STEPPING off the Heathrow bus at Gloucester Green, Leona walked eastward first on George Street, then on Broad Street passing Trinity College, then on Hollywood Street before turning north on Mansfield Road. She passed the sports ground before arriving at her destination, Excelsior College at the University of Oxford.

Professor John Blair stood up from behind his desk to greet his American visitor. Beneath the ear hooks on his glasses, bushes of graying temple hair sprouted out like feathers, giving him the appearance of Winged Victory. He was dressed in a short-sleeved Tommy Bahama aloha shirt, plain white with a palm leaf pattern.

"Thank you, Doctor Blair, for receiving me on such short notice. I have some questions," said Leona.

"My pleasure, Doctor Foxx. I am always ready to discuss my research and other topics that could be of mutual interest. Won't you sit down?"

Leona placed herself in an armed chair angled in front of the modest desk while Blair sat, swiveled, and leaned back in his desk chair. Soon they were engaged in a back 'n' forth. Blair restated his position, namely, that intelligence consists of a quantitative advance in computational capacity and that, whether in AI or IA form, it's just around the technological corner. With this theory in mind, research should press forward toward the expansion of access to information.

"I'm just baking," announced Leona, grabbing each elbow with the opposite hand and twisting slightly. She then picked up a tissue and wiped a couple of beads of sweat off her forehead.

"Oh, should I turn on the AC?" asked Blair. Before receiving an answer, the professor reached toward his window unit, turned a dial, and paused until the air conditioner sent out its cooling breeze. "Now, that's better, isn't it?"

"Much better," responded Leona. "I don't know what the thermometer reads in Centigrade, but I'll bet it's 90 degrees Fahrenheit."

"'Tis a scorcher, isn't it? A bit unusual, this weather."

"Indeed," emphasized Leona. "Now, Doctor Blair, may I press you on one point? It seems to me that what we experience as intelligence is more than the accumulation of information. We human beings and perhaps other intelligent creatures, it seems to me, are capable of having insights. Rather than merely calculate, our minds make leaps. We imagine hypotheses and then we try to confirm or disprove these hypotheses by rallying evidence. Isn't this more than super-calculation?"

"Just a complex form of calculation, I believe. Existing computers can answer human questions by searching a data base, parsing nuances, weighing possibilities, and providing a precise response. Today's computers can do this better than most humans, even most scientists."

"But," Leona insisted, "we humans are capable of counter-factuals. We can imagine things that do not exist. We can imagine an orange elephant with two trunks, for example. A calculator, no matter how much information it has access to, is not capable of this. Am I right?"

"Imagining counter-factuals is not the same thing as knowing things. To be intelligent is to know things, true things. Smart computers know more things. The posthumans of the future will know so many things that we today will look to them like cave men look to us."

"The problem with your theory, Doctor Blair, with all due respect, is that it does not account for our ability to think non-literally. Artificial intelligence is strictly literal, strictly factual, not intersubjective. Let me give you a case in point. A few minutes ago I said something that was a flat lie. I hinted that I was freezing. You immediately knew that I was uncomfortable due to the 90-degree temperature, so you turned on the air conditioner. Had you taken me literally, you would have turned up the thermostat on the furnace. How can artificial intelligence distinguish between the truth and a lie at the literal level in order to deal with knowledge at the extra-literal level? Now, doesn't this capacity make human intelligence superior?"

"I don't see how a lie or any other counter-factual statement could in itself be a mark of intelligence. Or, at least an indispensable component of intelligence. Perhaps literal truth-telling by future cyborgs will mark a posthuman improvement over today's lying by an untrustworthy human species. Posthumanity could mark a leap forward in honesty, don't you think, Doctor Foxx?"

Leona paused. "What about jokes, Doctor Blair? Computers are more literal than fundamentalists. Unless you can see multiple meanings buried in the context, nothing appears funny. Let me try on an example. Are you a member of the Church of England?"

"Yes, of course."

"Here's how I define a member of the Church of England. An Anglican is a person who worships God, loves their neighbor, advocates justice, strives for world peace, protects our environment—and does all of this without being tacky."

"Tacky? What's tacky?"

"Oh, it's just an Americanism."

"Doctor Foxx, I do not consider humor a mark of intelligence."

Leona smiled. "I can see that. Please let me change the subject,

Professor Blair. Tell me, just how much hope do you place in TaiCom to lead the field of AI? And how realistic do you think the Transhumanist vision for the future is?"

At the mention of TaiCom, Blair winced. He paused. Then, he selectively ignored the TaiCom reference. "I believe that the Transhumanist vision is founded on solid computer theory and that advances in nanobiotech will eventually enable us to transcend our biological substrate and attain cybernetic immortality or, at least, radical life extension. Now, if you'll excuse me, Doctor Foxx, I have some other appointments I must attend to."

After cordial good-byes, Leona departed and headed for Heathrow. She boarded the airport bus. Leona turned her head slightly when she felt something. Some kind of activity seemed to be taking place within her brain. Before her mind's eye there appeared a note. To her surprise, she could read the note. It was a message. "I've found you," said the note. It was signed, "Khalid."

Had other bus passengers been looking at the Chicago pastor, they would have seen her silently laughing to herself.

CHAPTER 83

HEIDELBERG

ON THE MORNING of the 24th Graham departed his hotel on Bismarck-platz and entered the *Hauptstrasse,* the equivalent of Main Street in every nineteenth-century American small town. But Heidelberg's cobble-stone main street has been pressed down by the feet of pedestrians for eight hundred years. The American visitor was now in the oldest part of the romantic city, the Altstadt. His stroll took him past Perkeo, a coffee shop and restaurant named after a dwarf who once tended the giant wine cask in the castle. On his right he paused to admire the architecture of the German renaissance Hotel zum Ritter—a hotel for knights. Across the street from the Ritter stood the fifteenth-century cathedral, the *Heiliggeistkirche,* surrounded today by tourist booths selling Chinese-made baseball caps and umbrellas with "Heidelberg" printed on them.

Having filled Leona's prescription for coffees with snowball pastries, Graham took his tray into the middle of Marktplatz and seated himself at a small round aluminum table. He sat facing the reddish stone of the fountain with his back to the Rosenthal fine china store. After a bite of pastry and a sip of coffee, he spread out the

Frankfurter Allgemeinezeitung. This American visitor had no idea what he was reading, being limited to his native English language. When he noticed three sips later that the coffee level was going down in his cup, he began to wonder: *when will Leona show up? Did I get the right day? The right time?* Graham checked his watch and his memory. *I think I've got it right.*

A girl swirled her damp rag around the top of a just vacated table next to him. Then she brought her tub of dirty dishes toward where Graham was sitting. She filled his cup with fresh coffee. He continued to study the undecipherable German language newspaper in front of him.

"*Fertig?*" she asked him.

Graham, with his head down sipping his coffee, mumbled, "What?"

"Are you done," she said in English with a tone of impatience.

"No. I'm still waiting for a friend."

"*Wo is die Bedingung?* Are you such a cheapskate that you won't leave a poor *Dienstmädchen* a crumby tip?"

Graham suddenly realized that this young woman wearing an apron with her hair folded into her cap was, in fact, Leona. The buss girl grabbed the full cup of coffee while still standing and took a swallow. She nibbled on her snowball *Kuchen,* relishing the stunned and confused expression on Graham's face.

"This snowball is not as tasty as I'd hoped it would be," she declared.

Graham simply stared at his presumptuous visitor.

"Did you read the article on the second page, near the bottom?" Leona asked the befuddled Graham.

"I don't read German."

"Whatya mean? You went to Princeton, for the sake of Bremerhaven! Didn't you have to pass a German exam?"

"Remember, Lee, I told you I substituted Spanish for German."

"Oh, of course. That's Princeton, I guess. I got my German at

Michigan State while doing my doctorate. I tried Russian too. Both are science languages. Gimmie *Deutsch* any day."

In Graham's mind he tried to sort out the conversation. *Should I pursue this?* He thought. *No. I don't want any more entanglement on this dumb stuff. Nor do I want to risk another insult.*

Leona spoke. "The article reports a police investigation right here in Heidelberg. They found the body of a mutilated woman at the *Hauptbahnhof,* the main train station. She was in two suitcases, half of her severed limbs in each. Do you recognize the M.O.?"

"Ugly," winced Graham. "Yes, I recognize it. No doubt Khalid Neshat's in town. All the worse for romantic Heidelberg." He looked up and made a feeble attempt to take control of the conversation. "Now, Lee, are you going to sit down? How long will you look like a table waitress?"

"We've got an appointment," said Leona with an impertinent sigh, setting her coffee cup back down. She removed her cap and with a head shake dropped her hair to its usual shoulder length. She removed her apron, crumpled it, and threw it on the table. "Let's go, Grammy. You can leave the paper here."

"Aye, Aye, Admiral." He saluted obsequiously.

"Shape up or you'll be shipped out!" she ordered. Then, as Graham rose to his feet, the admiral looked up and into his hazel eyes. She spoke softly. "Thanks for coming, Grammy. I'm so very glad we're together again." She stood up on her toes and kissed the standing Graham on the cheek.

Graham felt all the ice inside melt and run down and out his shoes.

CHAPTER 84

HEIDELBERG

"WE'RE HEADED FOR UNIVERSITÄTS PLATZ," Leona announced, while placing her right arm in the fold of Graham's left. The two walked a few yards with a shared bounce, Leona smiling wildly. As they approached *Augustinergasse,* Leona spoke again. "The Augustinian monastery used to be located here. Martin Luther defended his position against indulgences on April 26, 1518. Didya git this at Princeton?"

"What happened at Princeton just doesn't matter, Lee. You're simply a better historian than I am."

"Well, for that little lack in your memory you get to go to jail. See that door over there?" she asked, pointing. "That's the student prison. For the two centuries prior to the First World War, misbehaving students were incarcerated. The culpable misbehavior was standard, of course: drunkenness, pranks, missing exams, and forgetting important historical facts such as the date of the Heidelberg Disputation. I now arrest you!" Leona was chuckling out loud.

"Take me to your prison. Please!" Graham laughed in a silly manner.

"Not today. You'll just have to suffer by staying free. We've got business ahead of us. See that white building? It's the New University. By 'new' the Germans mean it was refounded in 1805. The first founding was 1385, making it the oldest university in Germany. The first founder was Prince Elector Ruprecht the First, and the second was Karl Friedrich of Baden. That's why it has the sorta dumb hyphenated name, Ruprecht-Karl Universität."

"Who thinks the name is dumb?"

"I do. I don't like names with hyphens."

"Who cares what you think?"

"Well, certainly nobody here does." Leona looked up and pointed. "Once into the courtyard we'll turn to the building on the left. That's where we're going."

"Do I get to ask where and why?"

CHAPTER 85

HEIDELBERG

TEN MINUTES later they were seated in the faculty office of Professor Hans-Georg Welker. On the way in, Graham had joked in a whisper about this hyphenated name, but Leona didn't take the time to laugh. In one movement, so it seemed, Professor Welker rose out of his chair and swept effortlessly around his imposing desk with an open hand of greeting. At sixty-one, his gait and shake were firm. His robust barrel chest was covered by a navy, camel, and cream argyle sweater vest, which in turn was partially covered by a beige tweed jacket. No necktie. Most striking were his sparkling blue eyes, looking out above his half spectacles sitting just above the end of his nose. The neatly trimmed gray mustache stretched nearly half an inch beyond each corner of his mouth, giving the impression of a nineteenth-century countenance.

All three then filled their chairs along with their tea cups and proceeded with the appropriate introductions. Leona thanked the Heidelberg professor for his willingness to make time for this appointment. She explained that the two visitors wanted to gain a better grasp on the theoretical issues surrounding Transhumanism.

This understanding could, she said, have significant consequences. She did not specify those consequences.

Heidelberg is a good place to speculate about such matters. *Homo erectus heidelbergensis*—that's Heidelberg Man—was discovered in a gravel pit near here. This suggests our near-human ancestors enjoyed this romantic location along the Neckar River six hundred thousand years ago. Heidelberg Man gave birth to Neanterthals, Denisovans, and us, modern humans. I suppose he had help from Heidelberg Woman too, but we have not found her remains. Yet.

"Now, we're speculating about the future of our species. Among other fields, we study neuroscience here. We study how the brain works, how it provides the capacity for intelligent reasoning. Past and present—prehuman and posthuman—both here in romantic Heidelberg."

Graham and Leona purred appropriately.

"It's almost time for lunch," announced the professor. "What we're talking about is too important to drop now. Let me walk you to a student locale, where we can enjoy some beer and bockwurst. I have a bit more to say, and it will come out better if I have a lubricated voice."

CHAPTER 86

HEIDELBERG

Graham and Leona readily accepted the invitation. The three marched through the narrow streets with the professor's guidance. The group walked past Karlsplatz, past Zum Zeppl, and turned in at Zum Roten Ochsen—the Red Ox—an old student beer hangout. A hostess seated them near the front wall at a wooden table. The table's surface was covered with graffiti, with carvings and etchings from inebriated youths who were either about to enter the student prison or who had just been released. From the ceiling dangled ram horns. On the wall shelf stood a row of artistic beer mugs, upside down. A complex coat of arms with the word 'Pfingsten' was carved into a sidewall. Other walls were covered with photos. One large photo dated from 1887 and showed two young princes arm in arm: Prince Max and Prince Ludwig. The professor ordered beer, sausage, and sauerkraut for their table. Soon the conversation re-commenced.

"The problem with the Transhumanists is threefold," announced Professor Welker. "First, they overlook a firmly established theological principle, namely, a creation cannot be more intelligent than its creator. Our world, said the medieval scholastics, demonstrates intelligence. It simply could not have come into being at the hand of any creator who is less intelligent than its creatures. It took an intelligent God to create a rational world. No one would expect worldly intelligence to exceed divine intelligence."

"But many Transhumanists are atheists," interjected Graham. "They don't believe in divine intelligence. The only intelligence they believe in is human."

"I'm well aware of this," grumbled the professor. "Still, this was Darwin's mistake, and it's one of the reasons Darwin's otherwise informative theory has prompted such vigorous opposition. Darwin thought that over time simple organisms could give rise step-by-step to complex organisms; rocks could evolve into brains. And, Darwin added, all this could happen by natural selection without the guidance of an intelligent creator. Until someone demonstrates that an unintelligent creator can bring an intelligent creature into existence, I for one cannot believe it. If it's never happened before, I don't see how Transhumanists can be confident they'll be the first to accomplish it."

"Are you a member of the Intelligent Design school that denies Darwinian evolution?" asked Graham.

"Oh, gosh no!" responded Welker. "I believe Darwin's theory of species evolution via natural selection is the best explanation we've got. It's good science. Even so, only intelligence can beget intelligence, even if it takes a long time to develop."

Graham and Leona looked intently at the professor, waiting for what would follow.

"And, secondly," Welker continued, "we have learned from history what can go wrong when a misguided society tries to create the superhuman. Nietzsche and the Nazis tried to create the *Übermensch*, the Superman, recall. Once this ideal was projected, then every average or below average person was dubbed inferior. To be less than the *Übermensch* meant your life is not worth living. A doctrine arose: persons with *lives-not-worth-living* should be met with death before they can make babies and pass their inferiority to the next generation. Gas chambers became the place for those who might retard our progress toward the superhuman. That was the Nazi way. I want to avoid seeing this happen again."

A waiter showed up to distribute the lunch. Leona took a second look. He was obviously Chinese, but his German sounded authentic, and the name "Klaus" was written on his restaurant badge. Klaus was wearing antiseptic plastic gloves. Once sausage, kraut, and beer had been placed on the wooden table, Leona asked Welker, "So how does all this apply to Transhumanism?"

"Here's how: I believe we can safely forecast that Transhumanists will not succeed at creating a posthuman creature that is more intelligent than they are."

"What about Watson?" asked Graham.

"Oh, do you mean IBM's Watson, the Jeopardy winner?"

"Yes, that's the one."

"Watson is only a computational machine with access to an immense library of data. Watson is not intelligent in the same sense that a human being is intelligent. Despite three quarters of a century of advances in computer technology, we still do not have a single example of machine intelligence."

"So," Graham attempted to sum up, "if Transhumanists think they can make a race of beings more intelligent than we are, they're whistling Dixie."

"Dixie?" said the German professor with a questioning look on his face.

"Never mind. It's just an Americanism," remarked Graham, shaking his head. "You said the problem with Transhumanism is threefold. You've told us the first problem is that it fails to recognize that a creator must be more intelligent than its creature. You said, secondly, that when this was tried in the past that it failed. Okay. So, what's the third problem?"

"The third insurmountable problem Transhumanists face—or refuse to face!—is good old-fashioned sin. Despite what Plato believed—that the more rational we are the more moral we are—the facts show otherwise. Even the smartest, most rational people we know can choose to do bad things. The greater the intelligence, the greater the potential for evil. Those who led us into World War I and World War II were smart people. The Nazis were smart people. And millions of people died. As the modern world advanced in science and technology, our capacity for wreaking violence and bloodshed advanced proportionately. The most intelligent people among us are working daily to make smarter and smarter weapons, leading ineluctably not only to genocide and but even ecocide."

"So, a posthuman world will not be a better world," interrupted Graham. "Is that what you're saying?"

"Yes. We cannot evolve ourselves into goodness. Posthumans, who will allegedly be more intelligent than we are, are likely to spread wanton violence and destruction beyond Planet Earth to other heavenly bodies. So, no matter how much our Transhumanist friends may accomplish in improving our ability to reason intelligently, the potential for evil will not dissipate, but rather will grow proportionately."

"How come you know so much about this?" asked Graham. "You're not a scientist."

"That's right. I'm a philosopher, not a scientist. But philosophy is a field-encompassing field. We've got to know what the scientists think they know so we can out-think them. In many ways the scientists—and especially the techies—are quite naive about what they think they know. Someone needs to teach them about reality. Once in a while it means we have to prick their balloons and let the debris fall back to *terra firma*."

While the conversation ensued, Leona sensed that something was happening in her head. German words, not English, penetrated her consciousness. *"Totschlagen!"* A brief moment passed. Then, again. *"Vernichtung."* This was followed by *"Mord begehen dreimahl, Washington und Foxx und Welker."* Then, the sensation dissipated.

CHAPTER 87

HEIDELBERG

WHILE SAYING their good-byes on the sidewalk in front of the Red Ox, the professor asked his American guests if they had yet seen the sites of romantic Heidelberg. Leona and Graham reported that they planned to walk off their lunch by climbing the hill to the Philosophenweg on the far side of the Neckar River.

"The now century-old house of Max Weber, the originator of the sociology of religion, is up above the philosopher's trail, sitting in the physics college. Maybe you'll notice it while walking," commented Professor Welker. "Poets such as Holderlein used to stroll the Philosophenweg, waiting for their inspiration. Maybe you'll get the inspiration you need to solve these Transhumanism problems. Good luck. Good bye."

Leona put a finger to her head. It fell on the spot of her implant. The finger had no impact on her mind, of course. Yet, she wondered almost out loud. *Could I have received a satellite transmission intended for someone else? Who would want me to murder someone? Who would want to murder me? Graham? Professor Welker? Anybody here?*

"Have we been spotted yet?" Graham asked Leona.

"No way of knowing for certain. Suppose we assume we're still incognito and enjoy ourselves for a little while. We can get back to the spy business later."

"Okay with me. Shall we head for the Philosophenweg? There we can pretend we're Hőlderlein or Weber. We can filter what Professor Welker just said, looking for clues. Or, I can simply hold your hand like Cupid does."

CHAPTER 88

HEIDELBERG

The two spies walked as if they had no mission. They sauntered with deliberate steps over the brick surfaces of the roads and alleys, winding their way toward the Neckar and the old bridge, die Alte Brücke. With Leona's arm tightly hooked through Graham's elbow, the couple wandered through the arches just below the raised cast iron gate. The Romans had built a wooden bridge on this spot, but three centuries ago the Heidelbergers constructed this now magnificent monument to premodern human engineering. During one of their pauses at the bridge's edge to study the flow of the Neckar below, the couple looked up and remarked on the beauty of the castle on the hill framed above by forests and below by red tile roofs interrupted by church spires.

"Does beauty count as rational, as a product of intelligence?" asked Graham rhetorically. "Will more intelligent posthumans create greater beauty? Will they appreciate beauty more than we do?"

Leona nodded without speaking. Soon the couple was again walking toward the far side of the river, this time holding hands. As they neared the far side, with only a few yards to go before departing the bridge, they stopped for one final view of the water with its rapidly moving crew boats manned by rowing students.

"Doesn't that guy back there look like our waiter?" Graham quizzed.

Leona focused. "It's Klaus. Did he follow us?"

Less than forty yards to their right, Klaus was leaning on the bridge's stone rail, aiming a gun in their direction.

"Down!" Graham exclaimed. Leona and Graham dropped to their knees. A puff of smoke from the gun and the sound of a ricocheting bullet affirmed they had taken the right diversionary action. Up and running, the couple raced eastward and across the street to the steep hill's foot. They raced for the Schlangerweg—the snaking path leading to the Philosophenweg—turning a fence corner to block any straight shots that might follow. Again, they could hear bullets ricochet.

The winding and climbing path, like the streets of the old city, was surfaced with century-old brick ends. But on either side were ten-foot-high stone walls, giving the Schlangerweg a tunnel effect. The unforgiving reddish brick road led upward, supplemented occasionally by sections of steps. When he hit a straightaway section, the assailant stopped to fire his weapon at the fleeing couple above. The running targets escaped by taking the next turn, denying the shooter a clear shot. During a brief respite, Leona and Graham looked downward at the blind corner behind them. Leona pulled out her Kimber and aimed it.

"Suppose I shoot the stone wall," she said. "Then the slug would ricochet around the corner and hit Klaus."

"Now, that's dumb," retorted Graham, unholstering his hand gun.

Leona looked up at her partner, registering insult. "Dumb?!"

"Yeah. It's dumb like a hyphenated name. Bullets don't connect stone walls with targets very well. You keep going, Lee. Let me see if I can get behind him."

Graham scrambled up the inside wall. Leona fired her ricochet shot anyway. Even if she missed, her pursuer would have to pause to wait for the ambush to clear. As soon as Graham had disappeared into the overhanging grass above, Leona pressed on up the hill. Soon the follower with gun drawn entered the straight section to occupy the position just vacated by Graham and Leona. The Chinese waiter pressed upward. Once the gunman had made the next turn, Graham descended again to the path level. He followed. The hunter was unknowingly now caught between his prey.

After a few more turns, the gunman caught sight of Leona's trailing foot ducking out of sight ahead. He fired at the spot where he had last seen the running Leona. In the momentary silence following the shot, Graham, with two hands aiming his Glock 19, hollered: "Freeze. Drop your weapon."

The thug was stunned. The two hands of the Chinese Klaus were raised, the gun hanging limply from a trigger finger. Leona now descended and made herself visible in front. Klaus' facial expression registered his newly gained knowledge: he was surrounded. Escape was hopeless.

"I said: drop the weapon!" Graham screamed with both authority and impatience.

The Chinese gunman suddenly dropped to his knees, regained a firm grip on his pistol, and aimed it at Leona. Graham fired. Skull and brain fragments splattered the path's stone wall, and Klaus' body slumped slowly down to the brick surface.

Graham and Leona were stunned at the turn of events. Nothing moved for a moment. Graham caught his composure first. "Do you see what I see?" asked Graham. "There, on his left hand. A snake tail tatt."

Leona nodded. "Look at that Chinese character."

功率

Graham's hand slapped about the corpse. He drew a cell phone from the dead man and quickly checked the text messages. The most recent, only minutes previously, was addressed to "Khalid," and read: *"Washington und Foxx werden bevor Tea Time gestorben sein."* Graham showed the message to Leona, then pocketed the phone.

"Let's get outa here," commanded Leona.

CHAPTER 89

HEIDELBERG

"What I have is the electronic invitation to this evening's banquet and contract announcement," Leona told Graham, handing him a single page computer printout. "It's from Holthusen's office." The two had just escaped with their lives from a treacherous gunfight on the Schlangerweg. Leona's room at the Hotel am Schloss was now the venue for their little respite from the *Sturm und Drang* of international intrigue. Actually, it was no respite. Because even when they were not getting shot at, they were still talking about shootings, shootings in the past and shootings in the future. Once a spy, continually a spy, or so it seems.

Graham read the printout. "It says here that *Deutsche Technische Institut* and *Tehran Technologies Incorporated* have agreed to a major partnership. This merges German high tech with Iranian high tech. If I make this out correctly, together these two will marshal the world's masses and march the planet straight into the Singularity. DTI's president is Dieter Dietz. TTI's president is—get this, Leona—none other than Khalid Neshat. I'm holding in my hand here a confirmed invitation for two persons to attend tonight's announcement and celebration to be held at 20:00 in the *Kŏnigssaal* [Kings Hall] at the Schloss Heidelberg. Huh. I thought the castle was just a ruin."

"It is a ruin," offered Leona. "It's ancient. Dedicated in 1534. But some quarters have been refurbished and are still used today. Especially the *Kŏnigssaal*. It's a great place to throw a party, at least according to Wikipedia. If you look out my hotel window, you'll see the path that leads up to the castle entrance. At least according to Map Quest. We'll be on that trail this evening."

"What! You're not thinking about going to this event, are you?"

"Yes, indeed."

"But Khalid Neshat is going to be there. He'll probably be master of ceremonies."

"Yes, we *are* going, Graham. And we're going to scare the shit out of that bastard, Neshat! He thinks he bumped us off this afternoon. We're not out to make converts. But when he sees us, he just might believe in resurrection."

CHAPTER 90

HEIDELBERG

AT 7:30 THAT EVENING, Graham was back in Leona's room at the Hotel am Schloss to pick up his date.

"You look spectacular!" he exclaimed.

"How do I rate such a handsome prince to take me to the Castle?" Leona handed Graham a small plastic bag. "These are my heels. Would you please be a prince and carry them for me?" She pointed to her feet, shod in Nikes.

Graham and Leona trudged up the Schlosseingang, another snake trail winding its way up the mountainside on harsh bricks. Because the Schloss Heidelberg was built and destroyed and rebuilt multiple times over multiple centuries, it is a hodgpodge of architectural styles. The only continuity is found in the color, a rustic red that almost glows from within the sandstone. After arriving in the courtyard at the foot of the Baroque façade built by Frederick IV in 1607, which Leona recognized from the photos now lodged in her brain, she tugged on Graham's arm, signaling him to cease walking. He stood still and firm, while Leona stripped off her Nikes with one hand and replaced them with high heels. Once she had adjusted her skirt, she signaled that the march to the Kings Hall could resume.

As the American couple entered the hall, they were each given a glass of freshly poured champagne, what the Germans call Sekt.

"Let me show you something," said Leona. She guided Graham gently through the mingling crowd toward the rear of the Kings Hall, toward a curtain. She knew just where to go—she was guided by that huge database that had been downloaded into her head. "Behind this curtain is where the kitchen staff work," she said.

Leona pulled the curtain aside just a few feet, uncovering a most unusual cast iron contraption. Two vertical rods stood in parallel. They began at the floor and stretched to a height above their heads. "This is a pump," announced Leona. "It leads to a very large barrel of wine in the floor below us. Centuries ago the servants could retrieve an endless supply of the purple liquid to make certain the king's parties would not lag."

"Sometimes, Leona, I think you've got wine on the mind."

Leona smiled. "Maybe I do. Down below are a couple of wine barrels, giant casks. The largest is called the Great Tun or Grosses Fass, built in 1751 by a guy named Carl Theodor. It holds over 58,000 US gallons. It took the trunks from 130 Oak trees to make it. It was guarded by a local hero, Perkeo, a dwarf. Interesting, huh? I've got more."

Graham looked a tad impatient.

"Perkeo was the court jester, a short guy who came from Tyrol. That's in the Alps. It is alleged that he only drank wine. He died because someone bet he couldn't drink a glass of water. He took the bet, drank the water, and died on the spot."

Graham's impatience was becoming too much. "So, Lee, why are we standing here with you giving me a history lecture?"

"Because I want the time to see if we're being followed," said the damsel looking over her date's shoulder.

"Are we?"

"No. Not yet."

"Good."

"No, not good."

"You mean you want us to get followed again and murdered again?"

"Followed, yes. Murdered, no. I see that everyone's seated now. In a few seconds we'll migrate to our table. We'll walk right past the head table, where Neshat can get a good look at us."

In moments the couple was walking slowly across the front of the dining room, passing the high head table on a raised platform to their left. Graham stood tall and cavalier, a posture befitting a royal knight. Leona nearly pranced in her high heels, broadcasting the features of feminine pulchritude that draw admiring stares from all directions. The speakers and dignitaries at the high table were momentarily distracted from their engrossing conversations, each reviewing the not-so-subtle enticement below them.

Khalid's eyes met Leona's. His face flashed confusion and disorientation followed by scorn. He faked a continuous smile, barely hiding a seething anger. Leona turned on one of her heels, swinging her left earring out. It flashed in the chandelier light. Even from this distance, Khalid could see that it was Kelly's earring on Leona's left ear. Outsmarted, outwitted, and outmaneuvered, the Iranian felt dragon's fire rising into his mouth from within.

Soon Graham and Leona were seated in the second row of tables. Following a pair of invocations by local clergy—the first to the Holy Trinity and the second to Allah—the dining began. Then, the program. The featured speaker was a philosopher announcing that a new and higher stage of human evolution would begin during the lifetime of many present this evening. The speaker was not, to be sure, Hans-Georg Welker. Rather, it was a local philosopher who frequently quoted John Blair.

This address was followed by personal and official remarks by representatives of both DTI and TTI. Khalid's toasting glass held fruit juice made from imported oranges, while those of his colleagues were filled with sparkling Sekt, made from a dry white Burgundy grape. During a moment of audience applause, Khalid called an aide —a broad-shouldered Mongolian wearing a tuxedo—to his side and whispered something serious and emphatic.

DESSERT AND COFFEE finished the sumptuous meal. A tuxedoed waiter showed up at their table with an envelope. The name "Rev. Leona Foxx," was written on the front. After waving it in front of Graham, the addressee opened it and removed a note card. "Dr. Khalid Neshat respectfully requests your presence immediately following this event at the Great Tun to discuss matters of mutual interest." Leona turned the text so Graham could read it. The tuxedoed messenger waited.

"Please inform Mr. Neshat that my answer is yes. We will meet him shortly downstairs in the giant cask room." The messenger bowed and departed.

Graham noticed Leona fidgeting and rumbling under the table. "What're ya doing?"

"Removing my heels and putting my Nikes back on." Leona looked directly at Graham. "Shortly before I go down to the Fass Zimmer, you should disappear. Take my blue leather bag."

"Why? So I can escort your heels? I'd rather escort your feet."

Leona glared, then continued. "The bag also contains my heat, my Kimber. Please listen. Next to the Great Tun is a set of toilets. They're in large rooms. Enter the one for Herren, obviously. Find an excuse to remain there until you hear activity in the Fass room next door. Then, come out and cover me. Okay?"

"Do you want to take Neshat alive?"

"The bastard doesn't deserve to live another second."
"That doesn't answer my question: dead or alive?"
"We have no right to serve as his executioners."
"You're still not answering my question, Lee."
"Woman's prerogative."

CHAPTER 91

HEIDELBERG

As Leona descended the dank walkway to the wine cellar, her Nikes kept a secure grip on the brick. Once in the wine cellar, she was greeted again by the tuxedoed messenger. "Mr. Neshat would like to engage you in conversation, Rev. Foxx. He is waiting for you on the top of the Great Tun."

Leona followed the rickety wooden stair case to the right, climbing up the side of the giant wine barrel. Atop this unofficial Wonder of the World, she found a flat wooden dance floor surrounded by a low rail to prevent drunken polka dancers from plummeting over the side.

"I'd like to offer you a glass of Silver Oak cab," announced a voice filtering through the dim light from a chair in the shadows. Khalid Neshat was sitting with his back to the barrel's front edge, a hundred feet above the basement below. Leona was entering the platform from the rear. Neshat continued. "But, with your uncanny refined tastes, I fear you might discern a slight change in viticulture recipe. This recipe is one I like to offer my guests, especially my beautiful guests. But it does not pass your discriminating taste test, does it, Reverend Foxx?"

"It's a lethal recipe, isn't it, Dr. Neshat? Like euthanizing cattle, you serve your girlfriends a Mickey Finn and then finish them off with a knife to their throats. Mickey Finn mixed with cabernet sauvignon plus murder as a chaser is a cocktail taste I prefer to do without."

"But you ran away before we could get to know one another. My heart was broken, Madame Pastor."

"I'd rather your heart get broken than my throat get slit. Why do you do such things? Kelly was such a dear friend. Miss Detroit did nothing to harm you. And I bet that poor young assistant in Taipei, what was her name?..."

"Yang. Lilly Yang. I remember my victims. My victims don't really die if they live on in my memory. It's a kind of objective immortality, so to speak. What the Transhumanists want, of course is different. They want subjective immortality. They want to enjoy consciously their everlasting life."

"What is it that you want, Khalid?"

"I want Iranian immortality. I want Cyrus to live forever in the memories of the history books. Well, we no longer read books, do we. I want Cyrus of Persia to live on in the cloud. I want the emperor to rule space. And he will when consciousness emanates from Earth to fill the universe. Cosmic consciousness will someday be Persian consciousness."

"Khalid, you're a physicist. What is all this consciousness nonsense? Don't tell me you believe in the Singularity? Intelligence Amplification? Post-biological consciousness? Do you?"

"John Blair has established the theory. It makes good sense to me."

"While Hans-Georg Welker disputes that theory. Who's right?"

"If we eliminate Professor Welker, then there will be only one theory remaining, right?"

"No, just one less theoretician. Ideas live on even when their inventors don't. They live on in the world of ideas."

"See, Leona, you have just proved my point. I believe in the Cloud. So do you."

CHAPTER 92

HEIDELBERG

"As you can see, Reverend Foxx, I simply cannot proceed with all my ambitious plans if you're alive to obstruct them. But I find you damned hard to kill. You don't like to die. And when you appear to die you don't stay dead."

Leona cocked her head and emitted a victorious smile.

"I'm puzzled about a matter, Pastor Foxx. I know you have a chip implant. I know you receive my satellite transmissions. But I receive no response. I cannot track you. Why?"

"Because the reverse transmission feature has been disconnected. Simple as that," said Leona, again triumphantly.

"Why don't you just do what I tell you?" he asked.

"Oh? You've not heard of free will?" she asked sarcastically.

Neshat looked bewildered. He paused to process what he had just heard. "Be that as it may, I still need to kill you and Graham. But I'm finding it more difficult than it should be. Now, just what am I to do?"

"Why do you ask me to solve *your* problem? I've got a problem with you. You've developed the addictive habit of seducing and murdering members of the fairer sex. You kidnap and kill to get your way. You can kick the habit, you know. You could free yourself from all the evil you plan. As I see it, you've got two options: repent or die. I'm here to hear your confession. I might even offer to help you mend your ways, Dr. Neshat. Or, if you'd prefer, I could help you with the other option."

"Do you mind if I smile, or even laugh? You have no weapon. I've got you surrounded with my men, my Mongolian Guards. As soon as I snap my fingers, you drop from existence into non-existence. That's the power I have, and the power you lack."

"Have you noticed any shaking on my side of this conversation? No, I don't think so. I'm not anxious. You've been trying to harness the hurricane winds of non-existence for quite some time now with your murders and rumors of murders. The non-existence of others has been your gift to so many in our world. But I think this is a gift that should stop its giving. Tonight! Tonight, your soul will be required of you."

"May I laugh even louder, Reverend Foxx? Perhaps you don't get it. I'm the one here with the power of life and death, not you. It's you who's been given a death sentence." He snapped his fingers and two of the imposing Mongolian Guards stood up on their feet.

"Okay. I'll snap my fingers." She snapped. Nothing appeared to happen.

"Ha. Ha." Neshat was laughing. "The lady pastor doth bluff."

"No bluff. I now have a gun cocked and aimed right at your excessively large head. It's time to repent, Dr. Neshat. Or else…"

Neshat turned to his right. Then down.

"Look to your left," said Leona.

Neshat turned cautiously around on his chair to look over the rail at a wooden landing only a few feet below the giant cask top. There he saw Graham, standing erect, holding a gun with two hands, sighted directly at him. A momentary expression of terror took over Neshat's face.

"Should I simply say the word 'fire'?" quizzed Leona.

"How did he get there? My men? I had guards? Where are they?"

"I'm sure Graham has made them comfortable," quipped Leona. The two Mongolian Guards rose and walked to the opposite side of the platform. When they saw Graham in command, they inched their way backwards.

"Now I'm the one with power, Dr. Neshat. But I don't covet power the way you do." She hollered, "Graham, drop the gun to your side. But keep it handy, just in case."

A look of puzzlement overtook Neshat's face.

Leona walked in a small circle with her eyes staring into those of Neshat. She then took control of the conversation. "You like power, don't you, Khalid?" She'd switched to using his first name. "You wallow in power. You bathe in power. You lie awake at night dreaming and conniving and planning to get more power. Am I right, Khalid?"

"Yes, you're right, Leona. When I flirt with a beautiful woman and I perceive that she's beginning to give her heart to me, I get a head rush. Then, once she's given herself totally to me, I assume the role of a god. She worships me through sexual surrender, and I decide whether she lives or dies. And this is exactly what I plan for Europe and Europe's descendants in North America. I will seduce Europe through its lust for technological innovation by offering the promise of the most radical innovation, human transformation. Then, it will be my turn to decide whether Europe lives and thrives, or whether it dies the death of a thermonuclear holocaust. All of Europe if not all of our planet will want to pay me tribute. Then, once again, Cyrus of Persia will rule the known world. It won't be my power alone, Leona; it will be the power of a rising Iran."

CHAPTER 93

"Actually, Khalid, you are a religious man. As it turns out, power is not something we own. We don't *have* power. Rather, we channel it. We become the vessel for power to flow through us. This is what makes the lust for power so religious: we want to become the vessel through which something greater can flow. For you, Khalid, Iran is your actual religion, not Islam."

"I find it uncanny, Leona, that you think of me as a religious man. Do you think of me as holy?"

"By no means, my Persian friend. You are demonic. You have chosen to worship an idol, Iran. And through this idol you plan to establish yourself as a god with the power to grant or withhold existence to innocent young women, and even to all of Europe. You've sold your eternal soul to Satan for an ephemeral moment of triumph in Earth's paltry history. This is self-destructive. And somewhere in that consciousness of yours is an awareness of just how evil it is."

"So, you never stop being a preacher, do you, Leona. I do believe that right now you're trying to save my eternal soul."

"That's right, Khalid."

"Well, if, as you say, I've already sold my soul to Satan, then it's too late, isn't it? No one is going to buy it back."

"It's not too late."

"Oh, yes it is."

Suddenly, all lights went out. Graham's gun sounded and flashed in the darkness. But it hit nothing. It lodged in the room's ceiling.

Leona raced to her right and down a short flight of wooden stairs. In seconds she had arrived at the landing where Graham stood. They touched and then ran together downward toward the cask room's bottom floor. Ambient light from distant sources made it possible to see the shadow of someone scaling down the front of the *Grosses Fass*, first gripping the wooden baroque emblem of Carl Theodor, then falling to the basement floor. The figure leapt up and out of the *Fass Zimmer*. Graham, scrambling down stairs, could not get off an accurate shot.

No doubt the two Mongolian guards are either still atop the barrel or en route down the wooden stairway on the far side, speculated Leona. She and Graham ran in the direction they believed Khalid Neshat had gone: into the courtyard fronting the façade of the Frederick IV building. While on the run Graham passed the Kimber to Leona's hand.

The two turned left and ran through the archway onto the terrace overlooking the old city and the Neckar River. The shadow they were following led them up a castle wall to the so-called Fat Tower, *der dicker Turm*. Built first to withstand the assault of attacking armies, the Fat Tower was re-constructed in 1619 to hold a theater—similar to Shakespeare's Globe Theater—when the German Prince Frederick V brought an English bride, Elizabeth Stuart, home to the Palatinate. The French later dynamited the *dicker Turm*, leaving room for today's rocky lawn across which Khalid Neshat was now running. All this ran through Leona's mind uninvited.

Neshat reached the outer edge and then stopped to catch his breath. A Glock 17 dangled at his side. Had he been in the mood for sightseeing, he could have appreciated the orange glow of the lighted Alte Brücke spanning the Neckar River hundreds of feet below. But this was not a time for appreciating beauty.

Leona would not allow such recreational time, as she announced in a loud voice, "Khalid, I suggest you drop that weapon!"

The cornered Neshat froze. He allowed time to pass. Leona's mouth had begun to open to repeat her command, when Neshat spun toward her and raised his Glock. He did not have time to pull the trigger. From the darkness on the opposite arc of the round tower's interior, a flash of light was accompanied by the loud crack of another Glock. Graham was firing. Three dime-sized red spots suddenly appeared on the left side of Khalid's skull. Each grew and the blood oozed out. The already dead body of the would-be Cyrus of the twenty-first century turned slightly as the legs gave way. He fell torso first over the Fat Tower's edge and into the night breeze filling the otherwise empty void below. By the time Leona and Graham had reached the tower's precipice, they saw Neshat's body slam into the unforgiving red bricks on the pavement.

CHAPTER 94

THE CLOUD

LEONA LEFT Graham to engage with the onrushing Heidelberg Police Department. She ran against the crowd to the dining hall, to the seat she recalled Neshat had occupied at the banquet's head table. She found what she was looking for. She grabbed the laptop, still in its case, and ran for the Schlangerweg. Down she ran, with gravity helping her to take giant leaps. After some minutes she arrived at the Hotel am Schloss.

Once in the privacy of her hotel room, Leona hastily opened Neshat's computer. It did not take her long to find the controls for satellite reception and transmission. She found the list of implants in place. Choong Lo's name with two others in parentheses, Helmut Klein and Charles Worthington, appeared first. Her own name was missing from the list, but she noted an independent icon with the initials, L.F. *Whew.*

When she came across Moshe Bisk and Tsvi Sechbach, she said to herself, *must be Mossad's men.* With a few clicks, Leona found herself ready to transmit updates to their respective implants. *Hmmm. What shall I say?* Leona set to thinking, thinking without calling to mind the library of knowledge awaiting her access in her own implant.

Once she had finished sending the final transmission to both Bisk and Sechbach, Leona turned to the satellite program itself. In minutes, she had changed the password to something only she would know. The new password consisted of sixteen nonsense symbols with no ordered sequence. She deliberately decided not to reread it. Not to memorize it. Then she logged out. The satellite surveillance and transmission system turned off. Leona closed the laptop lid.

"I'm in Heidelberg," Leona told Noel over her cell phone. "I'll be coming home in a few days. Do you think you could remove that chip we placed in my brain?"

"Of course, dearie. I'll have my appointments nurse call you and set it up. I think we could just do it in my office. I'll give you a mild sedative, so you might want to ask Graham to drive you home. Easy peasy."

"Thanks, Noel."

CHAPTER 95

JERUSALEM

MOSHE BISK THOUGHT he heard his alarm clock buzz. After opening his eyes, he realized that was a mistake. What had awakened him was in fact a satellite transmission received by his implant.

In his mind's eye Bisk could envision a man dressed in clerical vestments. He was an Armenian Apostolic Priest dressed in a full black robe, black phiro on his head, and a silver Armenian cross draped on his chest. What was distinctive was that the priest was also wearing a wide green belt. The image was accompanied by a message. According to the message, this would be the disguise of an Iranian spy in the Armenian Quarter of Old Jerusalem. It would be Bisk's task to assassinate the masquerader.

Bisk quizzed the satellite sender, "Has the disinformation problem been rectified?"

"Yes," was the reassuring answer. The satellite transmission followed with a logistical plan. He, Bisk, should dress in exactly this set of vestments. So dressed, the true Iranian spy would mistake him for another Iranian spy. This would allow Bisk to get close before pulling the assassin's trigger. The assassination was scheduled for midday, three days hence.

It was nearing noon on August 27 when Bisk began to stroll through the Armenian Quarter in the Old City of Jerusalem. He paused to visit a silversmith shop, examining the craftsmanship. He picked up a Jerusalem Cross with four equal sides. Each quarter of the cross represented one of the four Gospel writers: Matthew, Mark, Luke, and John. In the middle of the cross was mounted a tiny lamb, the lamb of God whose blood was shed for the salvation of the world. Bisk had no idea what he was looking at. He was concentrating on movement he'd caught with his left eye.

When Bisk turned he found himself face to face with the spy he had been looking for: black alb, phiro, cross, and green belt. He put his right hand under his robe and withdrew his Glock 17, invisible because hidden by the robe. He fired through his robe at the Armenian Cross on the chest of that Iranian spy.

At precisely the same moment, Tsvi Sechbach fired his pistol in the opposite direction.

ALSO BY TED PETERS

Click HERE to continue the adventure!

Blood sacrifice. Could there be anything more evil? What happens when the symbols of grace get turned upside down? Are we left without hope?

Set in the Adirondack Mountains, the clash between good and evil escapes its local confines to threaten the nation and even engulf the globe. The selling of souls to perdition fuels the fires of hell so that we on Earth cannot avoid the heat.

Discover Leona's Law: *You know it's the voice of Satan when you hear the call to shed innocent blood.*

Get *The Moon Turns to Blood* today
at **https://books2read.com/Leona-Foxx3**

Made in United States
Orlando, FL
16 April 2022